The Lost Tribe

THE BOOK OF MORMON SLEUTH 2

The Lost Tribe

C.B. ANDERSEN

BOOKCRAFT

SALT LAKE CITY, UTAH

Library of Congress Cataloging-in-Publication Data

Andersen, C. B. (Carl Blaine), 1961-
    The Book of Mormon sleuths 2 : the lost tribe / C.B. Andersen.
       p.   cm.
    Summary: Following a plane crash en route to Alaska, a Mormon family is captured by a primitive tribe somewhere in Russia and must rely on their knowledge of scripture to plan their escape.
    ISBN 1-57008-842-X (pbk.)
    [1. Aircraft accidents—Fiction.   2. Survival—Fiction.   3. Mormons—Fiction.
4. Book of Mormon—Fiction.   5. Russia—Fiction.]   I. Title: Book of Mormon sleuths two.   II. Title: Lost tribe.   III. Title.
    PZ7.A51887 Bp 2002
    [Fic]—dc21   2002002194

Printed in the United States of America   7973-6972
Bang Printing, Brainerd, MN

10   9   8   7   6   5   4   3   2   1

For Shari, who taught me how to love life
Thank you for your laugh
Thank you for our family
And thank you for believing in me

Contents

Preface

This is a work of fiction. Its purpose is to entertain but also to help young readers become more familiar with scriptural teachings. In this case, I have focused on peoples of the world, past and present, who have dedicated themselves to living by these teachings.

Do I believe the lost ten tribes of Israel are in northeast Asia? There are at least ten separate references in the standard works of The Church of Jesus Christ of Latter-day Saints that speak of the gathering of Israel. Third Nephi 5:24 states: "And as surely as the Lord liveth, will he gather in from the four quarters of the earth all the remnant of the seed of Jacob, who are scattered abroad upon all the face of the earth."

Other references specifically mention "the isles of the sea" (1 Nephi 19:16) or "the north countries" (Ether 13:11). Rather than gathering an entire group or nation, which has been hidden from the knowledge of the rest of the world, perhaps part of this gathering will proceed as Jeremiah prophesied: "I will take you one of a city, and two of a family, and I will bring you to Zion" (Jeremiah 3:14; see verses 12–19).

More important than the *location* of the lost tribes, is this: that if we will seek to understand the prophesies found in the scriptures, we will develop a deeper appreciation for the sacrifice of our Savior, Jesus Christ. May we exercise as much faith in that unparalleled event as did so many who lived before it even happened.

CHAPTER 1

Alaska Is No Place for a Cruise

June is my favorite month of the year. School is finally over; the weather is warm, but not too hot; and there is still a lot of time left before I even have to *start* worrying about homework taking over my life again. Basically, there is plenty of time to do all those things I wanted to do during the school year but never had time for.

So what was I doing the first Saturday in June to enjoy all this glorious, free time? Well, for two hours straight, I'd been sitting on an airplane, staring at the back of the seat in front of me. I stared at it so long that I am able to give a perfect description of it. The fabric somewhat resembled a checkerboard, except for the fact that it looked like the lines and squares had been colored by my four-year-old brother. The squares were arranged in a pattern that included six different colors: green, blue, and four different shades of purple. The seat was exactly 21 squares wide at the top and widened to 27 squares at about my shoulder height. I counted 343 full squares and 216 partial squares covering the back of the seat. Of course, that didn't include the space where the elegant, fine-dining, fold-out, plastic dinner tray was.

Perhaps I should explain my situation a little more bluntly: I was *way* bored. In fact, I was more bored than I had been at any time during the previous nine months in Mrs. Hardy's eighth-grade English class. And after two hours, I could think of nothing better to do than count the little squares on the seat in front of me. I

1

couldn't listen to my CD player because our plane was still sitting at the airport terminal, and the pilot and his helpers had *each* made it *very* clear that "no electronic devices are to be in use" as long as we were sitting there. Apparently they were as bored as I was and didn't have anything better to do than sneak through the plane pouncing on owners of electronic devices that were "in use" against the rules.

When the pilot walked past, he tried to explain the importance of the rule by putting one hand on my shoulder and saying in this very official voice, "Son, the pilot of an aircraft is in constant contact with the airport tower when taking off or landing." I was going to ask which one we had been doing for the past two hours— taking off or landing—or how he managed to maintain "constant" contact with the tower as he was walking through the cabin, but he continued before I could decide which question to ask first. "*Any* interruption in that *vital* communication," he said, "could lead to potentially *extreme* consequences for *everyone* involved, both in the air and on the ground due to unforeseen changes in weather or other relevant conditions." He emphasized the word *extreme* by forming a fist with the hand that was not gripping my shoulder and moving it firmly to his heart as he directed his gaze slightly upward. He didn't move for a couple of seconds, and his pose was so perfect that I had this uncontrollable urge to glance around, looking for the guy who must have been taking his picture. I did wonder for a moment if our pilot wasn't living just a little too close to fantasyland for me. I never found the photographer, but it would have been a great picture, given our pilot's full head of thick, white hair and matching, shiny, white teeth.

I began affectionately thinking of the crew as "Snow White and the Seven Dwarfs." But not out loud, of course. I had already identified several of the dwarfs' names. "Grumpy" was the one who did the best job of convincing me that I might actually lose possession of my CD player if I didn't keep it well hidden. "Sneezy" was the one with allergies that had "been acting up" ever since she'd arrived in Salt Lake City the evening before on a flight from Portland.

Once the dwarfs were gone, I wrapped my CD player in my coat and stuffed it back into the overhead bin. Yes, that's right: I had my coat. It was the first week of June, and I was packing a winter coat. Dad thought it might be "a little cold" when we first got to the airport in Alaska, so every single one of us was clutching a coat as we walked through the airport terminal on the way to the plane. It was *way* embarrassing. And, *no*, according to my dad, a light jacket "would not be sufficient."

I closed the bin and slumped back into my seat. I was sitting by the aisle with my four-year-old brother, Danny, next to me. Brandon, my other brother, is about a year younger than I am. He was sitting on the other side of Danny, staring out the airplane window, and he looked as bored as I felt. But for some reason Danny thought that *I* was the only one who had the ability to answer his questions—every *single* one of them.

"This is funny, huh, Jeff?" he asked me for about the fifteenth time. He was experimenting with his dinner tray and the two little toy cars he brought with him. He had spent the last twenty minutes trying to determine the exact angle to which he could raise the front edge of the tray before his cars would begin sliding sideways. He *acted* like he was trying to keep them from sliding all the way off the tray, but he was always either too slow, or he would drop the tray again so fast that the cars would bounce off anyway. Each time he would laugh almost uncontrollably as the cars tumbled to the floor of the plane. Then he would plunge headfirst after them, giggling the whole time.

"Jeff," Danny gasped loudly between laughs, "did you see my cars fall down? It's funny, huh?"

Danny would be starting kindergarten in the fall, and I was trying to imagine him sitting behind a desk for several hours at a time. Somehow I just couldn't see it.

We have three sisters who were sitting right behind us. Shauna, who just finished her junior year in high school, was in the middle and had been working hard to keep Meg and Chelsea entertained, both of whom are in elementary school. She had read part of a book to them, played a couple of games, and now she was making up some story about them being princesses going on a royal cruise, as she painted their fingernails. The smell of the nail polish made me rub my nose. I reached up and tried to open my air vent a little more, but it was evidently already maxed out, so instead I adjusted Danny's vent so it blew slightly in my direction. He didn't seem to notice. And neither did anyone else.

The flight attendant walked past and asked if there was anything else she could get for us, but we all admitted we'd had about all the soda and peanuts we could stand for the time being. "Are you sure?" she asked, practically bubbling over with enthusiasm. We were sure.

Because she repeatedly bombarded me with just about as many *smiling* questions as Danny did, she quickly became the dwarf known as "Happy." I figured she was giving me all the attention because the only passengers still on the plane were all in my family, and everyone but me seemed to be pretty much content with whatever they were doing. I looked back at Mom and Dad, who were on the same row as my sisters, but across the aisle. Dad was reading some book, and Mom was asleep next to him—which, by the way, is the *reason* why we were the last ones on this plane.

Apparently, there was some problem that had to be fixed before we could go anywhere. Two hours earlier, the plane had been about half-full when the pilot announced through the little, crackling speakers above our heads that "some of the navigation instruments in the cockpit do not appear to be working properly, although there are no problems with any of the plane's essential functions."

"Oh, great," Brandon had said to me, "so does that mean the

4

plane can fly, but if we take off we won't be able to tell where we're going?"

"Yeah!" I answered with disgust. "We'd be flying for about three hours and then he would do something like make an urgent announcement for everybody on the right side of the plane to watch out for a really tall, pointy mountain with lots of snow on it, 'cause that's where we're going to have to turn to get to the airport!"

Brandon laughed. "It could be worse," he said after a moment. "Remember Lehi's family was halfway across the ocean when the Liahona quit working in the middle of a storm. At least we're still on the ground." He smiled and turned to stare out the window some more. I have to admit that he had a point, but I didn't bother to mention it. I was too busy thinking about the fact that ever since Brandon had received a copy of the original edition of the Book of Mormon last summer when we visited our Great-Aunt Ella, he seemed to regularly come up with something relating to the Book of Mormon. It made me wonder how much he was reading it.

A few minutes after his first announcement, the pilot said they were sure the problem could be fixed before too long, but that the airline would be happy to move anyone who was interested onto a different flight. It turns out that *everyone* was interested in a different flight, except for *us!* In the following two hours, everybody else had gotten off, and they were probably already halfway through the in-flight meal on their new airplane. Brandon said he saw some airport guys with big blue headphones take a bunch of suitcases back out of the bottom part of the plane. He was sure he saw our stuff being hauled away with the rest. At this rate our luggage would be ready to come back home before our airplane even left the terminal in Salt Lake.

Actually, I think *certain* people in our family *were* interested in getting on a plane that showed some ability to move, but Dad was definitely not one of them, and he carried the ultimate executive veto power—at least as long as Mom was asleep.

"Mom was up all night packing," he had said. "She's tired. If she wakes up before the plane is fixed, then we can ask her if she wants to change flights."

Naturally, my first thought was to try to come up with some way to gently help her wake up, but I quickly noted two problems with that plan. First, in all my fourteen years, I'd yet to see anything gentle that helped Mom wake up. I think her condition can best be described as "she's not a morning person." The second problem was that Dad was between her and me. I turned around and flashed a plastic smile at Dad as I surveyed the seating arrangement. After staring back at me for a moment, he smiled hesitantly, with a look that clearly communicated that he wasn't sure if he should be worried about what I was thinking or not. I turned back around and pretty much gave up on the idea of trying to get us onto another plane.

As long as I'm on the subject of my dad, let me just say that he is *amazing*. Now before I give the wrong impression, let me explain what I mean by that. Every once in a while my dad comes up with some "grand" idea or another that he thinks is absolutely wonderful. He manages to convince my mom that it truly is a fabulous idea and then he springs it on the whole family. Of course, most of us eventually believe his descriptions of fun and excitement, and I admit that his explanations usually convince me, too. But I'm starting to learn that things never seem to *quite* work out the way he thinks they will.

What's *amazing*, though, is that something always happens that no one expects—especially not my dad. Just when his plan seems to be falling apart and nothing is going right and everyone is having a horrible time, something *always* seems to happen—something that makes everything far better than anyone could have imagined. And when it's all said and done, Dad never seems to think about it long enough to realize that none of what was so great about "his plan" had *anything* to do with what he had actually planned to start with. *That's* what's amazing.

As I sat on the airplane staring at the seat in front of me, I realized that it was happening again; we were now at the part where Dad's fabulous plan was falling apart. Let me explain where it all began.

A few months earlier, Dad had announced that our family had won a free vacation. We were going on an Alaskan cruise. Apparently, this airline (the one that so far showed no signs of getting anywhere near the air) had just opened up service in the Salt Lake International Airport and held a drawing for an all-expenses-paid trip for an entire family. And Dad won.

"Why would anyone want to cruise *Alaska?*" I had asked. "Isn't a cruise usually on *water* around some tropical islands? Alaska is land, right? Are we going to be cruising the Alaskan highways in the back of a semi with a hundred *other* lucky people? Do you think there will be windows? Or just a loudspeaker with the truck driver describing all the gorgeous things that we can't see?"

I was ignored, of course. Dad explained that we would be flying to Alaska, where we would board a cruise ship for six days and sail down the west coast of Alaska and Canada, docking in Vancouver and from there flying back to Salt Lake. He talked about all the cool places where we would stop along the way and showed us brochures with pictures of whales jumping and huge icebergs floating by. (I admit that when I saw the icebergs, thoughts of the *Titanic* entered my mind.) Apparently, the ship also had some video game rooms, several swimming pools, movie theaters, and more food than anybody could possibly eat in seven days. And everything on board was free.

Dad had done it again. He was his usual, convincing self, and he had made it sound fun. Eventually, I had started really looking forward to this. But somehow, enduring the smell of nail polish and listening to Danny laugh as his cars bounced to the floor over and over and over again had never been part of the fun things I imagined I might be doing on this trip.

Finally, though, the pilot announced that we had been cleared for takeoff, and the plane began to move. The jolting woke up Mom, who gave a wide yawn and asked in a loud, just-waking-up voice, "Are we there yet?"

Brandon turned to me with one eyebrow raised and said, "I thought Danny was supposed to ask that!"

I couldn't keep from laughing as Danny turned to Brandon with a puzzled look. Brandon laughed, too, because of Danny. I don't think either Mom or Dad figured out what we were laughing about because he was too busy explaining to her that so far the airplane had only moved about 35 feet and that had all happened in the last ten seconds. She responded by looking back and forth between Dad and the window several times. I think she was trying to decide whether to be confused or just not to care. She soon decided to close her eyes and settle in for the next two-hour, 35-foot stretch of the trip.

A moment later, Grumpy appeared in front of us with a little picture book explaining all the safety features of the airplane. The most enjoyable part for me was when she explained how the oxygen mask would drop in front of each of us in the event of loss of cabin pressure. She held the mask high in the air and then let it fall from her hand while she held onto the long, clear plastic tube that the oxygen comes through. The oxygen mask was a nacho-cheese-colored, plastic cup big enough to fit over your mouth and nose, with an elastic band for strapping it around your head. On the bottom of the cup, next to where the oxygen tube was connected, there was a clear plastic bag about the size of a sandwich bag. The sight of the nacho-cheese cup and the sandwich bag made my stomach growl. I was hungry—for something other than peanuts and soda.

Grumpy had a somewhat annoyed look as she watched the dangling mask swing back and forth in front of her face for a moment and then tried to demonstrate how to put on the mask without actually letting it ever touch any single part of her head. She looked like she'd just inserted her head into the dangerous part of a loaded slingshot, and I suddenly had this fear that she was going to accidentally let go and end up whacking herself in the nose. However, she managed to complete the show without injuring herself, for which I was grateful. I wasn't anxious to see her any more grumpy than she already was.

I thought about her little one-act play and how strange it was that she chose to look annoyed when she was pretending that the mask had just spontaneously dropped in front of her, instead of something more dramatic, like scared or surprised. She obviously wasn't hired for her acting skills—Brandon would have done a better job than she did. Of course, he'd basically been practicing his acting every day of his life whenever Mom was around. He could convince her of *anything!* The thought made me look over at Brandon and give him a little smirk.

"What?" he asked.

I laughed, realizing what I'd done and quickly said, "Nothing! Never mind."

He continued to stare at me with his eyebrows knit together for the next few moments, so I just closed my eyes and tried to get him to forget about it.

For the next little while things seemed to be going along pretty well. We took off from the airport with only a small scream coming from behind us as the plane left the ground. Meg giggled the name, "Chelsea!" as the plane started to climb, leaning us all back in our seats. I heard Shauna ask Chelsea if she was okay, to which she responded by panting loudly a couple of times and breathing a loud, "Uh-huh!"

Sometime later, after a snack that made school lunch seem like a banquet, the pilot announced that we were beginning our descent into Portland but that the stop would be quite short, since there was only one person scheduled to board and Sneezy was the only one getting off. I made a mental note of the fact that the *reason* nobody was getting off was that everyone who *would have* been getting off had been smart enough to get off several hours earlier and take another plane. I pivoted slowly to look at Dad, but his glance made it clear that he had absolutely no interest in hearing what I was thinking. A few minutes later the plane landed, Chelsea screamed, and Meg giggled Chelsea's name once more. This time Chelsea giggled, too—after recovering from her scream.

The guy who got on the plane looked like a mountain climber. He wore boots, a flannel shirt, and a backpack. He smiled at us as he came down the aisle, sat down a couple of rows in front of us, and pulled out a book to read. Brandon said the airport workers were loading metal boxes of various sizes under the plane. When the plane began to move, the guy listened politely as Grumpy performed the second showing of her little warm-up act but then immediately returned to his book. Apparently, he was just about as impressed with her acting ability as I was. Once we were in the air and the little seat belt lights above each of our seats had gone out, he came back to where we were and sat across the aisle from me, buckling his seat belt.

"Did I hear a scream and some laughing coming from back here?" he asked.

"Those are my sisters," I smiled with one side of my mouth, motioning with my head in their direction. "They've done that at each takeoff and landing so far. We're starting to get used to it."

He smiled and said, "Are you all together? You're the only other passengers on the plane."

"I know," I said flatly, after glancing back at Dad again. It looked like he was asleep now, too. "These are my two brothers, you've already noticed my sisters, and behind you are our mom and dad."

"Wow!" he said in near disbelief. "You're all one family?" I didn't really know how to respond because I was already well aware of the amazing size of our family. I didn't really have time to say anything, though. "I came back to apologize," he immediately continued, "for making you wait as they loaded all my gear onboard, but it looks like I'll have to catch your parents later."

"No need to apologize to them," I smiled. "Sitting in non-moving airplanes on the ground is apparently one of their favorite things. I don't know if this is a newly discovered pleasure or not, but I wouldn't worry about it if I were you. We spent about two hours waiting around in Salt Lake, and they seemed pretty content basically the whole time."

I think he wasn't sure how to respond, so he simply said, "Oh?" after a moment and sort of nodded his head a little bit.

"Were all those boxes yours?" Brandon asked. "And why are they all made out of metal?"

"Oh, I work for the USGS." He seemed happy to be able to move to a new conversation. "That's the United States Geological Survey. I study volcanoes. We had just finished taking some readings at Mount Saint Helens when we were notified that there's some new volcanic activity not far from Anchorage. I was sent out first, while the rest of my team finishes up at Saint Helens. Those boxes hold our equipment. A lot of it is extremely delicate—which is why it's all in metal boxes."

"I've heard about Mount Saint Helens," I said, "but I didn't know there were volcanoes in Alaska."

"Oh, yeah!" he answered. "There are quite a few—and several of them have been active in the last hundred years. Shishaldin Volcano was active just last May, and the place I'm going to investigate is called Crater Peak. It was active in 1992 and, I think, in 1953 before that."

"Really?" Brandon said. I looked over at him because I didn't know he had been listening. Danny had stopped playing with his cars on the dinner tray and was quietly checking this guy out.

"Yeah," he continued. "In 1992 it was spitting out huge rocks that were landing several miles away."

"Whoa!" Brandon and I each responded.

"I'm Tom," he said, reaching to shake our hands. "What are your names?" After we told him, Brandon and I continued asking questions. The guy was pretty interesting and ended up talking to us for the next hour or so about volcanoes and where the closest ones were that have been active in the last few years. I was amazed by the whole thing. I had no idea so many active volcanoes still existed in the world, especially so many just in Alaska.

The pilot announced that we were beginning our descent into Anchorage, noting that the weather was 61 degrees and cloudy, and that local time was 8:37 P.M. At this point, the USGS guy said, "Well, I guess I'd better get back up to my seat. It's been great talking with you," and then he went back and sat with his book.

A couple of minutes later, the pilot came on again and said, "Folks, I'm afraid that we have ourselves a situation here. I've just been informed that a volcano has erupted approximately 75 miles west of Anchorage and that the winds are moving the volcanic cloud over the Anchorage area. We will not be able to land at the Anchorage International Airport until we are certain that we can avoid getting any volcanic ash into the plane's engines."

I looked out the windows on both sides of the plane and could see nothing *but* clouds. "Looks like we're already in it!" I said to anyone who might be willing to listen to me.

"He said before that it was cloudy," Brandon reminded me.

"Yeah, but how can he tell the difference between the regular, just-rain-on-you clouds and the *much* worse, volcanic, burn-your-engine-out-so-your-plane-crashes clouds?" I challenged.

Brandon had no response for *that*. I looked down and was relieved to see that Danny had fallen asleep. I suddenly realized what a dumb thing that was to say when Danny might have heard me. At this point, I could feel the plane begin to turn left. Just as I was beginning to lean to one side to counteract the plane's turn, the plane quickly leveled off again. The jolting apparently woke up Mom, who asked in a sleepy voice, "Are we there yet?"

Before anyone could answer, the speakers suddenly crackled once again. This time it was the copilot. He sounded a little nervous.

"We've been informed that we are already too close to the volcanic cloud," he said. "We are changing our route again and as a precautionary measure, we will be descending as quickly as possible."

At this point it felt like the plane seat practically dropped out from underneath me. It reminded me of the roller coaster at Magic Mountain that I went on once—only once.

The copilot continued. "Please do not be alarmed," he said, "but as an additional precaution we will be deploying the oxygen masks for your use."

Before he even finished his sentence, the oxygen masks above every seat in the plane popped out and began swinging back and forth in front of our faces. Now I was sure that Grumpy was wrong to look annoyed by the oxygen masks during her demonstration— the correct feeling in a situation like this was definitely more like *panic*. And fear. The size of Brandon's eyes told me he felt the same way I did.

CHAPTER 2

A Ship without a Rudder

Realizing that this was the exact situation for which I had been trained, I made a mental note to thank Grumpy the next chance I got and then quickly inserted my head into the slingshot and let go.

"Put your masks on!" I heard Dad call. His voice sounded muffled and a little frantic. I turned and saw that he and Mom both had their masks in place and were looking over at the girls.

"I'm trying!" Chelsea whined from behind me.

"Let me help you," came Shauna's voice.

"Help Daniel with his mask," Mom said, looking at me. I turned back around and saw that Brandon was already trying to get Danny's mask around his head, but without much success. Danny was more than *slightly* perturbed that somebody was apparently trying to suffocate him in his sleep. He was throwing his head from side to side and pushing away every attempt by Brandon to get the elastic band behind his head. I turned my face toward him just in time to get whacked in the ear by the back of Danny's flailing hand. I put my arm up next to his shoulder and leaned toward the aisle in an attempt to avoid any more direct hits.

"Whoa!" I said, blinking and opening my jaw as far as it would go. "I think Danny just popped my ear. That one's been plugged ever since we left Portland! Thanks, buddy!"

I exercised my jaw open and shut several times just to make sure.

"Jeff! *Help* me!" Brandon complained excitedly. Even through the mask, his voice made it obvious that he was more than just a little bit frustrated.

"Danny!" I said softly, rubbing his chest and the top of his head. "Wake up! It's a game! Look, we all get to wear these cool masks!" He stopped throwing his head around and made his first attempt at opening his eyes.

"Huh?" he moaned, blinking and looking up at me.

"Look at these masks we get to wear," I said. "We all get to act like monsters!"

"I don't wanna be a monster," Danny mumbled, closing his eyes and trying to snuggle back into his seat.

"C'mon," I said. "We *have* to. Mom said."

"Okay," he sighed, looking back and forth from me to Brandon. I could tell that he wasn't too excited about the idea.

"Look at this," I laughed. By breathing hard in and out several times, I was able to make the little sandwich bag quickly blow up and flatten again, with a popping sound each time it inflated.

"I wanna try!" Danny giggled. He reached for his mask in Brandon's hand and said, "Let *me* put it on."

"That's what I've been *trying* to do," Brandon grunted with exasperation. He looked at me with bulging eyes and his head tilted to one side. His mask hid the rest of what I'm sure was a very pleasant scowl intended solely for me.

"You're welcome!" I smiled, then, realizing that he couldn't see my mouth, I added the happiest fake laugh I could manage. Brandon just continued to glare back at me.

Meanwhile, Danny had gotten his mask on and was doing his best to make his sandwich bag inflate. He was leaning forward with his hands on his knees, his elbows pointing outward, breathing in and out for all he was worth. After about half a minute he gave up, plopping himself against the back of his seat and letting his eyes roll back into his head.

15

"I can't do it," he breathed between long, slow blinks. Just then, Grumpy's crackling voice came out of the overhead speakers.

"We have experienced a slight drop in cabin pressure," she explained. "Please note that the oxygen masks have been deployed for your use."

Well, there's a revelation, I thought. Brandon and I looked at each other, wondering who would be the first one brave enough to say, "Duh!" out loud.

She continued by repeating some of the lines from her earlier visual demonstration. "Please place the oxygen mask over your mouth and nose."

"Check!" I said in response.

"Put on your own mask first and then help any children who may be seated next to you."

"Check! Check!" I said again, quite proud of myself.

"Remember to breathe normally," she continued, "to avoid hyperventilation."

"Uh–oh!" I said, slowly turning to look at Danny.

"Good *job*, Jeff!" Brandon said. "Next time you want to help, uh, maybe you ought to follow instructions."

I'm sure he *really* enjoyed saying that. I ignored Brandon and asked Danny if he was all right now.

"Yeah!" he panted slowly, "I—think so."

"Maybe we shouldn't try to blow up the bag anymore, okay?" I suggested.

"Okay," he said, then added, "I think that's a good idea."

"So do I," Brandon agreed, but I have *no* idea what expression he had on his face at this point, because I refused to look at him. It's amazing how quickly *some* people forget the favors they receive.

Grumpy continued a moment later. "The pilot has informed me that we will be descending as quickly as possible, so the oxygen masks should only be necessary for a few minutes."

"Why do we have to wear masks?" Danny asked after a moment. "Did something bad happen?"

"Just to make sure we're safe," I tried to reassure him. "It'll be okay." I didn't want him to get too worried about it, so I asked, "Do you want me to do something with you?"

"What?" he asked.

"I don't know. What's in your backpack?"

At Mom's suggestion, we had each filled our school backpacks with stuff to do on the trip. Dad added the requirement that we each include our scriptures, but other than that we were allowed to bring anything that would fit—and that we were willing to carry ourselves. Dad added that part, too, probably because he didn't want to end up getting stuck carrying some kid's mega-pack.

Danny had originally thought he might want to bring along part of his rock collection, but I used a practical demonstration to help him figure out that he might not want to carry his backpack around very much if it was full of rocks. He almost fell over when I put the straps on his shoulders and let go. "Besides, Danny," Shauna reasoned when she heard me laugh and saw what we were doing, "you'll need all the extra room for the *new* rocks you're going to find on our trip!"

Once Shauna gave him the idea of coming home with new rocks, he didn't want to carry *anything* he didn't have to. He removed everything other than his required paperback copy of the Book of Mormon. I laughed again as I realized that he had already forgotten about my practical demonstration; maybe he figured Alaskan rocks would be lighter than the rocks he already had. Last I heard, Shauna was trying to convince him that it would be a good idea to bring along at least a few things to play with.

Typical of how much he changes his mind, when I pulled his backpack out from under the airplane seat in front of him, I discovered junk protruding from each and every pocket and opening. He had cars and trucks, pencils and crayons, coloring books, picture

17

books, cards, and stuffed toys. Things fell out all over the place as I tried to search through his bag.

We eventually selected a coloring book, and for the next twenty minutes or so he colored while I kept watching out the windows on each side of the plane. Everything was still cloudy. The plane felt like it was flying pretty much level and straight, but the air seemed to be a lot rougher than it had been for the first part of the trip. But maybe it just seemed rougher because of how nervous I was. I could hear Shauna talking quietly with Meg and Chelsea behind us; she was doing a good job of keeping them preoccupied, but to me she sounded a little nervous, too. I could hear Mom and Dad whispering quietly, but I couldn't tell what they were saying.

Pretty soon I noticed the pilot coming down the aisle. He stopped and said something to the volcano guy, holding his hand out in our direction. Tom immediately removed his oxygen mask and stood up. The two of them then came back to where we were sitting.

"Hi," Tom said to me, as they approached us. "The pilot says that we don't need the masks anymore." He looked back at Mom and Dad and said, "I'm Tom. I met your children earlier."

There was a quick exchange of short greetings as we removed our masks and then Tom again sat in the seat across the aisle from me, in front of Mom and Dad. The pilot stood facing all of us with his hands perched on the seat backs in front of me and Tom, blocking the aisle.

"I've asked this gentleman to join us back here for a moment so that I can explain our current situation to all of you at once and in person." The pilot spoke in that same formal voice he had used with me earlier. I thought about my CD player and felt an urge to check and make sure it was still safely wrapped up in my coat. "We're at a low enough elevation now," he continued, "that the oxygen is no longer necessary, but we still have ourselves a situation here."

He paused, but no one else said anything. I began to wonder

how many more times I was going to hear this guy say that we "have ourselves" something.

"We've lost navigation again," he said. Brandon and I glanced at each other, obviously both thinking about the Liahona that quit working in the middle of the ocean. The pilot continued, "and the radio is inoperable. It's not unusual to lose radio capability near a volcanic eruption, because of the debris in the air, but it should have returned as soon as we were away from the area. It hasn't. So we have ourselves something of a dilemma."

He paused again.

"Do you have any idea what's wrong with the navigational system?" Dad asked.

"We did hear some thumps under the cockpit of the plane," the pilot answered, still using that formal voice. I was starting to think maybe that was the only voice he had. "We are not sure what that was, but one of our theories is that we actually flew over the erupting volcano and were struck by some small rocks that damaged both our navigation equipment as well as the radio."

Brandon and I immediately stared at each other. We were apparently no longer better off than Lehi.

"Is there anything else wrong?" Mom asked.

"Not that we know of," the pilot answered. "We have full control of the plane, but we're anxious for a break in the clouds so that we can have a better idea of where we are. Our last known heading was approximately northwest, and the latest weather report showed clear skies in that direction—so we're hopeful, because we do have ourselves a plan."

"So assuming there's a break in the clouds," Tom said, "what is your plan?"

"Thank you for asking," the pilot replied. "Judging from our last known heading we should be nearly in a direct line with a Russian military base along the coast of the Bering Sea."

"Russia?" Brandon asked in obvious shock. "We're going to Russia? I thought we were over Alaska."

"Brandon," Dad said reassuringly. "We'll be fine. Let him continue."

"Sorry, sir," Brandon mumbled to the pilot, somewhat embarrassed.

"That's no problem, son," the pilot nodded in Brandon's direction. "As I was saying, we believe we are heading almost directly toward this Russian military base. We are currently over Alaska, but there's not much between here and Russia. The truth is, we lost navigation just as we were beginning our westerly turn and so we're not exactly sure. We may be off by a few degrees."

"A few degrees?" asked Tom with raised eyebrows.

"Yes," nodded the pilot grimly. "And as you probably realize, the longer we fly, the larger the difference a few degrees can make. That is why we're anxious for the clouds to clear so that we can get a visual bearing."

"Won't that be a problem when the sun goes down?" I asked.

"Uh . . . ," the pilot hesitated. "Well, this time of year in this part of the world the sun is only down for about four hours each night. We still had about two hours of daylight left when we were approaching Anchorage. Combining that time with the fact that we are chasing the sun, we estimate that we should be approaching the military base at about sunset local time." The pilot gave a small smile.

"You act like you feel that's good," Dad commented.

"We believe it is," the pilot nodded. "It means that we can use the daylight to get our bearings relative to major landmarks such as mountain ranges and shorelines, but then we should be able to use the lights of the military base to make a safe and accurate landing. But we do need to get ourselves some clear weather as soon as possible."

I looked out the window and saw nothing but dingy-looking clouds.

"So for now, I guess we just watch and wait?" Tom asked.

"That is correct," answered the pilot. "We will let you know as soon as anything changes." He paused for a moment and then asked, "Any other questions?"

He was about to return to the cockpit when Danny raised his hand and asked, "Can I please go to the bathroom?"

Maybe he's ready for school after all, I thought. The pilot smiled and nodded. "Go ahead, son," he said. He then turned and made his way back to the front of the plane.

"I don't think that's the kind of question he was looking for," Brandon said to Danny as Danny unbuckled himself and hopped off the seat.

"Well, I was *wondering* for a long *time*," he explained dramatically.

"Do you want me to come with you?" I asked.

"I'm almost *five*, Jeff," was all he said before heading to the back of the plane. He rolled his eyes better than any teenage girl I'd ever seen.

Just as Danny returned a couple of minutes later, I heard Chelsea ask, "Dad, shouldn't we say a prayer?"

"I think that's a great idea," Dad said. Then, a little louder, he asked, "Would you boys like to join us for a family prayer?"

"Sure," we both said.

"Come sit on my lap," Dad suggested to Danny, who quickly took advantage of the offer.

I unbuckled my safety belt and kneeled backwards on my seat with my elbows on top of the headrest. After asking Dad if he approved of my technique, Brandon did the same. Dad offered the prayer. I was interested to hear what he would say. He always spends a lot of time mentioning things we're thankful for in his prayers, but this was one time when I figured he might get to the matter at hand a little quicker than usual. I was wrong. He spent what seemed like several minutes being thankful for things that I didn't know he even knew existed. Of course he mentioned each person in the family by name; he often did that.

I remember almost word for word the last part of his prayer. He said that we were thankful to be on this trip together. Then he asked that we be blessed to have experiences that would make us stronger, both individually and as a family and that we would be brought closer together. I was surprised, however, by the last thing he mentioned that we were thankful for. He said that we were thankful "for the trouble that we now found ourselves in."

I almost opened my eyes to see if anyone else was as shocked by this statement as I was. I'm glad I didn't do it, though, because I might have missed the next thing he said. He said we knew this would be a great opportunity to witness His power and that we were anxious "that the works of God should be made manifest" unto us. Then he ended the prayer.

"Thanks, Craig," Mom said.

"You're welcome," Dad smiled.

"Yeah," Shauna agreed. "Thanks, Daddy."

There were some more things said by some others, but I wasn't really listening. I was thinking about what Dad had said in his prayer. A couple of minutes later I asked, "Dad, what does 'manifest' mean?"

Danny was asleep on his lap, and Dad looked like he was fading fast, too. He looked over at me and said, "Uhmm. . . . It means to show or to prove. I was quoting part of a scripture in the New Testament."

"I have a dictionary, if you want to look it up," Shauna offered, reaching for her book bag.

"You have a dictionary?" I questioned. I couldn't believe it! "*Why?*" I asked.

"Why what?" she countered, reaching inside the bag.

"Why, when you can bring anything you want," I explained with obvious disbelief on my face and in my voice, "would you bring a dictionary on *vacation?*"

"So *you* can look up the word *manifest*," she smirked, holding out the beat-up, pocket-sized dictionary for me to use.

"Very funny," I said, taking the book and looking for the words beginning with the letter M.

"I think it's great!" Dad said. "And you don't have to tell us why you brought it if you don't want to."

"Well," Shauna explained, "I was talking to my English teacher at the end of the year about my grade, and I just told her how strange I thought it was that there's so much that we get taught about English that we don't really use. I told her that I already knew enough English to do everything I need to in life."

Dad had a wry look on his face. "You're talking about Mrs. Bailey, right?" He smiled. "I can just *imagine* what she thought of that! What did she say?"

"Yeah, it was Mrs. Bailey," Shauna answered. "Well, after I said that, then she said that if I watched closely, I'd notice words every single day that I didn't know or wasn't sure what they meant. And then she said that if I would keep track of it, then she'd give me an extra credit point next fall for every ten words I find that I didn't know before. But they have to be from normal conversation or road signs or something like that."

"So are you doing it?" Dad asked.

"Yeah," Shauna answered quickly. She acted almost as surprised about it as I was.

"You are?" I asked. I was ignored.

"How many have you found?" Dad asked.

"I've got 137 written down already," Shauna said, "and it hasn't even been a *month* yet. I can't believe it!"

Dad chuckled. I took this opportunity to read what I had found.

"Manifest means 'clearly apparent to the sight or understanding, obvious,'" I read out loud. "There's one you can write down, Shauny. Now you've got 138."

"I already knew that word," Shauna replied.

"No way!" I said. "Is that true? Or are you just willing to give up one tenth of an extra credit point just to make me feel like you're smarter than I am?"

"No!" Shauna laughed. "I would be willing, but in this case I don't have to."

"But I guess 'manifest' isn't part of everyday language, anyway," I continued.

"Sure it is," Dad said.

"What?" I exclaimed. "When was the last time you heard someone say 'manifest' who wasn't quoting scripture?" I asked.

"Just last week," Dad replied. "I was watching a late-night outdoors show where the guy said that if the fishermen take too many fish from the reservoir, the problem doesn't 'manifest itself until the next season.'"

"The New Testament is about fishermen, too," Brandon said. I didn't even know that he was awake. He yawned. "It sounds like the word 'manifest' is only used by fishermen."

Shauna and Dad both laughed.

"Whatever!" I said.

"Why don't you see if you can find the scripture I quoted," Dad suggested, still chuckling.

I gave Shauna back her dictionary and grabbed my quad from my backpack. I used to have a Bible that was separate from the other scriptures, but Mom and Dad gave me the quad when I was ordained a teacher in the Aaronic Priesthood when I turned fourteen. It was sure nice having all the Church scriptures together in one book now.

I immediately turned to the Index in the back and found the heading, "Manifest, Manifestation."

"Hey," I said after looking through all of the scripture references under this heading. "There isn't anything here from the Bible. Didn't you say you were quoting a scripture from the New Testament?"

"That index is only for the Book of Mormon, the Doctrine and Covenants, and the Pearl of Great Price," Dad said. "You have to find Bible scriptures in the Topical Guide."

"Oh, yeah," I remembered, turning to the middle part of my quad. After searching for a minute or two, I said, "It's not in here!"

"Are you sure you're looking in the Topical Guide?" Dad asked. "Check the top of the page."

"Oh," I responded. "No. . . . It says 'Bible Dictionary.' Wait a minute! I didn't need Shauna's dictionary; there's already one right here." After thinking about it for a minute, I said, "No, wait. 'Manifest' isn't in there. What kind of dictionary is this?"

Dad laughed. "It's not the kind of dictionary you're used to. It does have definitions of some words and phrases, but mostly it has explanations of people and places and other things in the Bible. It even has a chronology of events from Adam through the writings of the Apostles."

"What's a chronology?" I asked.

"It's a time table for when certain things happened in history," Dad explained.

"That's not a *dictionary!*" I said. "That's an encyclopedia! Mrs. Hardy gave us an entire test about reference material last year in English. Believe me—I *know* what I'm talking about!"

"You do, huh?" Dad smiled.

"Yes!" I said emphatically. "If *I* was going to make a Bible Dictionary, I'd make a dictionary of weird words that are used only in the Bible . . . like *manifest.*"

"Fishermen use it, too," Brandon reminded me, his eyes still closed.

"You *mentioned* that," I said. I also grunted loudly, making sure he realized how annoyed I was, since, with his eyes closed, he was not able to get the full effect from my expression.

"So start your own Bible dictionary," Dad suggested.

That caught me by surprise. It was sounding a little too much like homework to me. "I would," I hesitated, "but I didn't bring any paper." Then I added, "I think I'm on vacation from writing anyway—for the summer."

"I've got something you can use," Shauna offered, holding out a small purple notebook for me to take. The cover was worn, but the inside seemed unused except for a school-year calendar that was taped to the first page.

"I carried that silly thing around with me the whole school year," she laughed at herself, "and I never did use it for anything."

I flipped through the empty pages as she spoke.

"Hey," she said, "that calendar is still good for the rest of the summer! Now you can be sure to know exactly when school starts again!"

"Thanks," I said, faking a smile. "Okay, tell me the definition of *manifest* again." This was my way of getting her to look up the word for me, since I had closed her little dictionary before I gave it back to her. She's pretty cool, though. She found it again without saying anything else. I had a pen in my book bag, and I managed to find it while she was looking up the word. Here's what I wrote on the second page in the little notebook that Shauna gave me:

JEFF'S BIBLE DICTIONARY (*not encyclopedia!*)

Manifest—clearly apparent to the sight or understanding, obvious.

I read what I had written and thought about Dad's prayer again. That's when I remembered that this had all started with me trying to find the reference. I opened up to the middle part of my quad again, this time making sure that I was in the Topical Guide. The references under "Manifest" filled half a column and continued onto the next page, but just about five lines down I found where it said: "9:3 works of God should be made manifest in him." I had to look a couple of lines above the reference to find out that it was in the book of John.

I looked it up and found that it was a story about a man who was born blind and when the disciples asked Jesus if the man was blind because *he* had sinned or because his *parents* had sinned, Jesus said neither one had sinned, "but that the works of God should be made manifest in him." Then he healed the man so he wasn't blind anymore.

I thought about it for a minute, then turned to Dad and asked, "So Jesus said that the man was blind just so they could see God's power?"

"That's right," Dad nodded.

I was quiet for a minute before asking, "So in your prayer, you were saying that we're grateful for having a bad thing happen because it gives us the opportunity to witness the power of God?"

Dad nodded his head a couple times before saying, "I think you're with me."

I thought about what that meant for a few more minutes before writing this in my notebook, just below the definition of manifest:

John 9:1–7 Man born blind so that Jesus could heal him, making power of God manifest.

Nobody said anything else for a while, and I was beginning to feel sleepy, so I put my one-word Bible dictionary inside my scripture case and returned it with my pen to my backpack. For the next couple of hours, I dozed in and out. Each time I awoke, I looked out the windows. The clouds didn't look like they were getting any thinner. Some time later I woke up, looked toward the front of the plane, and saw Dad coming back to his seat.

"What's going on?" I yawned. "Did they find the military base yet?"

"No," Dad shook his head slowly. His face was grim. "We've been flying far too long, and now they have absolutely *no* idea where we are."

CHAPTER 3

A Night without Darkness

"No way," I whispered to myself. Then, looking up at Dad as he walked past me, I asked, "Is the radio working yet? Or anything else?"

"I'm afraid not," he answered, sitting down next to Mom. "All that has changed is that the sky is now clear, we're flying along the coast of something, and even though we've been flying for hours, the sun hasn't gone down."

"Hours?" I asked. "How long have I been asleep?"

"Quite a while," Mom smiled.

"But you said we're flying along some coast?" I questioned.

"*Some* coast is right," Mom answered, "but apparently no one knows which one."

"That's bad, right?" I asked.

"Well, it could be worse," Dad replied.

"If *this* isn't bad," I said slowly, "then what is?"

Before saying anything, Dad looked over at where the girls were sitting and asked Shauna, "Are Meg and Chelsea both asleep?" They were.

"Danny's asleep, too," Brandon offered.

"Well," Dad sighed, "in an attempt to be positive, let me explain what is *good* about our situation as the pilot and copilot explained it to me. First, the plane still seems to be working well, aside from the loss of the radio and navigation. Second, we still have several hours of fuel left, which gives them a lot of time to try to locate an acceptable place to land. And finally, the sky is clear, making it possible to see where we're going. If you want to try to imagine a *bad* situation, then imagine the opposite of each of those things."

No one said anything for a minute. I finally blurted out, "You mean *bad* would be when they *can't* steer the plane, when we have *no* fuel left, and when there are so many clouds we can't even see where we're going to *crash?*"

"Jeff!" Mom scowled at me, "Dad said to *imagine* those things!" Then shaking her head, she added, "Obviously, it's a good thing we made sure all the little guys are asleep."

"Sorry," I mumbled. I tried to make a small laugh, but nothing really came out.

"Thanks," Dad said. "But now compare our present situation with what you just described. What do you think?"

After pausing for a moment I managed to force half a smile. Dad raised his eyebrows slightly as he watched me. "Get it?" he asked after a moment.

"Got it," I said quietly.

"Good," he smiled slightly. I wondered how he could stay so calm.

"Do they have *any* idea where we might be?" Shauna asked hopefully.

"Well, the coast is on the left side of the plane," Dad explained, "with water on the right." Dad paused for a moment before adding, "They think that water is probably the Arctic Ocean."

"Wait, what?" Shauna said. That was her standard response for "you said something that confuses me and I don't want you to say anything else until you either explain it or I have time to think about it for a minute." Given the option, I was glad she just said "wait, what"—especially considering how *much* she said it.

"No way!" Brandon said.

"But I thought the Arctic Ocean was covered in ice and snow!" Shauna exclaimed.

"You're right," Dad agreed, "but according to Tom, the ice melts during the summer months, leaving a band of open water along the northern coast of North America, Asia, and Europe. And if you look out the window on this side of the plane, you can see it."

Brandon, Shauna, and I all jumped up at once and were each pressing our noses against the cold windows. Brandon and I were at the two windows just in front of where Mom and Dad were sitting, and Shauna was behind them.

I couldn't believe it. The sun was low on the horizon toward the back of the plane, reflecting brightly off the white snow and ice in the distance.

"So is this the northern coast of Alaska?" I asked.

"I don't think so," Dad answered flatly. "Remember the pilot said that our last known direction was northwest? So we're probably—"

Brandon didn't let him finish the sentence. "Russia?!" he exclaimed, whipping around to stare at Dad over the back of the seat. His mouth was gaping open. "This is the northern coast of *Russia?*"

"Probably," he nodded.

"Cool!" Brandon breathed, turning back to the window.

"Are you *nuts?*" I asked, turning in his direction. "I don't want to crash in Russia!"

"Jeff!" Mom glared at me. "Will you *please* use words that are a little less frightening."

"They're all still asleep," I protested, quickly scanning the seats where Meg, Chels, and Danny were to make sure I was telling the truth. I had to check fast, because I'd already said it. I got lucky on that one.

"Which is why you're not in a lot more trouble," Dad warned.

"*Now* is the time to practice speaking about our circumstances in an appropriate manner, please."

"Sorry," I mumbled. Then, quickly, trying to get the focus anywhere else besides on me, I added, "But I still think Brandon's crazy."

"How many people do you know that have seen Russia?" Brandon asked, without taking his gaze from the window.

"We don't even know for sure that it *is* Russia," I said.

"Well, it's *some*place we've never seen before," Brandon replied. "And I think it's way cool!"

"*Freezing* is more like it," I whined. "Wait till we're *stuck* down there somewhere!"

"Je-e-eff!" Mom said, putting at least three syllables into my name. "Enough!"

"Sorry," I mumbled again. "I'll be quiet now." I had just proven to myself—and to everyone else—that I didn't have the ability to "speak about our circumstances in an appropriate manner," so I figured I'd better just give up.

No one said anything for a couple of minutes, and I continued to stare out the window, watching the coast of whatever it was moving along below us. I couldn't believe the situation. *What did we do to deserve this?* I thought. Then, almost before I even finished the thought, I heard Dad's voice in my head saying, "that the works of God should be made manifest." I thought about this for a moment and tried to imagine how the power of God could change our situation. I came up with about six ideas almost immediately—and not one of them involved either a crash landing or spending any time in a foreign country.

"The pilot also said that the sun is on its way up again," Dad said, breaking the silence. "So instead of going down in front of us and to the right, it just sort of made a huge circle from left to right as it got lower, and now it's coming up behind us again."

"Oh, cool," Shauna said. "Look back this way, guys!"

31

With my nose against the window, I turned my head toward the back of the plane and looked at the location of the sun again. It did seem a little higher in the sky than it had been just a few minutes earlier.

"But why didn't it ever go down?" I asked, looking from the window toward Dad. "Didn't the guy say earlier that it was down for four hours at night?"

"Have you ever heard of the Arctic Circle?" Dad asked. Of course I had heard of it, but I had no idea what the question really meant, so I just stared back at him until he continued. "The Arctic Circle is an imaginary ring around the top of the earth where each summer there is at least one day when the sun never goes down because you're so far north. The farther north you are, the more days there are when the sun never goes down. So I think that means we're quite a bit farther north now than we were at the time he said that," Dad smiled.

"As long as we're awake, why don't we have our family devotional," Mom suggested.

"Well," Dad said, "it looks like we're going to miss church today. Starting off with a devotional first thing on a Sunday morning sounds like a great alternative."

Dad's plan was for us to find an LDS ward in Anchorage to attend on Sunday. We were supposed to be in a hotel both Saturday and Sunday nights and then board the cruise ship first thing Monday morning. *Dad's self-destructing plans are right on schedule*, I thought.

"Oh, yeah," Shauna responded to Dad. "It's morning—we usually do it first thing in the morning."

"What do you mean?" I asked wryly. "It's *way* past time for devotional. Aren't we usually *done* by the time the sun comes up? I thought it was a family policy that we only have devotional when it's dark outside." I added a little "Hee-hee" laugh and looked around for someone to join my current crusade against early-morning devotionals.

For some reason, Dad is convinced that the only acceptable time for family devotional is sometime between midnight and sunup. I think it's usually closer to midnight. I'm not sure, but I think he chooses that time because he figures that's when we have absolutely *no* chance of being disturbed by any living creature. Half the time I can't even see straight when it's my turn to read. Every few months or so we have yet another family council to discuss the best time for family devotional. It seems like we spend at least half an hour talking about the pros and cons of every time when we could possibly do it. My vote is always "any time that ends with P.M." I'm sure no one but Dad ever thinks morning is even a *good* time, let alone the *best* time, but somehow after hearing all the reasons why no other time slot will work, we all end up agreeing to it *again*. How does he *do* that?

Well, my comment about it being obviously too late to begin devotional was completely ignored by everyone as they began pulling out their scriptures, so I got mine out as well. Brandon and I sat sideways, facing each other with our feet hanging in the aisle so that we could all sort of see and hear each other.

We always start with a Primary song, and Mom suggested we sing "Families Can Be Together Forever." Personally, I didn't think it was a very good choice because I noticed during the very first line that it says we're "on earth," but we were obviously in the air at the time. I thought earth would have been nice, though. But then Meg, Chels, and Danny all woke up during the song, so I figured it was probably best just to keep that thought to myself. Danny had climbed over me and was now spread-eagle across Dad's chest. After Brandon said the prayer, Dad asked, "Does anyone remember where we are?"

"Alma chapter . . . twenty-y-y something, I think," Shauna answered.

"Well, I was thinking that while we're away from home, that maybe we could do something a little different," Dad said.

"Different!" I laughed. "Dad, we *always* do something different! I'm still waiting for the time that we do something the *same!*"

For as long as I can remember, Dad has always had some scheme or another going on during our family devotional. Monday through Friday we read from the Book of Mormon with each person reading one verse at a time as we go around the room. Reading a chapter or so a day, we're able to read the Book of Mormon about once a year. But he always does stuff like have a question posted on the wall the day before we read a particular chapter and anyone who reads ahead of time and knows the answer from the chapter gets a prize. Or else he'll tell everybody who the good guys and bad guys are that we're going to be reading about that day, and then everybody is supposed to yell "boo!" when the bad guys' names are read or "yea!" whenever we read the name of a good guy. Danny and Chelsea are *way* into that one. Sometimes Danny is still saying the "o-o-o" part of his big long "boo-o-o" when we get to the next verse or when everyone else is now saying "yea!" for the prophet or the angel whose name is mentioned a couple of lines later.

On weekends for our family devotional, we read one or two talks from the latest general conference. Mom says that the conference talks are supposed to be treated just like scripture, so she always orders extra copies of the conference report from the Church Distribution Center so that each person in our family can have their own copy. For these devotionals, Dad will have us name all the first presidency and apostles in order of seniority each time the word *prophet, seer,* or *revelator* is read. Or whenever the word *temple* comes up, then we have to name all the temples in the state of Utah in order from north to south, or something like that. We had to get out the map to find out where Vernal fit into the list of Utah temples. So that's why I said what I did about always doing something *different* for our family devotional.

"Well," Dad continued, "I was just thinking that maybe we could study some subjects that have to do with our vacation."

"Like what?" I asked. I honestly couldn't imagine what he had in mind.

"Like when we're on the cruise ship," Dad explained, "we could read every verse we can find about ships or we could just find scriptures about traveling or we could just pick a subject that sounds interesting and see what we could find." Then he smiled at me and added, "It's nothing *too* different, is it? I just thought it might be fun. What do you think?"

"Do you think we can find anything about being up a river without a paddle?" I asked.

Mom's mouth fell open, and she looked at me like she couldn't believe what I'd just said.

"Not that that's *bad*," I quickly added with the biggest smile I could fake while fearing for my status as a member of the family.

"There probably wouldn't be much about airplanes," Brandon said thoughtfully, as if he had spent some serious time pondering before coming to that conclusion, "so I think we should find everything we can about going north, since all we know is that we'll probably end up landing someplace that's farther north than any of us has ever been before."

I looked over at Mom to see if Brandon was going to get the evil eye for bringing up a *bad* subject, just like I had been doing regularly, but she just looked at Dad to see what he would say. I thought, *Hey, wait a minute!* I was about to complain about the fact that *I* seemed to be the only one getting in trouble for making "inappropriate" comments, but before I recovered from the shock of this great injustice, Dad said, "Works for me! So let's all find the word *north* in the Topical Guide."

Everyone started opening their scriptures, except for me. I was still being *totally* amazed. My mouth was hanging open, and I was just about to ask why *Brandon's* comment was "appropriate" and none of *mine* were, but something kept me from doing it. Luckily, I quickly realized that since he had successfully diverted Mom's attention before I'd actually gotten into trouble, I should just be grateful for small favors.

"Okay, let's each take a scripture from the list," Dad suggested. "Meg, you look up Genesis 28:14. Shauna, you take the one in Psalms, and can you help Chelsea find Isaiah 49:12?"

"Sure," Shauna replied, turning to help Chelsea. To me, Chelsea still looked too asleep to care, but Shauna began talking quietly with her and helping her turn pages in her Bible. Chelsea was blinking slowly, with her eyes never opening more than halfway. She held her lips together so tight that they bulged out as far as her nose.

"Okay," Dad continued, "Jeff, will you take the next one? Looks like it's Jeremiah 3:18."

"Why is it in parentheses?" I asked.

"That just means that it's similar to the scripture listed right before it. But sometimes there are some interesting differences, so let's go ahead and read it."

"I've got Jeremiah 4:6," Brandon said, as he began flipping through pages.

"So that means that Jeremiah 6:22 is mine," Mom said.

"Great," replied Dad. "I'll take Jeremiah 23:8. Meg, go ahead and read yours as soon as you have it."

"I'm trying to remember where Genesis is," she giggled.

"It's the first book in the Bible," Brandon said.

"Oh!" she giggled again. It only took her a few seconds to find the verse after Brandon's hint. Meg was a great reader for a nine-year-old and had no trouble with her verse, which read:

And thy seed shall be as the dust of the earth, and thou shalt spread abroad to the west, and to the east, and to the north, and to the south: and in thee and in thy seed shall all the families of the earth be blessed.

"Good job, Meg," Dad said. "What does that scripture tell us?"

Meg's eyes got big, her shoulders scrunched up, and she stretched out her mouth in a big straight line across her face before giggling, "I don't know!" After a moment she guessed, "That all the families on earth will be blessed?"

"That's right!" Dad smiled at her. "All the families on earth will be blessed because of one man. But the part you read doesn't say who that man is. Does anyone know?"

"Abraham!" I said. "We learned about the Abrahamic covenant in teachers quorum."

"Good answer!" Dad said, "but it's not right."

"Wait, what?" Shauna said. She had a confused look on her face. "We talked about it in seminary. It's not Abraham?"

"Well, you're right about that being one of the promises given to Abraham," Dad explained, "but see in the verse before it says 'I am the Lord God of Abraham thy father,' so he can't be talking to Abraham."

"Oh, it's Jacob, right?" Brandon asked.

"Right," Dad answered. "How did you know?"

"It says it in the chapter heading," Brandon admitted with a small grin.

"That's not fair!" I whined.

"Sure it is," Mom said. "It's not only fair, it's smart! Good job, Brandon."

"Is this the Jacob-guy that gets his name changed to Israel?" Shauna asked.

Dad nodded his head. "This is the very same Jacob-guy," he said. "And this is where the Lord promises him that his people will spread over the whole earth, just like Abraham's seed. So who are his people?"

"The . . . tribes of Israel?" Shauna asked.

"That's right," Dad replied. "So did they spread over the whole earth like Jacob was promised?"

"Most of them are lost, right?" Shauna asked.

"Right," Dad answered. "Roughly speaking, the tribe of Judah and half the tribe of Benjamin stayed pretty near Jerusalem. But the other ten and a half tribes broke away and went north, so now their descendants have been scattered over the earth."

"Daddy-y-y!" Chelsea whined. "You're talking too much! I've been waiting to read my scripture for a really long time!"

"Yeah, Dad!" I joined in, copying Chelsea's whine. "You're talking too much. I've been waiting, too!"

"Okay," Dad laughed at Chelsea. I noticed that he didn't look at or laugh at me—just her. "Shauna's next," he reassured Chelsea, "and I won't talk so much and then it will be your turn. Or do you want to read yours first?"

"I can wait," she answered, "but just don't talk too much on Shauna's turn."

"Okay," he agreed. "I won't talk too much this time. I promise. Go ahead, Shauna."

"I have Psalm 48, verse 2," Shauna said. It reads:

Beautiful for situation, the joy of the whole earth, is mount Zion, on the sides on the north, the city of the great King.

"This is talking about Zion being the city of God," Shauna explained. "And I didn't know what the 'north' part meant until I read the footnote. It says, 'there was in various lands a concept that the dwelling place of Deity was in the north.' So it's just talking about where Zion might be."

"What's Deity?" Meg asked.

"It's another name for God," Mom explained.

"Any other questions?" Dad asked.

"Yeah," I said. "I have a question: How come I never think to look at the footnote? And also, is that cheating or is it another smart thing like Brandon's chapter heading idea?"

"I only read them when it's talking about something I don't understand," Shauna said.

"That doesn't narrow it down too much for me," I laughed. "Especially in the Old Testament."

"Je-e-eff," Chelsea complained, "now *you're* talking too much!"

"Okay," I said quickly. "I'm done."

"Anything else?" Dad asked. "Or is it Chelsea's turn now?"

Chelsea got an excited look on her face and looked quickly at each person before asking, "Can I read mine now?"

"Yep," Shauna answered, pointing to the verse on the page for her. Isaiah 49:12 reads:

Behold, these shall come from far: and, lo, these from the north and from the west; and these from the land of Sinim.

Chelsea had just finished first grade, and she always took her turn during family devotional, so she was a pretty good reader. She only stumbled on the word *Sinim*.

"What's 'Sinim'?" she asked after Shauna helped her to pronounce it.

"I don't know," Dad admitted. "Anybody know what 'Sinim' is?"

"No," we all agreed.

"But I know where to find out," I smiled triumphantly. "And it's not using a cheater chapter heading or footnote. I bet it's in the Bible Dictionary that's really an encyclopedia."

I quickly found the word 'Sinim' and read this:

It is uncertain what country is meant, but it must have been one of the most distant lands known to the writer of the prophecy.

"So it just means a place that's as far away as you can think of," I said. Then I added, "like Russia!"

I tried not to look at Mom as I spoke. No one said anything for a moment, so I added a little, "Hee, hee!" fake laugh just to try to ease the tension a little bit.

"R-right," Dad said. "So this scripture is talking about Israel being gathered from the north and the west and from as far away as you can think of. Jeff, why don't you go ahead and read yours so we can see how similar it is to Chelsea's?"

Jeremiah 3:18 reads:

In those days the house of Judah shall walk with the house of Israel, and they shall come together out of the land of the north to the land that I have given for an inheritance unto your fathers.

"This is also talking about the gathering of Israel," Dad said, "but does anyone notice anything different about it?"

"What does it mean the house of Judah will walk with the house of Israel?" Brandon asked.

"Oh, I think I know," Shauna said. "Doesn't it mean that the Jews and Gentiles will both be covenant people in the last days?"

"Yeah," Dad smiled. "Good job, Shauna!"

"Score!" I called out, raising my hand so Shauna could accept the compliment with a high-five. And then, in my very best narrator voice I said, "May the genes that have made you such an outstanding specimen of scriptural intelligence be shared abundantly among your siblings."

Mom just looked at me like she had no idea *whose* genes were responsible for my apparently warped personality.

"No sharing. I don't want you wearing my jeans!" Shauna punned.

"Ouch!" Brandon responded in a pained voice.

"Check, please!" I said. Lately, that was my favorite response, whenever I felt it was time to be done with the current conversation.

"Woo-hoo, Jeff!" Mom said softly. "Come back! We're still having devotional here!"

"Sorry," I laughed under my breath. Then I quickly added, "I'm back."

"My turn," Brandon said and then he read Jeremiah 4:6:

Set up the standard toward Zion: retire, stay not: for I will bring evil from the north, and a great destruction.

"This is a warning to Jerusalem to be prepared for the destroyer," Dad explained.

"Yeah," Brandon said, "but it says the evil is coming from the north. Is it talking about the lost tribes of Israel?"

"I don't think so," Dad answered. "Remember that Jerusalem was destroyed right after Lehi's family left? They were conquered by the Babylonians, who came through Syria from the north."

"Mine's about the tribes of Israel," Mom said.

"Let's hear it," Dad said.

Mom read Jeremiah 6:22:

Thus saith the Lord, Behold, a people cometh from the north country, and a great nation shall be raised from the sides of the earth.

"So the tribes of Israel will return from the north and build a great nation," Mom said.

"Yeah," Dad agreed, "and my scripture says where they will build it." He read Jeremiah 23:8:

But, The Lord liveth, which brought up and which led the seed of the house of Israel out of the north country, and from all countries whither I had driven them; and they shall dwell in their own land.

"So where will they build their great nation?" Dad asked.

"In Jerusalem," Shauna answered.

"That's right," Dad said. "We learned a lot about 'north,' didn't we? Good choice, Brandon. Any other questions or comments from anyone?"

"How come there aren't any scriptures about 'north' in the Book of Mormon?" I asked.

"There are," Dad answered. "Check the Index." As I turned to the back of my quad, he added, "The Topical Guide doesn't have every scripture listed."

There are several references listed under "North" in the Index to the Book of Mormon. The one I thought fit the best with the other ones was Ether 13:11. The middle part of the verse says:

. . . and they are they who were scattered and gathered in from the four quarters of the earth, and from the north countries . . .

"Thanks, Jeff," Dad said. "Let's have a closing prayer now."

"Mind if I pray with you?" came Tom's voice. I looked up when I heard him and saw that he was standing in the aisle between Dad and Shauna. He was apparently on his way back to his seat.

"That would be great," Dad said, looking up at Tom. Brandon and I pulled our legs out of the aisle and returned to our same praying positions from earlier, kneeling backward in the seat with our elbows on the top of the headrest. I left the aisle seat empty for Tom.

"Thank you for joining with us," Dad smiled at him. "If you don't mind, I would like to offer a prayer to God, our Heavenly Father, in the name of Jesus Christ."

"I am Christian," Tom replied to Dad as he knelt next to me. "And I am honored to be joining with you. Please go ahead."

The way that Dad explained how he was going to pray made me think a little bit. I had never been in a group prayer before where some people belonged to different churches. At least not that I knew of. Since Dad described it the way that he did, I was curious to see how he would pray differently. I think I was a little nervous, too. I'm never quite sure how to act or how to talk about religion when I'm with people who have different religious beliefs than I do.

I listened closely and was prepared to make mental notes, but I was surprised at the end when I realized that Dad hadn't prayed any differently from any other time I'd heard him pray. He addressed the prayer to "Our Father in Heaven" and thanked him for a long list of blessings, including family and friends, the mercy of God, and the things that he mentioned to me earlier that were good about our current situation. Then he asked for a blessing upon the pilot and copilot that they would be inspired and guided to land safely. He closed the prayer in the name of Jesus Christ.

The prayer must have lasted close to five minutes. About three or four minutes into it, I started to think, *C'mon, Dad, we've got a guest—don't blow him away.* When it was finally over, I was both anxious and scared to see how Tom felt about Dad's prayer. I wanted to look at him, but I didn't want him to feel like I was checking him out, so I turned my eyes as hard as I could to the side without moving my head. Since he was right next to me, it was kind of hard to see him at all. Very slowly I began turning my head toward him until I realized that he looked like he was still praying. His head was bowed, and he wasn't moving at all. Nobody said anything for several seconds after Dad finished his prayer.

Finally, Tom lifted his head. Only when it was all the way up did he open his eyes and look at Dad. "Thank you," he said quietly, but with firmness. "I appreciate that fine prayer." And then nodding his head slightly, he added, "And I know the Lord has heard us."

"You are quite welcome," Dad smiled. "Thank you again for joining with us."

"Thank you for allowing me the honor," Tom smiled. "I am truly grateful."

"It was nice to have you, Tom," Mom said. "Or is it Thomas?"

"Either is fine with me," Tom said. "Most people call me 'Tom,' but it is nice to hear my given name once in a while."

"Then 'Thomas' it will be," Mom smiled again. "You have a fine spirit about you. You said that you are Christian?"

"Yes," Tom replied. "I'm on the road most of the time, so I don't really attend church services anywhere, but I enjoy reading from the Bible, and I pray regularly. Some scientists allow their pursuit of science to diminish their faith, but the more I see of the perfect complexities of our earth, the stronger my belief in a Supreme Creator grows."

"I agree," Dad nodded. "In my mind, there's no way all this could just be an accident."

"You have a wonderful family," Tom said. "Looks like the little guy didn't quite have the juice to make it this morning," nodding toward Danny who was still zonked out. His comment about "morning" made me think about the sun, and I noticed it shining through the windows from the rear of the plane. Everyone else continued in conversation for another couple of minutes as I moved to the window and surveyed the earth below.

We were still flying along the coast of something, with a narrow strip of open sea water separating it from the unending snow and ice on the north horizon. It seemed like it was a little harder to see than before. I think it was because we were flying a lot lower than we had been earlier.

"Hey," I called to anyone who might be listening, "it looks like we're getting really close to the ground."

"That's right," said Happy, who was just coming down the aisle from the front of the plane. This was the first time that I thought her name didn't fit. She seemed a little tense and worried. "The pilot has asked me to have each of you return to your seat and fasten your safety belt. He is planning to attempt a landing along the coast."

Attempt? I thought, not daring to say it aloud. "Attempt" wasn't really what I would describe as a confidence-building word at this point. It took everything I had not to blurt out, *If the "attempt" fails, do we get a second shot at it?*

"I thought we were going to keep flying until we found an airport," Brandon said.

"We're almost out of fuel," Happy replied with a sad look, "which means we're almost out of options."

CHAPTER 4

Airplanes Don't Float

"Please put your son in his own seat with a safety belt," Happy said to Dad.

Danny remained asleep as Mom moved over next to the window, and Dad strapped him into the seat between them. Happy was hastily retrieving pillows from the overhead bins for each one of us to keep on our laps. Danny immediately wrapped his arms around his pillow without opening his eyes and snuggled into it comfortably. He smacked his lips a couple of times as though he was having a dream about his favorite dessert.

"When we land," Happy explained, "each of you should lean forward with the pillow held tightly to your face. The pilot will announce over the intercom when we're close to the ground."

Without another word to us, she walked briskly forward, following Tom back to his seat. She gave him a pillow and then disappeared somewhere at the front of the plane.

No one said anything for the next couple of minutes. I watched quietly as the ground came closer and closer. I couldn't imagine how we were ever going to be able to land there. There was no beach to speak of, and there were rocks and rolling hills everywhere.

"Dad," I said quietly, "why don't they try to land over there on the ice cap? It looks really smooth."

"I don't know," Dad said. "I'm sure they have training for situations like this. We can ask him after we land."

45

"Unless none of us . . ." I stopped myself before saying something that would get me into a whole lot of trouble. "Unless none of us . . . *remembers* to ask him because we're all so excited about how well this all turns out," I quickly corrected myself. Dad raised his eyebrows but didn't say anything. Mom just stared at me with a blank expression.

Just then the pilot's voice crackled over the intercom. "Prepare for an immediate landing!" he called. "I repeat! We are landing immediately."

As soon as he finished speaking, the plane felt like it took a nose dive. Meg and Chelsea both screamed. And there was no giggling this time. We were going down so fast that I was having trouble keeping my face down against the pillow.

"Hold on to your pillow!" Mom called.

For the next few seconds, the plane continued to drop quickly and rocked abruptly back and forth. Suddenly, there was a huge thud, and my head and pillow bounced hard against my knees. We seemed to be floating for a couple of seconds when there was another loud thud, and my head bounced into the pillow again. This time we floated for just a second or so before we hit the ground with one more thud and then we finally seemed to stay landed.

The plane was shaking violently, swaying back and forth and bouncing wildly. The engines got really loud, and I felt myself thrown forward against my safety belt, making it really hard to breathe. The top of my head was scrunched against the seat in front of me. Even with all of the bouncing around, I noticed that the plane seemed to be leaning to one side. Suddenly, with one of the big bounces there was a loud cracking sound, and everything leaned even harder toward the side of the plane that had already been lower.

Books and toys and stray pillows started bouncing in my direction from the other side of the plane. I could feel myself being pulled closer and closer to the window. As this was happening,

I noticed that the plane started turning sideways. The plane continued to jolt us around for another few seconds and then finally came to a stop.

No one said a word. Everything seemed amazingly still and quiet after the incredible shaking and pounding that had been all around us moments before. I didn't even dare move for a few seconds. I looked up to see that some of the overhead bins had popped open and there were straps hanging from them that were now swinging slowly back and forth. I could hear the soft sound of water splashing as it lapped gently up against the side of the plane where I was sitting.

Danny was the first to speak. "Mom," he said sincerely, "I don't think I like airplanes anymore." After a pause, he added, "I don't want to do that again."

"I don't want to do that again, either," Mom said. "But planes aren't supposed to do that. This one had something wrong with it."

"Oh," he breathed, "but is the plane okay now?"

"I don't think so," Mom said softly, "but *we're* okay now, and the plane's not going to be moving anymore."

"Good," Danny said quietly, "I don't think this plane should go up in the air anymore."

I looked over at Brandon, who had a wry smile on his face. "I don't think we need to worry about *that*," Brandon said to me.

I looked back at the girls, and each of them had wide eyes and sunken cheeks. Chelsea looked like she was about to cry, but she never got the chance.

"Everyone to the emergency exit!" yelled Happy as she came charging down the aisle toward us. She stopped at a window opposite to where Tom was seated and pushed open the emergency door. "As soon as it inflates," she instructed, "slide down the ramp as fast as possible!"

"We get to go down a slide now," Mom said to Danny, in the

happiest voice I think anyone could have come up with at that moment.

I looked out the window on my side of the plane and could see nothing but water.

"Let's go quickly," Dad said. "Everyone grab your coat and your book bag and get to the door!"

I unfastened my safety belt and leaned against the window to look out. The plane was sitting in clear water at the edge of the ocean. It looked like we were on the edge of a cliff that was just under the water. Past the edge I could see nothing. Wanting to share what I had discovered but afraid of getting into trouble for speaking "inappropriately," I simply said, "Dad, I think we'd better hurry."

I was scared, and I think he saw that in my face as he looked at me. He shot a glance out the window and then back at me before saying, "C'mon, everyone. Let's go as fast as we can. Don't put your coats on—just grab everything and move." He spoke quietly, but his voice was tense.

"I've got Danny's coat and book bag," Brandon called over his shoulder as he hurried toward the exit.

"Give me yours, Meg," I said, following Brandon's idea. "Let's go!"

Shauna helped Chelsea with her bag, and we all ran forward. By the time I got to the door, Brandon was already on his way down the huge, inflatable, yellow slide. Tom and Happy were at the bottom ready to catch him. Grumpy was at the door and helped Meg get into a sitting position. Meg screamed as Grumpy gave her a push that sent her whooshing down the ramp.

"You're next!" Grumpy said to me, grabbing the book bags and tossing them down first. I sat down and pushed off as fast as I could, clutching my coat in my arms. I probably could have enjoyed the ride if I hadn't been so scared. As soon as I reached the bottom, Tom and Happy each took an arm and yanked me to my feet. Our book bags were in a heap on the rocky ground a few feet from the bottom of the slide. Brandon and Meg were standing next to the pile, staring blankly back up the slide.

"Well done," Tom said briskly as I handed Meg her coat.

"Put those coats on," Happy instructed as Tom caught two more book bags and tossed them onto the heap. Tom and Happy then immediately readied themselves to catch Chelsea and Shauna, who were on their way down together. Chelsea was wrapped in Shauna's arms. Next came Mom, followed by Mom's and Dad's bags. Then came Dad with Danny.

"Normally we wouldn't let anyone bring their carry-on bags from the plane," said Happy, glancing back and forth at our surroundings, "but considering the situation, I'm glad you brought them."

As I looked back up at Grumpy at the top of the slide, I heard Brandon say from behind me, "I think the plane is moving."

This was the first time that I had thought about where the plane was perched since getting out of it. And Brandon was right—the rear of the plane was starting to slide toward the water.

"Hurry!" Tom yelled. "It's going into the water!"

With that, Grumpy launched herself from the plane and landed about ten feet down the slide. She was soon followed by the copilot. The plane continued to slide slowly into the water and there began to be a loud scraping sound of metal against rock. No one else stood at the top of the slide.

"Where's the pilot?!" asked Tom tensely. Then, looking around he asked, "Is anyone missing other than the pilot?"

Happy and Grumpy turned quickly to Mom and Dad. "Our family's all here!" they said.

"We're all here, but the pilot!" Tom said.

"Where did he go?" Happy asked Grumpy.

"He said he'd be right back!" Grumpy replied, shaking her head.

The plane began moving faster, and the tail started to go under water. Just then the pilot appeared at the doorway with an armload of blankets.

"Jump, Neil!" yelled the copilot.

"Get ready to pull the release!" the pilot called back as he jumped onto the slide, clutching the blankets. The copilot grabbed onto a red strap that ran along the side of the slide from the bottom all the way to the top. By the time the pilot reached the bottom, the slide was almost level because the plane was going under fast.

"Pull!" he yelled. The copilot yanked on the strap as hard as he could, and the top of the slide pulled away from the plane.

We all watched in silence as the plane continued to sink into the water and finally disappeared from view in the early morning sun. There was a huge splash that jostled around the end of the slide that was in the water. The pilot remained seated on the slide, twisting his body around to look at where the plane no longer was. His face was red, making his hair look even whiter. The copilot still held the release strap tightly in both hands and stared at the water with obvious shock on his face. Bubbles continued to rise almost silently from the sunken airplane. The only noticeable sound was the panting of the pilot and the pounding of my heart. We all continued to stare at the water for several moments.

Again, Danny, was the first to speak. "What are we doing?" Danny asked. Several of us turned to look at him, trying to decide how to answer his question.

"We're *celebrating!*" yelled Grumpy suddenly. "You *did* it!" she said emphatically, reaching for the pilot and gripping his shoulders. "Nobody could have landed that plane like you did! You're amazing! You saved us all!"

The pilot just stared blankly back at her and blinked several times. "But we've lost the plane," he said finally.

"Who cares?" Grumpy laughed. "That was a lousy plane anyway!"

"She's right!" Happy agreed. "That *was* a lousy plane! And you did save us. We're all safe because of *you*," she smiled. "You were great! Thank you."

Then we all got into the act. Everyone was congratulating everyone else about the whole thing. It turns out that every one of us was either brave or a hero or some other fantastic thing we had never imagined before. That's when I heard a sound that I had never heard before and can never adequately describe, no matter how hard I try. Happy was the one who made the sound. It was an amazing combination of a cheer and a whoop and a ten-second-long yodel all rolled into one. She completed her yell by charging straight at the copilot and grabbing him around the neck with enough force to throw him over backward onto the slide while she landed next to him, at which point she planted the biggest kiss I have ever witnessed in real life—right on his mouth.

After a few seconds of them kissing and us all watching in either horror or complete disbelief, she turned to the pilot and said, "And my husband thanks you also!"

"Yes, I do!" said the copilot. "I especially thank you for not letting her ever do *that* to me in your presence before."

"You're married?!" I asked with astonishment.

"I should hope so!" Brandon responded.

"Now you know why we keep him locked in the cockpit," the pilot said.

"And now you know why she's always so happy after she's been to the front of the plane," Grumpy laughed. Everyone else laughed, too. Everyone, that is, except Danny.

"*Now* what are we doing?" he asked as the laughter died down.

"Now," said the pilot soberly, standing for the first time since his frantic ride down the slide, "we need to assess our situation here and get ourselves a plan."

The way he said it made a chill go up my spine. I caught myself zipping my coat up the rest of the way without really even thinking about it. It was the first time I'd really noticed what the weather was like. The air was still, but cold. The sky was clear. The sun was bright, but still low on the horizon. My nose felt cold as I sniffed.

"I'll try to be as delicate as possible," the pilot continued, "because we have children here." He nodded with a slight glance toward our family. "Honestly, I believe we will be fine. But it may be a while before we are found, because we have no way of contacting anyone. We have to assume that we are some distance from any major civilization. The plane has an emergency satellite-linked beacon, but it is impossible to tell how well it is working from its present location." He glanced toward the ocean as he made that last statement.

"Hopefully," he said, "the beacon was broadcasting correctly once we escaped the volcanic cloud, and though it may not be working now, the authorities should have a good indication of where we are. It is quite possible that we could see a rescue plane flying overhead in just a short time."

"But we should prepare for an alternate situation," Tom cautioned.

"Precisely," agreed the pilot. "Therefore, I suggest that we take an immediate inventory of our supplies and determine what needs we may have in the way of food and shelter." After a short sigh, he smiled and said, "By the way, my name is Neil, and I would be happy to have each of you call me by that name." Turning to Danny and leaning over with his hands on his knees, he added, "Even you, son."

"My name is Danny," he said.

"Hi, Danny," he said. "It is very nice to meet you."

"Hi, Mr. Neil," said Danny, at which we all laughed a little.

"Just call me 'Neil,'" he chuckled.

"Okay," Danny said. After he said it, he just sort of stared at Neil for a minute like he was trying to figure something out. His lips were squished together, his mouth was stretched from side to side, and the corners of his mouth were sunken into his chubby cheeks.

Then, without warning, he said, "Neil, did you know that airplanes don't float?"

Everyone laughed and then Neil said, "I had *heard* that, but until today I really didn't know for sure."

"I think they should make airplanes float," Danny said sincerely.

"I agree," answered Neil. "When we get back I'll tell them. Okay?"

"Okay," Danny agreed.

"And what is your name, young lady?" he asked Chelsea, who was next to Danny. She backed herself against Shauna's legs.

"I'm Chelsea," she said shyly, shrugging her shoulders and dropping her chin, so she had to strain her eyes upward to look at him.

"It's nice to meet you, also," Neil said.

He paused there, smiling at Chelsea just long enough to give her the courage to ask, "Why did you want to save the big, yellow slide?" Before he could respond, she added, "I think it would have been better for you to save the airplane!"

"You're right," Neil smiled, nodding his head. "It would have been better to save the airplane, but just *look* what I can do."

With that, he went to the slide, grabbed the red strap about in the middle, tilted the whole thing on its side, and then lifted it over his head. It was a struggle for him, but he managed to balance it for a second or two before it fell to one side, and he let go.

"I couldn't do that with the whole airplane!" he panted as he came back to where Chelsea was standing, now with her chin up and mouth open.

"Who-o-oa!" Danny giggled. "Neil is strong, huh, Jeff?"

I just smiled at him and nodded, avoiding the urge to ask him why he was asking me and not any of the other people standing around.

"That slide," explained Neil, "can now be used as a raft or a boat!"

"Oh!" Chelsea smiled. Still looking up at Neil, Chelsea reached backwards and tapped Shauna's leg several times. "Her name is Shauna," Chelsea said, as she tapped.

Neil looked at Shauna and asked, "You're Shauna?"

"Yes, sir," she smiled.

"Call me Neil. It's nice to meet you."

"It's nice to meet you, too, Neil."

Neil continued in the same way with each member of the group and soon everyone else was doing the same. It started to sound like a big party with everyone talking at the same time and practicing each other's names. It turns out that Happy's name was really Nancy, and Jo was the one I'd been calling Grumpy. I was glad to learn her real name, because the other one just didn't seem to fit anymore. The copilot's name was John, and he really was Nancy's husband. As the introductions were dying down, I found myself watching him for a minute or two.

John had the most interesting gum-chewing technique I had ever seen in my life. I found myself almost mesmerized by the rhythmic motion his chin made approximately every two and a half seconds. He would be perfectly still and then suddenly his chin would move quickly down to one side at an angle and then it would make a large, sweeping, circular motion from there back up around to the other side. The amazing part was that his chin seemed to drop about two inches in the process, but his lips never separated. It was fascinating, and I must have watched him for about two minutes before I realized I was staring.

Once introductions were complete and all the adults had had enough of practicing all the kids' names in our family, then we took "inventory." Luckily, everyone had a coat. I remembered to thank Dad for that one. Other than our family's carry-on bags (which contained nothing much, other than books and toys), all we had was the stack of blankets that "Mr. Neil" had grabbed at the last moment and a box full of emergency meals that Jo brought with her. They figured we had enough food for at least two days.

"I'm a little hungry now," I said.

"The word *food* may be a bit of a stretch," Jo admitted. "I know you've all heard people complain about airplane food, but that's just because they've never had *emergency* airplane food. This stuff . . . ," she paused for a moment as she tried to think about the best way to say it, "is like petrified granola bars. You'll have to be a lot more than just 'a little hungry' in order to be able to stomach one of these."

No one had a response for that. I wondered if what she said was true or if it was just her way of making the meals last longer by destroying everyone's appetite.

"Next," announced Neil, pointing to an area between two large hills that were nearby, "I suggest we set up a temporary shelter just inside that crevice over there. We can use the slide to protect us from the sun and any rain for as long as we're here."

I looked in the direction Neil had indicated and for the first time noticed something other than the ocean and its rocky shore. I slowly scanned the area as Neil spoke. The landscape was an eerie combination of soft, rolling hills and jutting, ragged rocks. In the distance I could see a huge mountain, which looked rocky and rough, much of it covered in snow. The area between the base of the mountains and the rocky shore where we stood was covered with mile after mile of rolling hills. The hills were covered with short, mossy grass and tiny white and purple flowers that didn't look like any I'd ever seen before. Tom saw me looking at the surrounding area and said to me, "This kind of landscape is called tundra. It's beautiful in its own way, don't you think?"

I didn't want to disagree with him, but it didn't look at all beautiful to me, so I didn't say anything.

One of the hills close to us had a rocky opening in it which created a tall, narrow passageway leading into darkness. I was surprised that there wasn't more snow everywhere else: this was not how I had imagined the shore of the Arctic Ocean. The place looked pretty harsh and barren.

Tom volunteered to make the shelter, and Brandon and I were assigned to help. Others were gathering loose rocks in an attempt to make a large "SOS" sign on the shore, which could easily be spotted by a rescue plane. As Tom headed toward the hill, I looked at the dark opening and asked if anyone might have a flashlight. No one did.

"Is this really the Arctic Ocean?" Brandon asked Tom as we walked. "Shouldn't everything be covered with snow?"

"This is quite typical for this time of year," Tom assured him. "Remember that the sun never goes down and depending on how far north we are, it could be that way for weeks. It's still very cold now, but that's because it's still very early in the morning. By mid-day, it could be warm enough that you may not even need much more than a light jacket. Snow melts quickly in temperatures like that."

"I had no clue," Brandon said. "I thought the entire Arctic Ocean was completely covered with ice all the time. At least until Dad said something different when we were on the plane."

"Yeah," Tom smiled. "A lot of people think that. But notice how short all the undergrowth is. This ground is buried in snow for probably eight or nine months out of the year. Anything that grows has to do it quickly. That's why those flowers are so small. They grow and bloom as fast as possible, because the season is so short."

"Is that why there are no trees or bushes?" I asked.

"Yes," Tom nodded.

As we neared the opening, I felt myself getting a little nervous. I realized that I was not the least bit interested in being one of the first to go into this cave in the middle of nowhere. "What kind of animals live around here?" I asked, slowing my pace a little.

Tom stopped and thoughtfully answered, "Well, in those mountains, I imagine that moose and some types of deer are pretty common, and uh . . . maybe musk ox—unless they only live in North America—I'm not sure about that. And a couple of types of bear—like polar bear. As for smaller animals—"

"What's a musk ox?" Brandon interrupted.

"Forget that!" I exclaimed. "What about the bears? And before we get any closer, doesn't that cave look like a *perfect* home for one?"

Tom looked at me with a half smile. "I wouldn't worry too much about it," he said. I wanted to ask what could *possess* him to say something so *ridiculous*, but I was still way too shocked to speak, and I didn't get the chance before he answered Brandon's question.

"A musk ox is a small ox with large horns and long, thick fur," Tom explained. "They look prehistoric. It would be fun to see one."

With that, he disappeared into the crevice. Brandon and I just stared at each other.

"Do you wanna go in?" Brandon asked.

"Are you *nuts?*" I retorted.

"What could happen?" Brandon said and followed Tom into the darkness.

I could think of about fourteen things right off the top of my head that could happen, all involving fear, pain, and large animals with either claws or horns. Within a few seconds, Tom and Brandon returned to where I stood.

"That should work," Tom said. "It looks like the opening goes all the way up, but we should be able to wedge the raft between the walls above our heads to keep rain off."

"Did you find anything alive in there?" I asked. "Did you go all the way to the back?"

"Guys, be quiet!" Tom whispered unexpectedly. He was staring past us, up the slope. I turned quickly, afraid of what I would find. Just a few yards away was a large, light-brown animal moving slowly with its nose to the ground. We all stared in silence. The animal looked sort of like a deer or elk, but its head was quite a bit bigger, shaped more like the head of a horse. It wasn't like anything I'd ever seen before. It seemed oblivious to us and to the noise down at the shore being made by everyone else.

"Ever seen a real reindeer before?" Tom asked so quietly that I almost couldn't make it out.

"A reindeer?" I mouthed, afraid to make any noise. Tom nodded and smiled.

"Yeah," Tom whispered. "They're common both in Alaska and in northeast Asia."

We continued to watch for a couple of minutes. Finally the reindeer lifted its head, sniffed the air, and moved quickly and quietly out of sight around the side of the hill.

"Guys, guess what we saw?" I called as we ran back to where the rest of the group was.

"A reindeer!" Brandon said, before anyone else had a chance to answer.

Everyone thought it was pretty cool, but Danny was by far the most intrigued. He had the most excited look on his face that I had seen since he found out that we were going on an airplane.

"A reindeer?" he asked with twinkling eyes. His mouth continued to slowly open wider and wider after he spoke. "One of Santa's reindeers?" he asked. Then, almost too afraid to hope, he asked quietly, "Is Santa here, too?" His eyes darted about as he waited for an answer.

Everyone tried not to laugh. "I don't know," I said. "He might be—but we didn't see him. We only saw the reindeer."

Danny stared into the hills for a moment before asking, "Can I see Santa's reindeer?"

"He's already gone," Tom answered, joining us, "but the next time we see one, we'll be sure to come get you so you can see it."

"What's that?" Chelsea asked, pointing toward the hills. We all turned to see what she was pointing at. Walking slowly along the edge of a hill, biting at the ground was a reindeer. I couldn't tell if it was the same one or not.

"There's your reindeer," Tom smiled, stooping down between Danny and Chelsea. "I guess he came back just so that you could see him."

We all watched for a moment until suddenly the animal stopped short and lifted its head. It was perfectly still for several seconds and then bolted straight toward us without warning. Tom quickly stood and waved his arms, causing the reindeer to turn sharply and scamper down the shoreline for quite a distance before it again turned abruptly and disappeared behind a hill.

"Why did he go?" Danny asked.

"Something must have scared it," Dad answered.

And just then we saw what it was.

Moving slowly over the top of a small hill came ten or twelve men. They stopped at the top, standing in a single line facing us. They were close enough that I could have thrown a rock and easily hit them, if I dared. They looked like warriors from another time, several of them holding spears in an upright position. They were dressed in long, heavy robes that hung past their knees. They had leather shoes or boots that came up past their ankles. Most of them had hats that looked like small, thick towels wrapped around their heads. Many of them had bushy beards. Their faces were hard and stern.

"Hello!" called Neil, taking a couple of short steps forward. He stopped short as his greeting hung in the air for several seconds. "We need help!" he called out, again waiting for any sign from the men in front of him. The only movement I could detect from either group was John's slow, rhythmic chewing. Everyone else was frozen. I felt my throat get tight as the tension grew.

CHAPTER 5

The Salt of the Earth

After at least thirty seconds of silence, I was half expecting Danny to ask again what we were doing. But the silence was broken by a short yell, which came from down the shore. Everyone in our group looked to see who had made the noise. There was a lone man, some distance away. It looked like he was dressed as the others, but with the sun behind him, it was difficult to make out much detail. I looked back at the other men. They continued to stare at us without moving or without looking toward the man on the shore.

The man yelled something again. This time it was not just a single sound as was the first noise he made, but it sounded much more like several words or a sentence—but it made no sense to me. I had the distinct impression that no one else understood him, either. No one, that is, in our group. But the men on the hill seemed to understand and responded by moving toward us. As they came closer, their spears began to drop until they pointed straight at us. Within half a minute, they had surrounded us in a large half circle. I noticed that a few of them looked like they were still in their teens, but their shoulders were broad and their hands were wide and rough.

One of the men yelled something strange at us and thrust his spear in the direction of the other man. They were close enough now that I could easily see how sharp that spear was. Two or three others with spears started doing the same thing and making similar sounds that none of us could understand.

"I think they want us to move," whispered Tom.

"I think you may be right," replied Neil, who was backing up to be closer to the rest of us. Then he pointed to himself and thrust his hands toward the man who had first yelled. "You want us to move?" he asked, repeating the motion.

The spears were again thrust in the direction of the other warrior.

"Let's move slowly," Dad suggested, reaching down to pick up Danny and beginning to move down the shore toward the other man.

I scooped up my book bag as we started to move, but John quickly suggested, "I think it would probably be better to just leave that here. We don't want them to think that we have weapons."

"Good idea," replied Neil as he began following Dad. "Perhaps we should just leave everything here for now. We do not want to create a situation for ourselves."

"But what if we don't get another chance?" I asked quietly but intently. "I think we already have ourselves a situation." I looked around for a moment until it was obvious that no one planned to respond.

I dropped the bag to the ground, and several others put down whatever they were carrying or working on, and we all moved slowly toward the man who stood motionless with the sun behind him. This seemed to be what the warriors wanted because they quit making noise and just followed behind us with their spears pointed at our backs. Everyone stayed pretty well bunched together. Neil took the lead. I wasn't sure if that was because he wanted to be the leader or if he just wanted to be as far away as possible from the guys with the spears.

Within a minute or two, we had almost reached the man who was by himself. "He must be the leader," whispered John, between chin rhythms. I looked at the man and decided John must be right; everything about the way this man stood and acted said that he was in charge, and he wanted everyone to know it. As we got nearer to him, he yelled something else that we obviously didn't understand.

"Watch it!" I heard John call from behind. I turned to see him stumble after being pushed with the handle of the spear by one of the men who was following us.

"Maybe we should move a little faster," suggested Tom.

The leader then yelled something else and scowled at us as we drew near, thrusting his hands further down the shore. I wondered how long he was going to keep yelling words at us that we obviously didn't understand. I thought, *I should have saved the name Grumpy for this guy—or maybe Dopey.*

"Keep moving," Neil whispered. "And perhaps we should try to pick up the pace a bit."

Walking past the leader, I was able to get my first good look at one of these guys. He had a thick bushy beard like many of the others. His robe and hat looked like they were woven from a thick, uneven wool. He had a worn, leather belt tied at his waist. He was husky and strong, and his skin looked leathery and rough.

We walked along the shore for close to ten minutes, before anyone else from either group said anything. I was shocked that neither Chelsea nor Danny was asking questions about what was going on. I decided they were probably too scared—just like the rest of us. I began to worry about how far the men were planning on taking us, thinking we should have just grabbed our food and other stuff and taken our chances. These guys probably would have made it very clear if they didn't want us to bring anything. Their gestures had seemed to make all their other demands clear enough so far.

Suddenly, the leader came rushing past us. He had disappeared behind his men after we passed his position, and I had been wondering if he was still standing back there somewhere. He dropped to the ground in front of us and began yelling again. This time he seemed furious. He scooped up some sand and brought it over and thrust it at Neil. I guess he had decided that Neil must be the leader of our group because he was the only one who had tried to approach them so far. I was a little surprised to see sand, because so far every-thing along the shore had been pretty much solid rock.

"What is it?" Neil asked. "What's wrong?"

The leader yelled again, shaking the fistful of sand in his face and pointing with the other hand into the sky. Then he opened his hand, holding it up close to his own nose and took a deep sniff. Immediately he grimaced and jerked his hand away from his face, thrusting it at Neil again. This time Neil got the idea and leaned forward to smell the sand. Neil let out a quick cough and pulled his face away. The leader yelled again, shaking the fistful of sand one more time.

"What's going on?" asked John.

"I think I might know," answered Neil, moving forward and stooping down. He scooped up a handful of sand and carefully smelled it two or three times. Then he took a pinch of it with his other hand and placed it on his tongue.

"Salt," Neil said, without standing or turning to look at us. Then he stretched his hand out, waving it back and forth over the sand. "This is a salt deposit."

"So what's the problem?" asked Dad.

"The problem is," Neil replied, "the salt that this guy has in his hand smells like jet fuel."

"Oh, no!" breathed John.

With that, Neil took a couple of steps further away, scooped up another handful and brought it to his nose. He didn't even look like he sniffed before coughing and quickly dropping it to the ground again.

"I'm afraid that we have contaminated the salt," said Neil with a nauseated look on his face. I wasn't sure if his look was due to the smell of the jet fuel or simply from the thought of what had happened.

"But our plane cra—I mean—landed—way back there," I grunted. "How could jet fuel get from there to here? The water hasn't even been up here. It's dry."

"I'm sorry to say," admitted Neil, "that we made a fuel dump just before landing. It's standard procedure in an emergency, to reduce the risk of fire."

"I thought we were almost *out* of fuel," Brandon said.

"Yeah, me, too," I agreed.

"We were," said Neil, "but you must remember that 'almost' is a relative expression in a case like this."

"What does 'relative' mean?" I asked warily.

"It means," said Dad, "that compared to how much the plane can hold, there wasn't very much left."

"We probably dumped a couple hundred gallons of fuel," explained Neil. "And, unfortunately, it looks as though it must have landed right on this small salt deposit." He closed his eyes and let out an exasperated sigh. "So we have ourselves a problem," he concluded.

"It looks to me like these poor people are the ones with the problem," said Jo. "Can you imagine how valuable this salt must be to them? It's got to be irreplaceable for preserving food and cooking and who knows what else."

We all just stared at each other for a moment, each summing up the situation in his own way. Finally, Neil turned to the leader, with an expression on his face that was now sad and sorrowful. Before he had looked stern and determined.

"I am so sorry for your loss," Neil said. With that, he bowed his head and held his open hands out toward the leader. "I am so sorry," he said again.

I watched nervously to see what the warrior's reaction would be.

He just stared sternly at Neil for several moments, I guess trying to figure out what he meant.

"I am *so* sorry," Neil repeated. "Please forgive us."

The leader's expression didn't change for a few seconds before he finally let out a yell and acted like he was about to slap Neil across the face with the back of his hand. Several people from our group gasped as he swung—I think all of them were female. But the hand didn't touch Neil, and Neil didn't move from his bowing position. The leader yelled at Neil a couple more times, but Neil never moved. Finally, the leader yelled something at his men, and they started pushing us to move again. This time they moved us farther away from the shore along the edge of the salt deposit, toward the hills.

For the first time, I noticed several long, triangular wooden racks about halfway between the salt and the edge of the hills. The racks were made of tree branches and logs and were covered with what looked like long strips of meat in various sizes and shapes.

"What's that?" Meg asked quietly.

"It looks like they're drying food in the sun," Dad whispered back.

"That's food?" Meg asked, making a face.

"Yes," Dad answered. "It looks like strips of meat and fish."

We continued to walk in silence past the long racks. Once Dad explained what it was, I could tell that the meat hanging on the different racks was in various stages of drying. I was amazed at how much meat there was. It looked like more than this group could possibly eat in a year.

Not far from the drying racks, we came to a small camp between two low hills. There were probably about twenty tents that looked sort of like the tepees you see in old American Indian movies. There were poles leaning together with animal skins wrapped around them. Each tent only had five or six poles, and the skins were covered with short, dark fur.

We were all forced to sit together on the ground not far from the group of tents. Four of the men stood in a circle around us, each about ten or fifteen feet away. They were each looking us over one by one. I figured they must have been assigned to guard us, because they each had a spear that they pointed directly at us. I had no idea what they were thinking because their expressions never changed.

"What are they going to do with us?" Meg asked Dad.

"I don't know," he admitted. "But we've made them very angry because we ruined their salt. We'll just have to wait and see."

"Are they going to hurt us?" she asked.

"I don't think so," Dad reassured her.

"But we have ourselves a hidden card up the proverbial sleeve," interjected Neil with a confident nod.

"Huh?" Meg grunted, with one side of her nose wrinkled up. She looked back and forth between Dad and Neil several times.

"He means that we have a surprise that they don't know about," Dad explained.

"What is it?" Meg asked with excitement.

"Yeah, *what?*" asked John with disbelief. He looked like he couldn't imagine how we could possibly have a surprise for anybody in a situation like this. He even stopped chewing his gum as he stared at Neil.

"The rescue plane," smiled Neil. "These men and their work are all sitting in plain sight. When that plane comes looking for us they may not see *us* right away, but they'll know someone is here." He plastered that same smug look on his face that he had shown when he was first telling me about the vital communication between the plane and the tower. I was sure there was no photographer this time.

I noticed other groups of men were also glancing in our direction as they went about their work at the drying racks. The men had large knives they were using to cut long strips of meat from a large, dead animal of some kind.

"What is that thing they're cutting up?" Brandon asked.

"I have no idea," Dad admitted. "It looks like a huge fish of some kind, but I'm no expert on marine life."

"I believe it's a narwhal," Tom offered.

"What's that?" I asked.

"It's a small whale, indigenous to the Arctic Ocean," Tom explained.

"A *whale?*" I asked in astonishment. "How did they catch it? How did they get it up here? That thing's huge!"

"I don't know how they caught it," Tom admitted. "If it was wounded or sick it probably was staying close to shore where the ocean wouldn't be as rough. And you know that whales breathe air, so it would stay close to the surface."

"Whales breathe air, like us?" Chelsea asked.

"Yep," Tom nodded, "through a hole in the top of its head. Cool, huh?"

Chelsea's mouth was open, and her eyes were wide as her head bobbed slowly up and down.

"But as for how they got it up here, I couldn't say," Tom continued, turning back to me. "It looks like it was dragged, because you can see the trail. It's hard to tell from here, but it also looks like there are lots of footprints along the trail where it was dragged. But it's over ten feet long and must weigh several thousand pounds. I can't imagine these guys being strong enough to drag it even a few inches, let alone a couple hundred feet."

We all watched in silence for a couple of minutes as the men continued to cut strips of meat from the narwhal and place them in a growing pile next to them. Soon a couple of other men came and each removed a strip of meat from the pile. There were several large leather-looking bags on the ground. The new men reached into one of the bags and pulled out a handful of something that they began rubbing into the strips of meat they had just pulled from the pile.

"What are they doing?" Brandon asked without taking his eyes away from the workers.

"I can't be sure," Tom answered, "but I would say they are probably rubbing salt into the meat."

"Why?" asked Meg.

"As a preservative," replied Tom. "It makes it so they can keep the meat for months without refrigeration. Drying also preserves the meat. It will be interesting to see if they do both to all of it or if they only use the salt for some of it."

"Of *course*," Jo breathed. "*That's* why they're here, and *that's* why they're so upset about us contaminating it. Those bags are probably all full of salt."

"What do you mean by 'that's why they're here'?" John asked.

"I'm sure the main reason they come here is because of the salt deposit," Jo explained.

"Come here from where?" John asked again.

"You don't think they live right here, do you?" Jo asked. "Look at those huts," she said, gesturing toward the tepees. "Those aren't permanent. And did you notice that there are *no* women or children? These men *obviously* don't live here. They're probably just here on an expedition. They collect bags of salt to take back to use at home. And as long as they are here, they also gather some meat and rub salt into it and dry some or all of it."

"But there are more people here than we've seen," said Tom.

"What makes you say that?" asked Dad.

"Because we've only seen about twelve men, but there are at least twenty shelters up there," Tom explained.

"Oh, you're right," Jo agreed.

"So maybe the women and children are off somewhere else," I suggested.

"I don't think so," Tom said. "Not all the meat on those racks came from marine mammals. And the skins on those huts definitely came from land animals. I would guess that the rest of the group is doing some hunting and will return soon to add more meat to the drying racks."

The thought of having even more of these strange foreigners around didn't excite me too much. I looked around and saw several of the adults looking kind of nervous also. Then I realized that we were the ones who were the strange foreigners. This was *their* land, not ours. And we had made a mess of it.

I continued to look around, investigating our surroundings. There were several campfire pits with piles of charred wood and ashes in the center and various bundles covered in animal skins stacked nearby. Near each campfire there was also one or more small bird cages made of small sticks or tree branches. The birds regularly flapped their wings and rustled about, occasionally making different kinds of chirping sounds. The birds were of various sizes and colors; their bodies were mostly either black or a mixture of white and brown. The black birds had white and yellow areas around their eyes and the back of their heads. The white and brown birds had red tufts above their eyes. I saw no other live animals.

"Uh-oh," said Neil without warning. "We've got ourselves a situation here now."

I looked to see what he was referring to. Five of the men were coming up from the shore where we had originally been, and they appeared to be carrying most of our "inventory." One of them was dragging the big, yellow raft behind him, while the others carried our family's book bags, the blankets, and the emergency meals. It was sort of funny to see how they carried everything. The guy with the box of meals had it perched on top of his head with his hands balancing it in front and back. It seemed to me like he would have an easier time seeing where he was going if he would have put his hands on the sides, instead of having one arm right in front of his face.

Two of the men had our book bags looped over their heads and arms like sashes or military belts with two each hanging in front and back. They held their arms out from their bodies like they were afraid to let them touch the bags. The last guy had all the blankets, but instead of leaving them folded in a stack, he had them all draped over his shoulders in a pile so high that you almost couldn't even see his head. I snickered under my breath.

"Look at how they're carrying our stuff," Brandon laughed quickly.

I heard a couple of other people chuckle a little as well.

"Makes you wonder why they're bringing it over here, doesn't it?" John asked soberly.

The laughter was short-lived. We all watched in silence as the leader joined the men approaching the drying racks. Together they went through everything, item by item. It took them a while to figure out how to get into the box of meals and actually open one. The leader managed to figure out that it must be food and tried putting a piece of something in his mouth. Almost immediately he spit it out again and rubbed his open mouth and tongue against his sleeve.

It took them even longer to figure out how to open the zippers on our book bags. They got into Danny's first, probably because there were toys and stuffed animals hanging out from every pocket and none of the zippers was completely closed. Once they knew how the zippers worked, they each started opening different bags. The leader had mine. He reached in slowly and started to pull something out. Even from where we were sitting, I could tell that he had my quad in his hands. He placed his hands on the front and back of the book, opening it like he was ripping something in half. He stared at the open book for several seconds without moving. Then, suddenly, he let out a yell like he had done earlier when he was trying to get Neil to smell the salt. He quickly pushed the scriptures back into my bag and made everyone else drop what they were holding and move away from our pile of stuff. Then he came storming in our direction. He continued to yell directly at us as he approached. His fists were clenched at his sides.

"What did he find?" Tom asked.

"It was just my scriptures," I whispered. I didn't realize how scared I felt until I heard it in my own voice.

CHAPTER 6

The Gift of Tongues

The leader continued yelling as he stomped toward us. When he was only about thirty feet away, there was a loud, short shout that came from the hills and made him stop short. He looked angrily in the direction of the yell. We all looked, too, and saw a group of men and older teenage boys approaching. There were about fifteen of them, and they looked and were dressed just like the ones who had originally found us. The leader and the man who had apparently yelled from the hill were exchanging comments as the new group approached. It was strange to watch because the leader would say something in obvious anger, but the other man would reply each time in a much softer, gentler manner. He seemed quite unconcerned with whatever the leader was yelling about. The new man had a thick, bushy beard much like the leader, but his beard was completely white and hung to his chest.

"Santa *is* here!" Danny breathed in amazement.

"If that's Santa," Chelsea challenged, "then where is his red suit?"

"He only wears it at Christmastime," explained Danny, not taking his eyes off the man.

"If that's Santa," Brandon whispered out the side of his mouth, "then this other guy has *got* to be *Scrooge!*"

I thought it was funny, but I didn't dare laugh—or even move, for that matter. We all watched as "Santa" and "Scrooge" continued their strange argument. After a couple of minutes, Scrooge trudged quickly to where our book bags were, yelling the entire way, and showed my quad to Santa, thrusting it into his hands. Santa's replies continued to be soft and apparently unconcerned.

As this was going on, the older men from Santa's group made their way to others who had been with us all along and began having quiet conversations while looking and gesturing in our direction. The new group had several reindeer with them, all harnessed together with leather straps and dragging a large bundle of something behind them. *Maybe this guy is Santa after all,* I thought. In any case, I now knew how they had dragged that narwhal from the shore to the drying racks. The younger boys stayed with the reindeer, patiently watching everything else taking place.

I noticed a couple of men from the new group move toward the salt deposit and reach down to scoop up some salt. They were apparently at a place where the surface of the salt had formed a crust because one of the men used what looked like a small ax to strike the ground a couple of times. Then he reached down, picked up some of what he had broken loose, and carefully raised it to his nose. After a moment he held it out for the other man to smell. Neither of them acted like there was anything wrong with it.

With the ax still in one hand, the man then took the chunk of salt he had broken loose over to where Santa and Scrooge were still arguing. He said something to the men and held it up for them to examine, but Scrooge immediately knocked the salt from his hand to the ground and stepped on it. The other two seemed completely shocked by his reaction. But before either of them said or did anything else, Scrooge grabbed the ax from the man and threw it high over his shoulder. I saw what was coming as soon as he let go; the ax was headed straight for the big, yellow raft. I heard a couple of gasps, signaling that others were thinking the same thing that I was.

Our fears were immediately confirmed by a soft pop, followed by a hissing sound that faded quickly as the raft began to shrivel.

The three men turned to watch the raft deflate for ten or fifteen seconds until it stopped moving. It looked as though it lost about half its size.

"Oh, great," whispered John. "So much for that."

Santa walked over to the raft and stepped on part of it that still had quite a bit of air in it. That part of the raft instantly flattened to the ground. He and Scrooge exchanged a few more words, but Scrooge was less agitated and more quiet now. Then Santa walked over to the salt deposit and stooped down to examine it. He brought several samples from various places up to his nose; it was obvious when he found some that had been drenched with jet fuel. We continued to watch quietly as he walked in our direction. All of his people stopped what they were doing and watched also. When he was almost to one of the guards, Scrooge yelled something at him. Santa didn't turn to look at him but acknowledged him by simply raising his hand about waist high and holding it there until he reached the guard.

Santa said something gently to the guard while at the same time pushing the point of his spear downward until it touched the ground. The guard responded by looking over at Scrooge as if to ask for a second opinion. Scrooge didn't say or do anything. The guard turned back to Santa, and their eyes met for a few seconds before Santa moved quietly to another guard. Again he spoke something quietly while pushing his spear downward. The third and fourth guards had already dropped the tips of their spears to the ground when Santa reached them, so he just spoke to each of them for a moment.

"I wonder if this means we can stand up and move around now," Neil said, as he immediately began to test his theory. But as soon as he started to stand, Scrooge let out his loudest bellow yet, and two of the guards immediately raised their spears and took a step forward. Neil immediately dropped back to the ground. Raising his hands toward them, he said, "Sorry! I see we still have ourselves the same situation. My mistake." The two guards slowly lowered their spears again.

Once we were apparently taken care of, everyone except for the guards seemed to be busy with something or another, and the younger boys led the harnessed reindeer down to the drying racks. At this point, I was able to get a much better look at what they were dragging. It looked like a huge, fat ski or sled made from about a dozen long poles. The skinny ends of the poles were strapped together at the front, pointing slightly upward. The cargo was covered by a heavy animal skin that looked like it had thick, two-foot-long dreadlocks hanging all over it. As I watched, the animal skin was removed and closely examined by a couple of the men for a few moments before several others joined them, and they began looking at what had been uncovered.

"It looks like they've killed a musk ox," Tom said. "At least that's what the hide looks like. So I guess they do live around here—wherever we are."

The hide had been covering a pile of fresh meat, which the men began to systematically cut into thin strips with apparently very sharp knives. As had been done with the narwhal, these strips of meat were rubbed vigorously with salt and placed on the drying racks. As the men continued their work, the younger boys took the harnesses off the reindeer and led the animals to a place down the slope from the tents. I couldn't tell if they were tied up, or if they had just been left to roam and graze from the tundra grass.

After quite a while, one of the men, apparently under instruction from Santa, approached us with what turned out to be lunch. We were given a kind of bread that looked something like small, flat pancakes, but a lot heavier. Some dried fish was taken from one of the racks and passed around to everyone in our group also. Danny liked it, but Chelsea and Meg took a sniff and wouldn't even try it. I thought it tasted okay, but it was pretty salty. There were even a couple of the adults who weren't interested in the fish but just ate the bread cakes. Cool, fresh water was provided to us in a small animal skin pouch.

About halfway through the meal, Danny said, "Dad! I have to go to the bathroom!"

Dad looked a little unsure of himself, obviously wondering the best way to try to communicate this to our captors. Luckily, Danny took care of it for him: he stood up and started dancing around in the way that only a four-year-old can do. It was obvious to everyone who saw him *exactly* what the situation was. It was only a moment before one of the guards came toward him and gently pushed him down the slope, but in a different direction than the tents. Dad stood and went with him, with no apparent disagreement from the guard.

"Oh, I see," said Neil with a smile. "I should have danced around when I stood up earlier. I'm happy that Danny was good enough to show us how it worked before the situation got too desperate for anyone else."

"Speak for yourself," said Jo. "I'm next!"

When Dad and Danny returned, Jo immediately stood and began moving in the direction they were coming from. Fearful of how often we might be allowed to take this opportunity, everyone in our group took their turn when someone else came back.

"It's not pretty," Jo said, as she returned to her spot, "but it works."

The afternoon got quite warm as the sun reached its high point in the sky. It was strange to watch it just make a huge circle around us without ever getting straight above and knowing that it would never dip below the horizon. Neil spent the entire afternoon intently scanning the eastern sky for any sign of an approaching rescue plane. He never said anything, but I could tell that he was getting discouraged.

I found myself watching the sky also. I wasn't convinced that I would ever see a rescue plane, but I occasionally noticed brown and white birds flying through the air above the hills. They would never get very high, though, and didn't seem to go very far. Several times I noticed some small, brown, mouse-looking things that scurried around in a group of ten or twenty at a time and then would suddenly all disappear into a hole in the tundra.

"Look at that," I pointed out the second or third time I saw them. "Those mice are nutso!"

"Those are lemmings," Tom corrected me.

"Lemmings?" Brandon asked. "I thought Lemmings was the name of a Nintendo game."

"Where do you think the name comes from?" Dad asked.

"These little things are famous for following each other around in large groups and all doing the same thing," Tom explained.

"Oh," I laughed quietly, "that's where the game gets its name: you can only control one guy at a time and all the others follow until you change what a different guy does and then they all follow him. I had no idea that lemmings were *real*. That's cool!"

"I had no *clue*," agreed Brandon. It was hard to keep my mouth shut when he said it.

"How do you know so much about this place?" I asked Tom.

"Well, you know," Tom hesitated, "I travel around a lot in my job and see a lot of nature. I don't really have any close family, so I end up reading a lot. Especially about places I'm going or have been to. So I guess I just pick things up here and there."

For the next few minutes, we all watched the rolling tundra landscape, watching for any signs of more lemmings. Chelsea seemed the most excited by them, but Danny seemed bored.

Eventually, Danny said, "Dad, I'm tired of this. When are we going to get on the big boat and see whales and floating ice?"

"I don't know," Dad admitted.

"Is someone going to come looking for us?" Meg asked. "I mean, when we don't get on the big boat."

"I'm sure they're looking for us already," Dad reassured her.

"What about at home?" Brandon asked. "Will our friends know that we're lost?"

"Well," Dad sighed, "not for a while. I told the neighbors not to be surprised if we were gone up to four weeks. Whitney said she wouldn't be going to camp for a month, so she would be able to pick up the mail and newspapers until then."

"But, *why?*" I asked in amazement. "The cruise was only for a week!"

"Don't you remember that we were going to rent a van after the cruise?" Dad asked. "We were planning to travel through California for another couple of weeks after the cruise."

"Oh, yeah," I groaned. "I forgot."

We all sat thinking about this for a moment before Chelsea said, "I wish Granny was here." She sounded a little sad as she added, "Granny liked camping."

Granny was Mom's mom. She had lived with us for as long as I could remember, but she had died a few months earlier. Right before school started last year, we found out that Granny had cancer. I think it was in her stomach. She had surgery, but it didn't seem to help much, because she died just a few months later—right after Christmas.

"She didn't really like camping all that much," Mom smiled.

"She didn't?" questioned Chelsea.

"No," Mom shook her head back and forth. "She just liked being with the family."

Chelsea snuggled in under Dad's arm and stared at the ground. No one else said anything, and within a few minutes Chelsea was asleep. I think everyone was thinking about Granny. I certainly was.

Twice during the afternoon, we saw Scrooge and Santa having an argument over what we thought were probably bags of salt. They repeatedly gestured back and forth between the salt deposit and the bags being used for rubbing salt into the meat. As before, Scrooge was loud and angry while Santa was quiet and gentle.

As evening approached, we saw something unlike anything I'd ever seen before. My attention was caught as four of the younger, teenage boys went down to an area close to where the reindeer were grazing and returned carrying something that looked heavy but was covered with an animal skin. Two poles extended out from under the animal skin on either side, providing four carrying handles—one for each boy. There was a waist-high pile of rocks not far from the huts, pretty much in the center of everything else around. The pile was quite flat on top, and the boys carefully placed their load on top of it.

"What's that?" I asked quietly.

"I have no idea," Dad whispered.

Scrooge now approached the pile and stood next to it. On his signal, the four boys carefully removed the animal skin. We were some distance away, so it was hard to get all the details, but they uncovered what looked like a rough, metal box with no lid that was about two feet long on each side and about a foot deep. The handles that the boys had been carrying were actually two long poles that ran under the box to support it. Mounted on each corner of the top of the open box was a short horn pointing up and outward that looked like it came from a cow or an ox.

"That's an altar!" breathed Tom. "I think we're about to witness a sacrifice."

"I wonder what *kind* of sacrifice?" said Jo very slowly and very quietly.

"A *religious* sacrifice," whispered Tom.

"Yes," Jo answered, "but I'm wondering what kind of . . . I mean who—or *what*. . . ." She paused, trying to decide how to say what she meant, but finally she just whispered, "Never mind. We'll know soon enough." She sounded tense. I got the feeling she was trying to avoid making an "inappropriate comment." I looked at Mom to see what she thought. She was looking at Jo but gave no hint what she was thinking, so I turned my attention back to the altar.

The boys built a fire inside the box. Scrooge made many hand motions and seemed to be mumbling constantly as the fire grew. His hand movements above the altar caused interesting swirls in the smoke as it rose past him. After a few minutes, one of the older men approached the altar very slowly with his hands extended out in front of him. He was carrying what looked like a large, brown and white bird whose tail feathers extended back toward him and whose head was being held between the man's thumbs. The bird was squirming about and squawking unhappily. The man gave the bird to Scrooge and then stood next to him.

It was hard to see exactly what happened next, but it looked like Scrooge killed the bird with his bare hands by twisting its head off. Scrooge then moved his hands back and forth several times from the bird to each of the horns on the four corners of the altar.

"What's he doing?" I asked as quietly as possible. This whole thing seemed sacred, and I didn't want to disturb anyone. I noticed that all the other tribesmen had stopped their work and stood silently watching Scrooge as he worked at the altar.

"I think he's putting blood from the bird on each of the horns," whispered Tom, without taking his eyes from the scene. "I think this might be what's known as a burnt offering, but it's been a while since I've read the book of Leviticus."

When he was done with this, Scrooge began pulling the feathers from the bird. He gave each handful of feathers to one of the helpers, who carefully arranged them on the ground next to the altar. He had all the feathers removed within about a minute. At this point, one of the boys brought over one of the bags of salt. Scrooge reached in a couple of times and seemed to be rubbing salt on the dead bird.

"Oh-h-h!" said Jo under her breath. "They also use salt for their rituals!"

"Maybe they're just cooking it for dinner," whispered John. "Maybe it's for flavor."

Jo looked at him like that was the dumbest thing she'd ever heard. I think she couldn't tell if he was serious or not.

"I don't think so," Tom said finally. "Look."

Scrooge had placed the bird directly into the flames, which now reached several inches above the top of the fire box.

"No one will be eating any of *that* bird," John said, "unless they like it *really* well-done." He laughed a little as he said this, but no one else joined in.

Everyone else seemed to be going about their business now, but Scrooge stayed close to the burning bird. I noticed that there were now several other small campfires burning, and various groups looked like they were making preparations to cook a meal. I could see no other animals of any kind being prepared, just more of the small, flat, pancake-type things that we had been given at lunchtime. My mouth began to water, and I began to wonder if they tasted better hot than cold. I was anxious to find out.

Before anyone ate anything, however, I noticed the man who had brought the bird to the altar was now returning with a large stack of the cakes. He gave them to Scrooge with a long, slow bow. The man then walked slowly back to his own fire as Scrooge put one cake down into the fire with the bird. I could hardly contain my salivating as I watched Scrooge and his four helpers then systematically eat the large stack of cakes.

Soon we were served cakes, fish, and water, just as earlier. I decided that these little cakes definitely tasted much better hot than cold. In fact, I thought it tasted a lot like a biscuit from KFC, except this looked like the biscuit that got smashed under the bucket of chicken. Thinking of KFC biscuits made me think of other food from KFC.

"Why did they have to waste that chicken?" I asked no one in particular.

"Chicken?" Mom asked.

"Well," I stammered, "you know what I mean—that bird."

"I think Tom's right; it looked like a burnt offering," Dad said between bites. "Like what the children of Israel did. You can read about it in the book of Leviticus like Tom said or in the Bible Dictionary."

"I could if I had my scriptures," I said.

"That's what you get," Brandon said. "You should have been thankful for what you had instead of whining that the Bible Dictionary is really an encyclopedia." He had quite the smug look on his face as he took another bite of the heavy cake in his hand.

"*What?*" I grunted. "And I suppose *you*—"

"Jeff," Mom interrupted quietly but sternly. "That's enough!"

"How can it *possibly* be enough?" I asked indignantly. "You don't even know what I was going to say!"

"Was it something uplifting, that would make people feel better?" Dad asked.

"It would have made *me* feel better," I said.

Dad didn't say anything, and I could tell that I wasn't supposed to, either. I figured I ought to *at least* be able to make a formal protest about yet-one-more "inappropriate" comment from Brandon, but instead I just decided to save this in my bring-it-up-when-they-least-expect-it file. I took another bite of the cake I was holding and suddenly realized that it didn't taste *anything* like a KFC biscuit. I had the feeling that butter and honey wouldn't help either.

The after-dinner ritual looked very similar to how things had gone after lunch, and then we watched as the tribesmen began cleaning up in apparent preparation for night. Another night without darkness, that is. Part of the cleaning up included Scrooge's helpers solemnly cleaning out the altar and placing the ashes on the ground in the same spot as the bird feathers. I wondered if all the feathers were still there, and it made me realize that I hadn't noticed any wind the whole time we had been here, but it was starting to get cold again. The altar was again covered in animal skins and slowly carried back into its original spot near the reindeer herd.

At this point, we witnessed yet another argument between Santa and Scrooge. We got the impression it had to do with our sleeping arrangements, because as soon as they finished, Santa stood watching as Scrooge gave orders to some men who herded us immediately up to the huts. As we got closer, Tom said that the coverings for the huts looked like heavy bear hides.

Our entire family was pushed abruptly into a single tepee. I didn't think there was any way that we would all fit inside, but it turned out to be surprisingly roomy. It was also dark. When the flap was closed, the only visible light came from the very top. Feeling around we could tell that the floor was covered only with a thin animal skin.

"Well, I guess it's time to sleep," Dad said in his usual, obvious way.

It took a while to get everyone a place where they were reasonably comfortable. But just as we thought we were settled, Dad said, "We need to have a family prayer."

I expected serious complaints from Danny and Chelsea about just getting settled and then immediately having to get up for prayer, but I was wrong. No one whined a bit but simply moved quietly into kneeling positions and waited. Dad said the prayer again. Usually he gave everyone pretty much equal opportunities to pray, but lately it seemed like he was doing it all. The first part of his prayer was all about gratitude for our safe landing. Then he even said that we were grateful to have found people who were taking such good care of us. I had a little trouble with that one. Finally he mentioned what I think we all had on our minds: please help us to get home safely. I would have added something like "very soon," but he didn't say anything about when. He just prayed that we would be able to get the most from this "experience."

Quite a while later, after asking seemingly unending questions,

Danny, Chelsea, and Meg eventually all fell asleep. I think it had something to do with the fact that the most common answer to every question was "I don't know" followed by a reassuring "but Heavenly Father will take care of us." I could hear Mom and Dad whispering back and forth. Brandon and Shauna seemed a little restless, like me.

Then, without warning, the front flap of the tent opened just long enough for a small figure to dart inside, after which the flap immediately closed again. The unexpected light blinded me for the few seconds that this boy was in our tepee. From his voice, I decided he must be about my age. He spoke softly in a voice that had the same ring as the tribesmen, but for the first time I could understand what one of these people was saying.

He said very slowly, "Worrying ye not necessary." The word "necessary" sounded funny because he emphasized the second syllable instead of the first. Then he said, "Speaking I good English. Being everything well."

Before any one of us could react or even move, the flap flew open and closed again, and he was gone.

CHAPTER 7

The Interpretation of Tongues

"Who was *that?*" Brandon asked, breaking the silence at least five seconds after the figure disappeared into the sunlit night.

"You mean '*What* was that?'" I corrected him. "You're assuming that was something *human.*" I was not entirely convinced that what I thought had happened was actually real.

"I think," said Dad after a pause, "that whoever or whatever that was can best be described as 'good news.'"

"What makes you think so?" Mom asked, clearly not convinced.

"Because we have someone with whom we can *communicate,*" Dad said.

I stared into the darkness for a moment before stating, "But we don't know who it is."

"Did anyone get a good look at him while the flap was open?" Dad asked.

"No way," Brandon answered.

"It was way too bright," Shauna agreed.

"But he sounded young," Mom said.

"Yeah," I agreed. "He sounded like he was about my age, or maybe Brandon's."

"Uh-huh," said Brandon. "I think Jeff's right."

"Well, that should help," decided Dad, "because there aren't that many young men here."

"That's true," Mom agreed. "I only saw perhaps three or four who looked that age."

"Do you think he'll be back?" Shauna asked.

"I don't know," Dad admitted.

"Do you think the same thing happened to everybody else?" I asked.

"I don't know that, either," Dad said. "I doubt it, though. He acted like he was trying to get us a message without getting caught. So we should remember exactly what he said so we can tell the others in the morning—especially if we don't see him again before then. Can anyone remember?"

"The first thing he said was 'Worrying ye not necessary,'" I said, using the same funny pronunciation of the last word. "I remember because the way he said it kind of reminded me of this kid at school who's from the Middle East."

"Oh, you're right!" Brandon agreed. "I know who you mean—but I can't say his name."

"Me, either," I said. "We just call him 'Abe' for short."

"Okay," Dad said, trying to get us back to the point. "That was the first thing. What else did he say? It seems like there were two or three short phrases."

"He said something about speaking English really good," Shauna offered.

"That's right," Dad said. "But it was something like 'Speaking I English well' or 'Speaking I English good.'"

"The last thing he said was 'Being everything well,'" Mom said.

"Okay," said Dad. "Was there anything else?"

None of us could think of anything else, so Mom and Dad quietly repeated the phrases several times, trying to make sure they didn't forget them. When it sounded like they were done, I asked, "Dad, who do you think these people are?"

"I'm not sure," he said. "Their rituals are obviously ancient, and so is their clothing. I can't decide if they look like they've been exposed to anything modern or not. They didn't seem too surprised by the airplane and the fact that we could be associated with something so loud and huge flying overhead. And that harness of reindeer was very interesting. I know that some of the people in Siberia actually herd reindeer like we would herd cattle. And . . . uh . . . do you kids know what a woolly mammoth is?"

"Uh-huh," we answered.

"It's a really hairy, elephant-like thing that lived a long time ago," Shauna said.

"Right," Dad said. "Well, they have discovered a large number of woolly mammoths in northeastern Asia, which have been frozen for apparently thousands of years. I read an article a couple of years ago about an expedition of scientists from the United States and Europe who came to study a woolly mammoth that was discovered by a small Siberian tribe. I remember being surprised by one of the pictures showing a sleigh being pulled over snow by several reindeer harnessed together. It looked a lot like what these people have."

"Really?" Brandon asked. "That's cool!"

"Yeah," Dad agreed. "So there are things like that which seem to indicate some exposure to the modern world—not to mention the fact that at least one of them can speak some English—and yet they still seem to be so isolated. And they're not speaking Russian or anything that sounds Oriental or European. So it just makes me wonder. It's amazing to think about what it would take to keep them . . ." He paused. "It's like the Lord has kept them protected here."

"So why now?" Brandon asked. "And why us?"

"Do you think they *want* to be isolated?" Shauna asked.

"And more important than that," I added, "how far are they willing to go to *stay* isolated from the rest of the world? And to make sure no else knows they exist?"

"Do you think they may not want us to go back where we came from," Shauna asked, "for fear we'll tell the rest of the world?"

"Good questions," Dad sighed. "I wish I knew. But I think we're safe for now. We just need to listen for and follow the Spirit. If you had your scriptures, I'd ask you to find what Nephi said about being led by the Spirit."

"Do you mean when he said 'I was led by the Spirit, not knowing beforehand the things which I should do'?" Shauna asked. "That's a seminary scripture."

"That's the one," Dad said. "Good job, Shauna. That's what we should be doing all the time. Let's just exercise faith and follow the Spirit."

No one said anything else. We just let the silence take over. I was amazed to feel a warmth and a peace that wouldn't have seemed possible for any rational person in a situation like this. But Dad was right; I felt safe. I continued thinking about Nephi being led by the Spirit and how his family was led into the wilderness, away from their home and their comforts. *At least they knew why they were being led into the wilderness*, I thought. This was certainly no promised land for us. I almost laughed out loud as I thought it, allowing a small puff of air to escape from my nose. No one seemed to notice. I drew a deep breath and before falling asleep, I began thinking about Nephi and his family. That brought my thoughts back to the native boy who had flashed in and out of our tent. I began to have the same hope that Dad had expressed: maybe we'd finally be able to talk to someone. Not long after, I fell asleep with the sounds of the boy's voice repeating those three phrases over and over again in my head.

I was awakened by a burst of light and a confusing jumble of sounds that were probably supposed to be words. My first thought was that it was a typical Saturday morning when I felt it was my right to sleep later than usual, but Dad had some big project that he needed my help with. When you're just waking up, it seems like you can never understand the first few things that people say. It wasn't until I noticed several other people beginning to stir all within four feet of me that I remembered where I was and realized why I couldn't understand what had been said.

The words came again. They didn't make any more sense this time than before, but we all got the distinct impression that this guy was losing patience as he waited for us to wake up and come out of our shelter. I thought the sun had seemed bright the night before when our surprise visitor made his quick entrance and exit, but now it was almost unbearable. The sun was directly in front of the opening, and we each shielded our eyes with hands or arms or both as we stumbled out. Chelsea whimpered a little as she clung to Mom's waist and staggered along next to her. Danny just slowly smacked his lips together as if he had fallen asleep with a large spoonful of peanut butter in his mouth. The thought made my stomach growl.

We were all escorted out to the same place where we had spent most of the previous day. It was like having an assigned pew at church and being forced to be there all day every day. Mom and Dad exchanged short, quiet greetings with Tom and the airline crew as we all sat wearily on the animal skins. Danny began to express his displeasure with the situation when one of the guards quickly caught our attention by grunting and thrusting his spear toward the altar.

"I think we're supposed to be watching the ritual," Jo whispered, staring soberly down the slope.

Scrooge was there again, and the scene looked exactly as it had the night before. The only change I noticed was that this time a different man brought Scrooge a bird to be sacrificed. He brought a different type of bird also. This one was black with white and yellow feathers on its head. It looked a little larger than the brown and white one from the night before. Scrooge mumbled and waved his hands as before, again causing the smoke swirls. The bird was killed in the same way as the first one, and its blood was sprinkled onto each of the horns of the altar. We and everyone else watched in silence until the bird was left to burn in the fire, at which point each of the groups began cooking cakes at their own fires. Still, no one spoke until the man who had brought the bird returned to the altar with a stack of cakes.

As he had before, Scrooge put one of the cakes in the fire with the bird, before he and his helpers began eating the rest.

"So why does he burn the bird?" I asked, remembering that I never got much of an answer the night before.

"I think it's what Tom said last night," Dad whispered, not taking his eyes from the scene. "It's a burnt offering like the Israelites performed in the Old Testament."

"They burn the first portion of what they have as recognition that all things come from God," Tom explained.

"Oh-h," I breathed softly, finally understanding. "It's like tithing, isn't it? We pay the first ten percent of everything we earn to show Heavenly Father that we know that all things come from Him, huh?"

"Exactly," Dad smiled.

"You offer *tithes?*" Tom breathed in astonishment. "Is this just something you do on your own—I mean in your own family? What do you do with the money?"

"We're members of The Church of Jesus Christ," Dad said, "of Latter-day Saints. We believe that neglecting to give tithes and offerings is the same as robbing God."

"Yes, I—I know," Tom said quickly. "Near the end of the Old Testament that is stated very clearly. But you're telling me that you give ten percent of all you have to your church?"

"We give ten percent of our income to the Church as tithing," Dad explained. "But we also give other offerings to help those in need in our area or other parts of the world. We have different funds for the poor, for missionary service, and we even have an education fund to help church members in underdeveloped countries. Our church teaches that we are simply stewards over what we have received and that the Lord expects us to be generous."

"I believe that also," Tom said slowly, "but I've never heard of a church that so literally followed the principle that is taught so clearly in the Bible. You said it's The Church of Jesus Christ?"

"Of Latter-day Saints, yes," Dad nodded. "We are often referred to as 'Mormons' because in addition to the Bible we also believe in the Book of Mormon, which is the history of God's people in ancient America and is 'Another Testament of Jesus Christ.'"

Tom raised his eyebrows and just stared at Dad for a moment. His eyes darted back and forth between Dad's eyes. His mind was obviously churning. "Well then, you should be intrigued by these rituals of last night and this morning," he said finally. "Because, as you surely know, the ancient sacrifices performed by the Israelites were all about the Messiah, Jesus Christ. Everything is symbolic."

"That's right," Dad agreed. "The blood represents the blood of the Messiah, which we now know was spilled by Jesus in the Garden of Gethsemane and on the cross to pay for our sins. The horns represent the great power of Jehovah. They use salt to strengthen and preserve food, and so it symbolizes the power of God needed to keep us pure and uncorrupted."

"Right," Tom nodded.

"What I find most interesting," Dad said, "is that all this most likely means that these people may be still looking for the Messiah, much like the Jews of today."

"That's true," Tom said with a slow nod. He stared at Dad for a moment before asking, "May I ask how your church feels about the Jews?"

"Well," Dad drew a deep breath, "probably the best way to describe it is to tell you what it says in the Book of Mormon. The first prophet who writes in the book is named Nephi, and he is told that his writings will be brought to the world, and the world will say 'We have got a Bible, and there cannot be any more Bible.' Then it asks something like, 'How did you get a Bible if not for the Jews?'"

"I remember this," Shauna said. "Then doesn't it say something like we don't remember all the trials and pains of the Jews"? she asked.

"Right," Dad said. "And it also says we are wrong not to remember their diligence in bringing salvation to the Gentiles."

"Really?" Tom looked amazed. "So you are obviously very positive toward the Jews, then?"

"Definitely," Dad agreed. "In fact, the next thing the Lord says is something like 'ye Gentiles have not remembered the Jews, but ye have cursed them, and hated them.' The Lord says that he will return all these things upon the heads of the Gentiles, because he has not forgotten his people."

"Wow," was all Tom said at this point.

"So I guess the short answer is," Dad continued, "we are taught to be grateful to the Jews for giving us the Bible and to revere them for their diligence through so many generations of hardship. And the Lord still considers them his chosen people."

"So the name of your church is The Church of Jesus Christ of . . . Saints of . . . ?" Tom asked.

"Of Latter-day Saints," Dad added. "Yes. We believe that Christ has restored his church and priesthood to the earth, which is today led by living prophets."

"But you still believe in the Bible," Tom said.

"We believe the Bible is the word of God," Dad nodded.

"Do you follow the Ten Commandments?" he asked.

"Of course," Dad answered.

Tom paused with a slight smile on his face. "I've heard of Mormons, but only that you believe and do strange things," he said. "But it sounds to me more like you just believe that God hasn't changed. That his laws are still valid." He paused again. "I still can't believe you live the law of tithes. But you don't do sacrifices anymore, do you?"

"No," Dad answered. "The Law of Moses was fulfilled at Jesus

Christ's death. According to the Book of Mormon, that ended sacrifice by the shedding of blood."

"But we still believe in sacrifice," Shauna reminded Dad with a smile. "We talked about it in seminary."

"That's true," Dad smiled. "When Christ taught the people in ancient America after his resurrection, he said that he now wanted a different type of sacrifice from us, didn't he? Do you remember what it was?"

"A broken heart and a contrite spirit," Shauna answered.

"Whoa, whoa, wait a minute," Tom said. "Is that in the Mormon Book?"

"The Book of Mormon," Dad smiled. "Yes."

Then turning to Shauna, Tom asked, "And you go to a seminary? Are you planning to be a pastor or something? Does your church have female—preachers?"

"Well, in our church," Shauna explained, "all the kids go to seminary for four years, from ninth grade through twelfth."

"That's amazing," Tom said quietly. "I've never heard of such a thing."

"Jeff starts next year," Shauna said. "He's going into ninth grade."

"But I thought burnt offerings were with big animals," Brandon said, bringing us all back to where the conversation started. He was staring down at the altar, seemingly completely disconnected from what we had been talking about. "Like cows and sheep and goats."

"Uh, well, according to the Old Testament," Tom explained, "it depends on the type of sacrifice. I think pigeons were allowed for burnt offerings for people who were less affluent."

"People who were what?" Brandon asked.

"Poor," Dad explained.

"Right," agreed Tom. "But other sacrifices like the peace offering or the sin offering always required the larger animals."

"And they didn't all have to be male like the burnt offering," Dad added.

"Wow," I said, shaking my head back and forth, "how could you keep track of all of it?"

"Well, it's really well outlined in the book of Leviticus in the Old Testament and from what I've seen so far," Tom answered, "it looks to me like they've done a pretty good job of following what I remember to be the important things. I'm not sure about all of it, though."

"I'm not sure, either," Dad agreed. "It's been quite a while since I spent much time in that part of the scriptures, so I don't remember how it all works."

"Something else I noticed," Tom said, "is that all the tent doors face east. That was a common practice among the people of God in the Old Testament."

"Oh-h-h!" Brandon grunted. "So that's why the sun was such a killer this morning, huh? Why do they do that? It's like an anti-alarm clock. I can't think of a better way to keep me from getting up."

"It's another symbol," Tom explained. "Christ's second coming will be from the east."

"Most of our temples face east," Dad said to Brandon. Then, turning to Tom again, he explained, "Temples are our most sacred buildings." Tom nodded. Dad added, "I wonder if all this has just been passed down through the generations by word of mouth—or if they have some writings that they can refer to."

"It would be interesting to find out, wouldn't it?" Tom agreed.

"No!" I blurted out. Everyone stopped talking and just looked at me. Before Mom had the chance to remind me about "appropriate" comments, I tried to explain myself. "I mean, well, yeah, it would be interesting to *know*. But I really don't think I want to be here long enough to find out. It's all kinda cool, I guess, but I think I'd really rather go home now, if it's all the same to you."

Everyone just sort of stared at me. It was not my intent to kill the conversation, but Dad and Tom were acting more like we were spending the day at a live museum, than like we were stranded thousands of miles from home with no apparent hope of getting back there anytime soon . . . if at all.

"I think we all agree with you," Mom said, "but for the time being I don't think there's any harm in learning what we can about these people and their customs."

"It could come in handy," Tom agreed.

"*How?*" I gasped in total disbelief. I thought he was nuts, but seeing as how we didn't know each other that well yet, I did have the sense to soften my question just a little.

"Thomas is right," Mom agreed.

"We may learn something that will help us get home sooner," Tom explained.

I didn't really have a response for that, but it seemed to me that the most important lesson we ought to be taking from the Book of Mormon right now was how the Nephites planned and carried out their escapes after they had been captured. Apparently, no one else felt the same urgency that I did.

"Did you tell anybody about the boy who came into our tent last night?" I asked Dad, hoping this might get us closer to what I thought was the important problem at hand.

"Oh, that's right," Mom said.

"You had a visitor during the night?" Jo asked.

"Yes," Mom answered. "It was amazing."

She proceeded to explain about the boy who appeared without warning and disappeared just as quickly. Our whole family quoted the lines we had memorized in our tent after he had left. No one else had seen anybody in their tents during the night. Apparently, John, Nancy, Jo, and Tom were all pushed into a single tent, but Neil got one all to himself. I called it the "Executive Tent." Everyone was both amazed and encouraged by the fact that someone here knew how to speak English. Once we had passed on all the details of the encounter, everyone began looking around at the tribesmen, trying to figure out who it might have been. Obviously, there was no way of knowing for sure, but we did narrow it down to three or four teenage boys who seemed to be likely candidates.

The morning moved pretty slowly after that. We just watched as groups worked here and there around the camp, and our four guards just watched us watch them. They did seem a little less intense now than they had the day before. About every half hour or so Neil would make some comment about rescue planes and other such things that were nowhere in sight. It was starting to bug me a little bit.

We all watched closely a couple of times as Santa and Scrooge had what appeared to be short, angry exchanges. At least Scrooge appeared to be angry. After the second one, Santa came to Chelsea and Danny and handed them each something that was small, brownish, and looked sort of like a squatty, twisted carrot. They just looked back and forth between him and what they now held in their hands. He held together all his fingers and thumb on one hand, putting his fingers to his mouth. He seemed to smile as he touched his lips. I couldn't believe it! It was almost a shock to see something other than anger or just plain stern faces all the time. Dad figured out what he was up to and said, "I think it's something for you to eat."

With that, Danny immediately tried to take a bite of it, but it was apparently more than his four-year-old jaw could handle. "It's too hard," he complained, staring at it.

"Just lick it," Dad suggested.

Danny stuck it in his mouth like a Popsicle, slopped his tongue around it a few times, and then made a huge "m-m-m-m" noise that sounded like it came straight from a Campbell's soup commercial.

To this point, Chelsea had not even *considered* putting this ugly thing anywhere near her mouth.

"Is it good?" she asked doubtfully.

"Uh-huh," Danny said, bouncing his head up and down.

"What do you think it is?" I asked.

"It looks like a root from a plant," said Tom.

Holding it in front of Dad's face, Danny asked, "Do you want to try it? It's *really* good!"

Dad pulled his chin back and acted like it was too close for his eyes to focus on. After a moment he took a lick and said, "Wow! That's *sweet!* Do you like it?"

"Uh-huh," Danny said again, returning the root to his mouth.

"M-m-mm!" Chelsea agreed. "It tastes like candy!"

"Tell the man thank you," Dad said.

"Thank you," Chelsea beamed up at him.

"Thank you, Santa!" Danny said.

There were several soft laughs as Santa smiled and turned away. He seemed to understand what Chelsea and Danny meant. At least the "thank you" part—not the part about being Santa.

"I don't think he's really Santa," Brandon said quietly to Danny.

"Uh-huh!" insisted Danny. "He has a big, white beard, he has reindeer, and he gives candy to kids!"

Who could argue with that? Or who would want to? Danny paused for a moment with his mouth partially open. His eyes sparkled and darted about as he thought about what he had just said. With excitement and wonder, he finally began nodding slowly, a hint of a smile at the corners of his mouth as he whispered to me, "He *has* to be Santa Claus!"

"Okay," I smiled back at him. "He's Santa."

Things seemed a little more relaxed for a while and then something else amazing happened. We witnessed yet another exchange between Santa and Scrooge. This time Santa had a teenage boy at his side. Santa continued to reply quietly and confidently to each of Scrooge's angry outbursts. It ended with them staring at each other for several seconds before Santa turned toward us and walked briskly in our direction with the boy close behind him.

Mom was the first to say anything about it. "Look," she said quietly. "I wonder if that's the boy who came to our tent." I had been wondering the exact same thing.

As they approached, Santa slowed his pace a little and placed his hand behind the boy's back, gently pushing him in front. They both stopped about five feet in front of us. No one spoke for at least ten seconds. The boy looked anxiously from one person in our group to the next. He was dressed much like the others, but he, like the other younger boys, had more color in his clothing. There was a hint of dark green mixed in with various shades of brown. Santa just waited patiently as he watched the boy looking at us.

Finally, the boy spoke. "Calling ye me name of Aaron, son of Levi," he said slowly and deliberately. He really emphasized the o when he said his name, Aaron. He gestured toward Santa as he said "son of Levi." We were all holding our breath.

"Wanting my father, Levi, me telling ye: worrying ye not necessary." This was the midnight visitor all right. He said it just the same as the night before, emphasizing the second syllable of "necessary."

No one seemed to know what to say. The airline crew looked over at us as if we should be the ones to respond, due to our long-standing relationship with the boy, developed through three sentences from the night before.

"Understanding ye me," the boy said finally. I couldn't tell if this was supposed to be a question or not, but Neil treated it like one.

"We understand you," Neil said slowly. His voice was as formal as ever. "Thank you for speaking to us, Aaron." Neil tried to pronounce "Aaron" the same way the boy had, but it sounded funny when he said it.

Aaron didn't respond to Neil but turned his attention to Santa—or Levi—who was apparently his father. Levi nodded back as if the boy knew what he was supposed to do.

"Coming ye to this place for what reason?" Aaron said, turning back to Neil.

"We are lost," said Neil. "Our plane—our ship—is under the water, and we are waiting for friends to come find us."

At this point Aaron turned to look at where Scrooge stood some distance away. Aaron looked a little nervous, but I couldn't decide if it was because he didn't understand or because he didn't think Scrooge would like what he had heard. Aaron mumbled something to his father who responded with a short mumble of his own.

"Coming your friends to this place what day?" Aaron said.

"We do not know," Neil said. "We hope soon—today."

Aaron and his father again exchanged mumbles. This time they both looked toward Scrooge. Scrooge seemed to sense that something was going on that would not please him. I watched him move suddenly to our pile of belongings, remove my scriptures from my bag, and begin stomping up the slope toward us.

"Leaving we this place tomorrow," Aaron said. "Coming ye with us."

"No!" said Neil immediately. Then more softly, "We will stay and wait for our friends."

"Remaining ye here not safe." Aaron spoke more quickly now. "Coming ye with us to place with many people protecting ye."

"How not safe?" Neil asked. He was starting to sound like Aaron. Without waiting for a response, he asked, "Many people protect us from what? Animals? Weather?"

"Protecting us ye from other people," Aaron answered. He stared hard at Neil and then turned to look at Scrooge. I knew right then which "people" we needed to be protected from.

Scrooge began yelling and shaking my scriptures with both

hands as he approached. Aaron and his father listened intently to his ranting before Aaron looked quietly at his father, who seemed to nod in resignation.

"Telling thee us what this book contains," Aaron said to Neil.

"I do not know," Neil said to Aaron and then turning to us he asked, "Whose book is that?"

"It's mine," I admitted. "They're scriptures."

Aaron gave my answer to Scrooge, who blurted something back. Aaron turned back to me.

"Telling this book the way of sacrifices and story of Jesus like Bible of Christian?" Aaron asked. This was definitely a question. But it seemed obvious that Aaron already knew exactly what was in the book. I wondered if Dad still thought these people had been isolated from the rest of the world for thousands of years.

My mouth was dry. "Yes," I finally answered weakly.

Aaron and Scrooge again exchanged a quick conversation.

"Leading our people is man who Christian calls Jacob," Aaron said, gesturing toward Scrooge. "Performing Jacob all sacrifices of our people." I thought the name "Scrooge" fit better, but I figured I could go with "Jacob" too.

Jacob was impatient with the formalities and blurted something at Aaron. Aaron turned slowly toward us and seemed to be attempting to muster the courage to say what Jacob wanted.

He drew a deep breath. "Performing ye sacrifices of God and Moses found in Bible?" Aaron asked. His eyes were glued to mine, and his jaw was clenched. Neither of us blinked for several seconds as we stared at each other. I now understood why this Jacob-guy was so upset with my scriptures. He was obviously familiar with the Bible and probably thought that since we had one, we might be performing ordinances reserved for priests. Since he was the leader here and this was his territory, I figured he didn't like the thought that we might be a threat to his authority.

That's when I got more scared than I had been the entire time so far. A million questions raced through my head. What did they do to people in the Old Testament who performed sacrifices without authority? Was it one of the sins punishable by death? I felt my throat tighten as I continued to stare at Aaron.

What should I tell him? We obviously didn't do the animal sacrifices, but didn't we do other ordinances of God, like baptism and the sacrament? Just a week earlier, hadn't I helped to prepare the sacrament and watched as Brandon passed it to members of the congregation? Did that count? I knew we had authority, but what would Jacob do if I told them we did that? Not all of us were members of the Church, so would saying "no" really be lying? Wouldn't it be best to protect ourselves any way that we could?

My heart pounded in my ears as I opened my mouth to respond.

CHAPTER 8

Mountain of the Lord

Dad answered for me, but Aaron continued to stare at me as Dad spoke. My fear didn't lessen just because I was not the one being questioned. In fact, it even seemed to get more intense as I waited to hear what he would say.

"We believe in Jesus Christ," Dad said in answer to Aaron's question. Dad continued as Aaron slowly shifted his eyes to look at him. "We do not perform animal sacrifices because they were done away with the death of Jesus Christ."

Aaron continued to look at Dad for a moment and then turned to give the information to Jacob. But before he could say what he had learned, Dad spoke again.

"But we *do* perform other ordinances not done away because of the sacrifice of Jesus Christ," Dad said. Aaron looked back at Dad as he began to list ordinances. He said, "We perform baptism by immersion for the remission of sins, the laying on of hands for the gift of the Holy Ghost, the sacrament of the Lord's last supper, anointing, ordinations, and marriage for time and eternity."

Dad paused and Aaron began to turn to Jacob again, but turned back once more as Dad added, "Most of these ordinances are performed for both the living and the dead."

My attention was caught by Tom's obvious shock over this last statement. "Do you perform baptisms for the dead?" he whispered. "As spoken of in the New Testament?"

Dad answered quietly yet firmly, "Yes. We do." He was staring at Jacob as he spoke.

"I've never heard of a church that followed all those biblical teachings," Tom replied.

Then Dad quickly turned to Aaron and added, "I speak for my family only. Not for this man or for this crew." He pointed at Tom and the airline staff as he said this.

Aaron's eyes narrowed. Looking directly at Dad, he asked, "Performing ye animal sacrifices found in book of Leviticus in Bible of Christian?"

"No," Dad responded.

Aaron now turned to Tom and asked the same question in the same way.

"No," Tom answered.

"None of us do, either," Neil offered, then raised his hands in a questioning attitude and looked around at his crew as if he wasn't quite sure he'd given the right answer. "Do we?" he asked.

"No," they all agreed, shaking their heads from side to side.

"Nope," said Neil, "don't think so! We're clear here!" Neil continued to look from person to person, shaking both his hands and his head quickly back and forth.

"This is well," said Aaron finally, and he turned to speak with Jacob and his father, Levi. The three of them conferred for several moments together. Jacob's voice was loud, and he seemed skeptical. All of his actions looked like they were aimed at intimidating the boy. But Aaron remained calm and appeared to be responding respectfully and patiently to everything Jacob was shouting at him. His father had obviously taught him well.

The exchange ended with Jacob storming away but yelling to no one in particular as he left. I figured he was just trying to make it clear to everyone within the sound of his voice that he was still in charge. When this was over, Levi called to several young men who had been with him when they first arrived and gave them brief instructions. They immediately dropped what they were doing and moved off in the same direction Jacob had gone. Levi and Aaron then turned to our group again.

With instruction from Levi, Aaron told us what was going on. The young men had been sent to retrieve our belongings for us. For now we were still being asked to stay in our group because Jacob didn't trust us, but since we would be traveling with the tribesmen, we would later be expected to help with preparations to leave the next day.

Neil began to protest against the assumption that we would be going with them. Without warning, Levi spoke for the first time something that we could all understand. His face was hard and stern as he said very slowly and clearly, "Staying ye here being certain *death* for ye all."

We were all shocked to learn that he also spoke English—or at least some form of it. None of us knew what to say, but I wasn't sure if everyone's silence came from the surprise that he understood English or from the weight of the words themselves. It was probably different for each of us, but the word *death* was definitely foremost in *my* mind.

"Speaking my father also English," Aaron said, after it became obvious that none us had anything immediately to respond. He went on, "Nevertheless, fearing my father also the wrath of Jacob. Angered is Jacob because of English and because of Christian. Fearing ye the wrath of Jacob being wisdom in ye."

"Okay," Neil sighed at last. "I suppose it might be better for us to stay with you." He sounded defeated. *Hello-o-o*, I thought. Shouldn't that have been obvious before now? From the very start *anyone* could see what a lunatic this Jacob-Scrooge-fruitcake was! But not just *any* lunatic—he was a lunatic with weapons, and his own gang, and delusions that he was Pharaoh over all that he could see—including us. As I was thinking this, I watched Neil look longingly at the eastern sky, scanning the horizon for any sign of the long-awaited rescue plane. He eventually gave up and looked down at his shiny, black, airline shoes instead. I got the feeling he was used to being in charge and having things go exactly as he expected. *Welcome to the new world*, I thought, *or more accurately, the old world.*

"We'll be happy to help in any way we can," said John. "Just let us know when and how you need us."

"Staying ye here until finish of midday meal," Aaron said. "Reading ye now from Bible like Christian for time of daily devotions."

By this time the boys had returned with our backpacks and other things. Even the punctured raft had been dragged to where we were sitting. Neil and John immediately began to check it out. As Aaron told us it was time for daily devotions, he reached into my bag, removed my scriptures, and handed them to me.

"Thank you," I said, looking up at him.

"It's definitely time for devotional," Dad said, passing out the bags to our family. Jo and Nancy began looking carefully through the box of emergency meals—I guess to see if they had been hurt or something.

"May I ask you something?" Tom said to Aaron as he started to walk away.

"Asking thee me anything at any time," Aaron said.

"How do you know English, and what is this you keep saying about Christians?"

"Living in village my people many years is Christian from United States America. Speaking Christian with my father and me each day English," Aaron smiled. This was the first time I had seen anything but a straight face from him.

"Oh," said Jo, "so that's what you meant when you spoke about the 'Bible of Christian.' This Christian in your village has a Bible with stories of Jesus and the sacrifices. Is that right?"

"Yes," said Aaron. He pronounced the word very emphatically.

"And you said that 'Jacob' is the name that the Christian calls the leader of your people?" Tom asked.

"Yes," said Aaron, again very firmly.

"Did the Christian give you the name 'Aaron'?" Jo asked. "And the name 'Levi' for your father."

"Giving Christian to my father name of Levi," answered Aaron. "Giving my father to me name of Aaron."

"What is the name of the Christian?" Mom asked.

Aaron thought for a moment before turning slowly to Levi and mumbling something. Levi mumbled back, to which Aaron responded by looking around at the other tribesmen, who all appeared to be busy with their own tasks. Aaron's eyes lingered for a moment on Jacob, who had his back to us. Aaron mumbled something else to his father without taking his eyes from Jacob. Levi paused for a moment before finally gesturing toward us.

Slowly, while still watching Jacob, Aaron reached his hands toward his own throat and then with a quick flick of his wrists removed a thin metal chain from around his neck. A small, flat piece of metal hung from the chain, which he cradled in his hand and held out for us to see. Several of us leaned in for a closer look. He stole one more quick glance toward Jacob and then pointed at the lettering that was stamped into the small plate of metal. The first line had "C A MORTENSEN" stamped on it, which he pointed to as he said the words "Christian—Anders—Mortensen."

"Oh," Jo breathed a soft laugh. "His *name* is Christian. We thought you were saying that he is a Christian by *religion*." Aaron just stared at her, and so she asked, "Do you understand what that means?"

Aaron again paused before saying, "Being Christian both by name and by religion." He paused. "Saying Christian Anders Mortensen to my father: Jesus is Christ and Messiah of world."

"So you know what it means to be a Christian?" Mom asked.

"Yes," said Aaron.

"Are you Christian?" Tom asked.

Aaron looked at his father. Levi looked back and forth between his son and Tom a couple of times and then mumbled something in their language. Aaron turned back to Tom and said, "Working we now on duties of this day. Speaking we later of these matters."

With that, both Aaron and Levi left us and went about their duties.

"This is *amazing!*" said Jo.

"Agreed," said John. "Those were dog tags! And they weren't new, either."

"What are dog tags?" Meg asked. "Do you think Christian has a dog, and that they took them from Christian's dog?"

"Dog tags are what men wear around their neck when they're in a war so that if they're killed people will know who they are," Dad explained.

"So why isn't he still wearing them?" Meg asked.

"I don't know," Dad said.

"But that explains how these people know English," Jo said. "They've had an American living with them."

"But what's strange," said Nancy, "is the *way* he speaks English. You would think that if he learned English from an American that he would speak more . . . correctly. It's strange."

"You're right," John said. "There's got to be more to this English stuff. But we may never figure out the whole story."

"Well, I'd sure like to talk to this Christian guy from 'United States America,'" said Jo, copying Aaron's words.

"Unfortunately," said Neil, "you may just get your wish. They seem pretty determined to have us tag along."

"It's for our own protection!" said Jo. "After watching how this Jacob-guy operates, I'm convinced we'll all be a lot safer if we hang tight with Levi and Aaron."

The adults all seemed to agree, even if it was a little reluctantly on the part of some of them. The kids just watched without really saying what we thought, one way or another. Neither seemed like a great option to me.

"Would you like to join us for a devotional?" Dad asked Tom and the airline crew.

"I would love to," answered Tom. Reaching for his backpack and pulling out a small black book, he added, "I also have a copy of the Bible with me."

"If it's all the same to you," Neil said, "I think I'd rather see about repairing the raft."

"Of course," Dad smiled.

Neil hesitated. "And after that last exchange," he explained, "it may be a good idea to show these people that we are not as much of a religious threat as they may fear that we are."

"We understand," Mom nodded.

"That's just fine," Dad agreed.

"I'll help you, Neil," John said, standing to follow him.

Jo and Nancy told us to go ahead without them; they wanted to complete an inventory of our emergency meals.

The rest of us sat down in a circle on the ground. "What shall we discuss today?" Dad asked.

"I'd like to read about burnt offerings," I suggested.

"So would I," Tom agreed.

"We generally begin with a prayer," Dad said to Tom.

"That's great," Tom replied. "Please go ahead."

Dad asked me to pray. I felt a little strange being out in the middle of who-knows-where, surrounded by people who had feelings about what we were doing that varied from intrigue (Tom) to fear (Neil) to hatred (Jacob). I glanced at each of these people and began to feel my chest tighten as my eyes rested on Jacob last of all. After a moment, I looked back at Mom and Dad. They each looked amazingly relaxed and calm. I couldn't understand how they could be that way. Tom looked the same as Mom and Dad. I felt myself begin to relax and decided that I should just do what I knew was right: I said the prayer.

I think I said the same things that I normally say in a prayer to begin our devotionals, but it felt different this time. Maybe I was just a lot more sincere when I asked for Heavenly Father to be with us. Maybe I was just more intent on wanting to feel the Spirit. I'm not sure. But it came. I felt an amazing sense of peace as I ended the prayer. I know it wasn't a very long prayer—maybe just fifteen or twenty seconds—but it was enough. It felt good.

We began reading the first chapter of Leviticus with each person in the circle reading a verse—except Danny, of course. It talked about burnt offerings and how to choose an acceptable animal and how to sprinkle the blood on the altar. No one made any comments as we read the first few verses until we got to verse 11. Brandon read that one. It says:

And he shall kill it on the side of the altar northward before the Lord: and the priests, Aaron's sons, shall sprinkle his blood round about upon the altar.

"Why do they have to kill it in front of everyone?" I asked. "Why don't they kill it first and then bring it to the priest?"

"Because it's a type of Christ," Dad answered.

"Wait, what?" Shauna said.

"Was Christ killed in private?" Dad asked.

"Oh-h-h!" Shauna said under her breath. "You're right! He wasn't, was he?"

"Nope," Dad continued. "He was killed out in the open for everyone to witness."

"Everything about these sacrifices is a type of Christ," Tom said. "The blood that is spilled to pay for our sins, the fact that the animal has to be male and without blemish."

"What's blemish?" asked Meg.

"A blemish is a mark or a spot or a flaw," said Tom.

Meg looked a little confused.

109

"It's the same as not having any sins," Dad explained.

"Oh-h-h," Meg nodded slowly.

"Did Jesus have any sins?" Dad asked.

"No," said Danny and Chelsea at the same time. They looked at each other and giggled.

"But why are these people using birds?" I asked.

"Yeah," Brandon agreed. "All this talks about is using cattle and sheep and goats."

"So far that's true," Dad smiled. "But let's keep reading."

It turned out that the last four verses of the chapter were all about using birds for a burnt offering. If I didn't know better, I would have thought that Jacob had read these words himself because what he did with the birds that the men brought to him sounded exactly like what was in the Bible. Verse 16 even talked about which side of the altar to put the feathers on after they had been plucked from the bird.

"I can hardly believe this," Tom said.

"What do you mean, Thomas?" Mom asked.

"These people are performing their burnt offerings exactly as they are described in here."

"Well," Shauna said, "they said that there's this Christian-guy who has a Bible that they've seen."

"Yeah," Tom said slowly, "but that Jacob character also made it clear that he was none too pleased about us having scriptures. I'm thinking that their ritual comes from somewhere else—and it seems far too precise to have just been handed down by word of mouth."

"Do you mean you think they have ancient biblical writings?" Dad asked.

"I don't see how else it could happen," Tom nodded.

We all just sat in silence for a moment.

"That means they might have some of the lost writings," Shauna said.

"What lost writings?" I asked.

"In seminary we talked about *lots* of different books," Shauna said. "I guess there are a bunch that are talked about in the Bible, but we don't have them anymore."

"I'll bet you'll find something about that in the Bible Dictionary," Dad suggested. "Try looking under the word *lost*."

As I began flipping pages, Tom looked confused. "What's a Bible Dictionary?" he asked.

"Not what you'd think," I smirked. "It's more like a really short encyclopedia for things found in the Bible." I continued to turn pages as I said, "So I'm creating my own Bible dictionary that defines weird words that I find in the Bible."

"Oh, really?" Tom asked. "How many words do you have?"

"Well, let's see," I paused, pretending to count on my fingers. "I think I'm up to . . . one."

Shauna rolled her eyes, but Tom thought it was funny. "Well, it sounds like you're off to a good start," he chuckled softly.

"Well," I said, "I just started it yesterday on the plane. Or was it the day before?"

"Did you find anything under the word *lost* yet?" Dad asked.

"Oh, yeah," I remembered, looking back at the Bible Dictionary. "Right here there's an entry called 'Lost Books.' Is that it?"

"Sounds like it to me," Dad replied. "So how many lost books does it mention?"

"Well . . ." I said, skimming through the first few lines, "oh, here's a list! The 'book of Wars of the Lord' and the 'book of Jasher' and the 'book of the acts of Solomon' and the 'book of Samuel the seer' and the 'book of Nathan the prophet' and . . . there are *tons* in here!"

"Why don't you just count them?" Mom suggested.

"Okay," I said, returning to the beginning of the list to count. "Whoa," I said after a moment. "It looks like fourteen or something like that. I had no clue!"

"So I guess you're starting to appreciate the Bible Dictionary now, huh?" Brandon asked.

"I never *didn't* appreciate it," I explained very calmly through clenched teeth. "I just said that it's *not* a dictionary."

The look on Brandon's face made it obvious that he *already* knew this but was taking deep satisfaction from his ability to aggravate me about it.

"Let's read the next chapter," Dad suggested in a blatant attempt to cut short Brandon's gloating. I made a mental note to thank Dad the next chance I got.

Shauna began reading the first verse of chapter 2:

And when any will offer a meat offering unto the Lord, his offering shall be of fine flour; and he shall pour oil upon it, . . .

There was more, but I didn't let her finish. "Hold on, wait a minute," I interrupted. "A *meat* offering is made of *flour*? What's the deal with that?"

"Uh-oh," Brandon said. "Sounds like it's Bible Dictionary time again."

I couldn't tell if he was serious or just trying to be a pain, so after staring at Brandon for a moment, I asked Dad, "Do you think there's something in there about meat offerings?"

"Probably," Dad answered.

"I've already got it," Shauna said. I think she was looking for it from the second I interrupted her. "It says here that a meat offering is more properly called a 'meal offering,'" she said, "and it says that it 'consisted chiefly of grain (or flour and cakes made from grain) and wine, seasoned with salt, and offered with incense.'"

"So somebody crossed the *l* in 'meal' and wrote 'meat' by mistake?" I asked. "Eureka!" I called in fake surprise. "I think we've discovered one of the places the Article of Faith talks about when it says 'we believe the Bible to be the word of God as far as it is translated correctly.'"

"R-right," Mom said slowly. Shauna rolled her eyes with a look that said, *Brothers are bad enough, but why do they have to be able to speak?*

"I slay myself!" I said.

"Well, crossing the *l* to make a *t* makes sense in English," Dad said, "but I think this was originally written in Hebrew."

"Oh, guess what," Shauna continued. "It says here that no burnt offering or peace offering was complete without it."

"So that's what those little cakes are that they gave to us?" Brandon asked. "Meal offerings to go with the burnt offering?"

"It looks that way," Dad said.

"This is amazing," Tom nodded.

"They know what they're doing, don't they?" Mom said.

Dad and Tom just nodded in response.

"Let's read some more," Shauna suggested.

Well, we ended up reading the rest of the chapter, and I learned a few more things about those cakes they made that we figured were the meal offerings. Part of it was supposed to be burned, and they couldn't make it with honey or leaven, because they weren't supposed to burn those things. I didn't know what leaven was, so I looked it up in Shauna's dictionary and added this to my Bible dictionary:

Leaven—an agent, such as yeast, that causes batter or dough to rise; fermentation.

Leviticus 2:11 No meat offering can be made with leaven.

I actually found two other words in the chapter that I added to my dictionary as well:

Memorial—serving as a remembrance of a person or an event.

Leviticus 2:2 The priest shall burn the memorial of it upon the altar.

Oblation—the act of offering something, such as worship or thanks, to a god.

Leviticus 2:4 Oblations of meat offerings must be made without leaven.

The verse that made me do the most thinking was verse 13:

And every oblation of thy meat offering shalt thou season with salt; neither shalt thou suffer the salt of the covenant of thy God to be lacking from thy meat offering: with all thine offerings thou shalt offer salt.

"So salt is really a big deal, isn't it?" I asked. I didn't direct the question to anyone in particular. No one answered, either. But they really didn't have to. We were all thinking the same thing, and no one wanted to say it out loud. These people made at least two offerings every day and *every* offering had to include salt . . . and we had just ruined what appeared to be their main source.

Rather than talk about the salt anymore, we decided to just keep reading. It was probably an attempt to keep our minds off of our situation, but because we chose to read about these sacrifices, I think it just ended up reminding us of our problem more and more. We kept reading for a really long time. Leviticus chapter 3 is all about "peace offerings." Peace offerings sounded pretty much like burnt offerings to me, but I guess they just did it whenever they were feeling at peace with God, unlike the burnt offering that they had to do every morning and night, no matter what.

The fourth chapter of Leviticus was all about "sin offerings." A sin offering was apparently required whenever they sinned without knowing it. Chapters 5 and 6 were about "trespass offerings," which were for sins against other people or for being disrespectful of sacred things. Trespass offerings were a big deal, I think, because not only did they have to give an offering, but they also had to make restitution of whatever they did wrong, plus another 20 percent.

"Wow," I said, "so if they got caught stealing something from somebody, then they had to give back what they took plus 20 percent more and then also give an animal for a sacrifice?"

"That's right," Dad said.

The whole thing seemed pretty severe to me.

"Dad," Brandon asked intently, "do you think that what we did to their salt would require a *sin* offering . . . or a *trespass* offering?"

I thought, *Well, now,* there's *a bad subject if I've heard one this entire trip.*

I looked at Mom to see what sort of deadly glare Brandon was going to get for that one. Instead I saw that Mom was much more worried about the truth of what Brandon had said than the fact that he had brought it up. I guess Brandon was the first one to think about it, because no one had an answer for him. In fact, no one even seemed interested in talking about it.

"I think it's time for a benediction," Dad said after a few moments.

Mom was the only one who responded. "I agree," she said.

Dad said the prayer, and we all quietly put our scriptures back into our bags.

Suddenly I got an idea that I thought might improve my standing in the "appropriate" department. "Does the Book of Mormon tell about how they did their sacrifices?" I asked, pulling my scriptures back out and turning to the index.

"It talks about performing sacrifices," Dad said, "but remember that they had the writings of Moses, so they didn't need to write down how they did them."

I was skimming through the references under "Sacrifice" in the index as he spoke. "Hey," I smiled, "I found Shauna's scripture." I turned to 3 Nephi 9:20 and read the first part out loud:

And ye shall offer for a sacrifice unto me a broken heart and a contrite spirit . . .

"Read the verse before that one," Dad suggested. I read verse 19:

And ye shall offer up unto me no more the shedding of blood; yea, your sacrifices and your burnt offerings shall be done away, for I will accept none of your sacrifices and your burnt offerings.

"I don't think that's something we want to be mentioning to these guys," Brandon said.

Dad just raised his eyebrows. No one said anything. As I put my scriptures away, Aaron and some of the other younger boys came to get our help. We were each assigned different tasks. Each of us, except for the girls and women, that is. They just stayed with our bags and stuff and watched the rest of us work.

Brandon and Danny and I were assigned to help Aaron. As we were going to hitch up two of the reindeer to one of the sleds, I noticed that Dad and Tom were helping take all of the dried meat from the racks and wrapping it into bundles. Aaron led the reindeer over by the drying racks and showed us how to take them apart and stack the logs onto the sled. Danny really had a great time. He was more interested in showing us how strong he was as he half dragged, half pushed several logs over next to the sled.

"Jeff!" he panted after each log. "There's . . . another one . . . for you to . . . put on it."

Then he would watch carefully as I picked up his log and inform me each time if he thought I had put it in a good place on the pile or if he thought it would soon fall off and tell me that I had "better do a better job."

We were less than half done when the sled looked like it had about all that it could hold. At this point, Aaron began to lead the reindeer down the shoreline in the direction we had come from two days earlier.

"Storing we this wood in cave in hill," he explained.

We soon discovered that he was talking about the cave that Tom and Brandon had explored right after our crash landing. Apparently they brought these logs with them from some other place for use during the summer and stored them in the cave during the long winters. Aaron wanted the logs carried as far back inside the cave as possible. Danny had absolutely no interest in going inside the cave, so he stayed outside and talked to the reindeer the whole time. I felt pretty much the way he did but didn't dare show it in front of Aaron.

After unloading the sled, we headed back for more. It took three trips and at least that many hours to get all the racks taken apart and stored in the cave. That was the first time in two days that I felt hot. We finished just in time for the evening ritual. It was great to be able to sit down for a while. I can't remember the last time I worked that hard—maybe because it had never happened before.

For dinner we were given some dried meat in addition to the cakes and water. It seemed really salty at first, but after a couple of bites, I really started to enjoy it. Danny really liked it, too, but I don't think Brandon cared for it too much; he gave his last piece to Danny who chomped it down like it was a candy bar.

After we finished eating, Aaron and Levi approached us.

"Leaving we for village my people on morrow in morning," Aaron said.

"How long will it take us to get there?" asked Neil.

"Traveling we three days," answered Aaron.

I could tell from the look on Neil's face that he didn't like the sound of that. And for obvious reasons. He was still hoping for a rescue.

"Are you sure that we can't just stay here?" Neil asked Aaron, glancing at Levi.

Levi got a look on his face like he couldn't believe we were discussing this again. His "certain death" comment was still ringing loudly in my ears.

Levi looked toward Jacob some distance away and then turned back to us. "Coming ye with us for safety of all your people," he said.

"Well, maybe we can talk to this Christian," Jo said to Neil, "and get a better idea of what's going on." Then she turned to Aaron and asked, "Does Christian still live in your village, or did he return to the United States of America?"

Aaron looked slowly over at his father and then back at Jo.

"Living Christian with my people three and fifty years," Aaron said. "Remaining Christian with my people to time of death. Saying

Jacob . . . Christian be never allowed to return to United States America."

"*What!*" breathed Jo. "*Why?*"

"Repaying Christian for trespass," Aaron said. The word *trespass* hit me like a fist in the stomach.

"Is the Christian still alive?" Jo asked.

"Living Christian not," Aaron replied. No one said anything for a moment.

"Have we trespassed against you?" Dad asked. "Must we repay you for our trespassing?"

Aaron didn't answer, and we all just waited and watched for a response.

CHAPTER 9

The Lost Tribe

"Coming ye with us," Levi said finally. "Taking we ye to place of great river of water with many travelers."

"Travelers?" Neil asked.

"Traveling men and women on large boats of great noise on river of water," Levi said.

"You said you wanted us to go to your village," Tom said. "Is your village near this river?"

"Going we first to village my people," Levi said. "Taking we meat to women and children in village."

"Then will you take us to the river?" asked Neil.

"Climbing we up high mountain and down high mountain to river of water with travelers," Levi assured us.

"We are not interested in remaining in your village for a long time," Neil said. "You understand that we are looking for just a short stopover on the way to the river. We do not even need to spend time to refuel, if you know what I mean."

I cringed as he said that. I thought, *Did you really have to mention fuel?*

"Leaving ye for river of water on next day from village," Levi assured him.

"Okay," said Neil after a pause. "We will go with you."

Right, like we have any choice, I thought.

"Leaving we for village on morrow in morning," said Levi.

"Sleeping ye now in preparation of travel." With that, Levi gestured toward our tents. We all understood that the discussion was now over.

"Thank you," Mom said. "Thank you for all your help and kindness."

Levi didn't answer. He just nodded gently and again gestured toward the huts.

"Before you go," Dad asked, "can you tell us what Christian's trespass was?"

"Sleeping ye now in preparation for travel," Levi said again.

"Yes," Dad responded. "I understand. I will not ask again. Thank you for everything." He headed for our hut, and we all followed.

"I think we're going to be okay," Tom said quietly as we approached the tents.

"I still don't like the idea of leaving the place where the plane landed," Neil grumbled.

That was the last I heard from any of the others as I climbed into our hut.

"Dad," Shauna asked, "do you think that going with these people is a good idea?"

"I do."

"Why?" Brandon asked. "Wouldn't it be better to stay close to where the plane landed, like Neil said?"

"Bra-a-an!" I hissed. "Don't you remember Levi saying something about . . . certain . . . *something* . . . if we stayed here!"

I was afraid to actually use the word *death* because I knew that I'd surely get in trouble for it. It was too dark in the tent to see anyone, so I could only hope that Brandon understood what I was trying to say.

"*I* think," Dad said after a moment, "that we should follow Levi's advice. He knows our surroundings far better than we do. He seems very kind and generous. And his idea about the boats on the river seems to be the best idea yet for actually getting out of here."

"What about the rescue plane?" Shauna asked.

"It's already been two days," Dad sighed. "I don't think there's a plane coming. I really believe we're going to have to find our own way out of here."

There was a pause. Then the silence was broken by Chelsea complaining about Danny's foot being in her face. Shauna said something about hoping there would be a place soon where she could shower. I was going to agree with her about her need but thought better of it. Everyone just seemed restless and irritated.

"Dad," Meg said softly. "Are we going to pray?"

"Of course," Dad said. So one more time, just after we were settled in our cramped sleeping space, we all wriggled back into a kneeling position. Mom said the prayer. I was surprised to hear her ask for the health and safety of the tribesmen more than she did for us. She also said something about them having all the salt they needed and asking for forgiveness for any hardship we may have caused them. She even asked that, if possible, we would be able to make restitution. Her comment made Aaron's voice resonate in my head: "Repaying Christian for trespass." After the prayer we all snuggled into the animal skins again. This time no one complained or said anything for a while.

I was almost asleep when I heard Mom speak softly to Dad: "I've been thinking about the way Aaron and Levi speak," she said, jarring me back from wherever my mind had been drifting—I think it had something to do with a large, flat bed and a soft pillow.

"It's strange, isn't it?" Dad said. Mom didn't respond, so Dad asked, "Is that what you mean?"

"Well, I was thinking about the two semesters of Hebrew I took in college," Mom continued. "I don't remember much about it, but I remember that the part of Hebrew that was the most difficult for me was the fact that the verbs always came first. I could never get used to that. But have you noticed how Aaron and Levi speak?"

She paused before answering her own question. "It seems like every-thing they say begins with a verb!"

"You're right," Dad said with a little bit of excitement in his voice. "Levi said, 'leaving we on the morrow' and 'climbing we a mountain.' You're right—I think you're right!"

"Don't forget 'repaying Christian for trespass,'" I yawned. In the dark, I couldn't tell if I was ignored or glared at. But I didn't care—I thought it was an important point.

"But there's more," Mom said. "Did you notice how at one point Aaron said that this Christian was living in his village and then later he said that the Christian was dead? It's like there's no differ-ence between past tense and present tense."

"Oh, it's probably just because English is unfamiliar to them," Dad suggested.

"Maybe . . ." Mom agreed. "But did you know that Hebrew doesn't have a present tense?"

There was a pause as Mom let her voice trail off at the end of the sentence.

"So are you saying that these people speak Hebrew?" Shauna asked.

"I don't know what I'm saying," Mom admitted.

"Well, what about how it sounds?" Brandon asked. "I mean, when they talk to each other does it sound like Hebrew? Do you remember how it sounds from your classes?"

"I don't really remember what it sounded like," Mom explained. "No one spoke Hebrew as an everyday language for hundreds of years until the last century. It was still used for religious services and for studying, but that was all. So there's no telling if it even sounds the same or not."

"That's *cool!*" Brandon breathed.

I grunted a soft but disgusted sigh. I thought he was nuts—he and everyone else, too. I wanted to stand up and shout, "This is *not* cool—this is *dangerous!*" But I didn't dare. Everyone was being so fascinated by the idea that we may have met people who had descended from the Israelites in the Old Testament, and yet I couldn't understand how quickly everyone seemed to forget about the fact that Old Testament people had no problem killing and enslaving their enemies. Levi and Aaron were nice, sure. But it was obvious that Jacob thought we were enemies. And it was also obvious that Jacob was the one in charge.

"Do you have something you want to say?" asked Dad in response to my grunt.

"No," I said, in the shortest syllable possible. Of course, it wasn't true, but I was tired of getting in trouble for reminding people about *reality*.

"We understand your worry," Dad said gently. "But again, the more we understand of these people, the better chance we have of keeping ourselves safe and figuring out how to get home as quickly as possible."

"We can try to *understand* the danger," Mom agreed, "without dwelling on it."

"I didn't say anything," I said.

"But it's apparent that you're unhappy with us talking about it," Dad said, "and we're just trying to help you feel better about what's going on."

I thought, *I'm not going to feel better until we're out of here*, but all I said was, "Okay." Again, as short as possible.

I know Dad could tell that I was still unhappy, but I figured he decided not to push it anymore. "Let's get some sleep," he suggested. "It sounds like we have a long way to go tomorrow."

The next morning we were again awakened by a burst of light as the flap to our hut was abruptly opened. *Obviously still facing east*, I thought as I squinted and covered my eyes with my forearm. Slowly, I tried to untie myself from the pretzel position I had ended up in. For some reason I felt a lot more sore this morning than I had the day before. We were escorted to our assigned pew and observed the morning's burnt offering. The only detail that differed from the other times was that yet another man brought the bird to be sacrificed. In all other aspects, everything about the sacrifice was exactly the same, at least as far as I could see.

After the offering, we were served cakes as before. I was beginning to get a little tired of them. Grape jelly or strawberry jam sounded really good. I decided that I shouldn't complain about lack of variety in our meals at home anymore. As soon as breakfast was over, Aaron and a couple of other boys about his age came and showed us how to dismantle a hut. I was amazed at how easily they came apart once you knew how to do it. I had not noticed before, but there were two poles quite close together which were apparently pinching one edge of the thick animal skin near the top of the poles. Simply pulling the poles away from each other at the bottom caused that edge to come loose at the top, and the entire skin fell to the ground in sort of a spiral motion around the rest of the poles. I was surprised to see that the poles were not tied together in any way but simply balanced and wedged against each other at the top.

The skin was laid out across the tundra as one by one the poles were removed from their standing position and laid across it. The amazing part about this was that they never made a sound. If we had been with my Scout troop, the sound of poles clanking against each other would have been heard for miles. When there were three poles left, Aaron showed us how to use one pole to push the other two just enough so that they almost stayed balanced before slowly falling toward him. As the last two poles began to fall toward him, he was able to silently lay the one he was holding on the pile and then reach up in time to catch the two that were falling—one in each hand—before they came crashing down on him or the pile. Again, there was not a single sound.

Aaron then rolled the skin quickly around the poles and wedged a couple of corners between poles so that it stayed in a tight bundle. When he was done he motioned for us to dismantle our own huts. I noticed that he used Neil's hut as the example. There were obviously rewards for being assigned to the Executive Tent.

Dad and Brandon and I began working on our tent while Tom and John started on theirs. I thought I had watched pretty closely and knew what I was doing, but it wasn't nearly as easy as it looked. I was holding the first pole as high as I could above my head and jumping up and down trying to get the top edge of the skin to come loose, but it was like it had been nailed in place or something.

"What *is* this!" I complained.

"I think you have the wrong pole," Brandon said. I noticed that he was standing far enough away from any work that he probably figured he had a pretty good view of the situation.

"It was right next to *that* one," I said, pointing to the other pole that seemed to be holding the skin in place. I forgot to quit jumping as I pointed, though, and so the first pole came flying down and whacked me on the shoulder before falling back into place.

"Are you all right?" Dad asked.

"Yeah," I moaned, rubbing my shoulder. Brandon gave me a look that said something like, "I could have told you that would happen." I ignored him.

"Let's try this pole," Dad suggested, and the skin immediately fell away from the top and did the cool spiral thing around the bottom.

"How did you *do* that?" I asked with exasperation.

He just smiled and asked Brandon to help him spread out the skin. Since I was now wounded, I was the one who got to watch. I was anxious to see how soon Brandon would lose that smug look on his face. It didn't take long. Dad was carefully removing the poles and handing them to Brandon to place on the animal skin. Of course, it never occurred to Brandon that it might be a good idea to put them on the part of the skin that was furthest from the slope or to turn them so they wouldn't easily roll that direction. The first two poles were okay until he sort of tripped on the edge of the skin and dropped the third pole with a loud "*crack!*"

Because of the noise, everyone in camp turned just in time to see the first two poles start rolling and bouncing down the slope. Brandon tried to jump after them but only tripped again, this time on the third pole, sending it spinning around himself and bounding after the first two. It took everything I had to keep from laughing. But no one else seemed to think it was as funny as I did. I wondered if the tribesmen even had the *ability* to laugh. They were obviously not amused by the situation, all of them just standing and staring in amazement. Jacob looked like he was completely disgusted by the incident, probably convinced that Brandon had certainly done it on purpose.

"Go help your brother," Dad said quickly.

Why is it that parents use the expression "your brother" or "your sister" when they're trying to get you to do something embarrassing? It's as if they're trying to make you feel some sort of extra responsibility for something you have absolutely nothing to do with, just because you happen to be related to someone who did something really dumb. I wanted to ask, but I knew it should probably wait until later. Instead, I scampered down the slope with Brandon right behind me. We moved as quickly as possible, bringing the poles back up to where they started. Everything seemed quiet, so I didn't dare look around to see how many of the tribesmen were still staring at us. But I had a feeling it was most of them.

By the time we got back up the slope, Neil and John had already finished their bundle and were helping Dad take down the last three poles from our hut. We just added ours to the pile—though not as quietly as I would have liked—and then helped wrap up the bundle. When we finished, I glanced quickly around and found that everyone seemed to have returned to whatever they were doing. Everyone, that is, except for Jacob. He continued to stare at us with a look of extreme distaste.

Within a few minutes, everything from the area was loaded onto the three reindeer sleds, during which time Brandon and I managed to keep from making any more major blunders. One sled held the stacks of meat, another the tent bundles and bags of salt, and the last held the altar and the caged birds for the sacrifices and several animal skin bags of fresh water. We were allowed to put our backpacks and other things on the second sled with the tents and bags of salt.

Then, without a word, the sleds began moving southward toward the mountains in the distance. Several tribesmen walked along each side of the reindeer, guiding them with just a touch on the side of the neck. I was sort of surprised that no one sat on the front of the sled with reins. As the sleds moved forward, I noticed that several of the men who had been guarding us on the first day came and stood behind us. Some held spears, though they were all in an upright position.

"Are we supposed to be following?" I asked.

"It certainly looks that way," Tom said as he began marching behind the sleds. We all followed.

"Let's go," Dad said with determination, putting one hand around Danny's shoulder and reaching toward Chelsea. "Would you two like to take turns riding on my shoulders?" he asked.

Just as Chelsea was saying, "Yeah," Aaron approached and said, "Riding small children to village." With that, he scooped up Danny, tucked him under one arm like a football, and did a funny little run/walk thing up to the front sled. Aaron then placed Danny gently on the back of the sled, facing backwards.

"Would you like to ride also?" Dad asked Chelsea as she stared at Danny with wide eyes.

She opened her mouth and raised her head as if she was about to nod and say "yes," but then she just froze there with eyes darting back and forth between Danny and Dad. Before she ever answered, Aaron was back. He grabbed her wrists and swung her around his body onto his back. Again he did the run/walk forward to catch up with the sleds. He placed Chelsea on the back of the second sled.

"Do I get to ride, too?" Meg asked. She pointed to the sled just in front of us and asked, "On this one?"

"I don't know," Dad asked. "We'll see."

Aaron returned to where we were walking and reached for Meg. She got a huge smile on her face and held her arms out toward him. Instead of picking her up like he had done with Chelsea and Danny, he walked just behind the last sled and motioned for her to catch up to him. As soon as she did, he placed his hands on the sides of her waist and swung her around onto the back of the sled. Her eyes sparkled as she settled into a comfortable position.

"Oh, man!" Brandon moaned. "One more sled, and I would get to ride, too, huh?"

"Do you think you qualify as a small child?" Dad asked.

Brandon didn't answer. Instead he just squished his lips together.

"I'm going to walk next to Chelsea," Mom said, walking quickly forward. She looked back over her shoulder at Dad and asked, "Do you want to stay with Daniel?"

"Of course," Dad said and immediately followed. "Will you three stay close to Meg?" he asked us over his shoulder as he left.

"Sure," we all agreed.

"I will stay with the children also," Tom offered.

And with that, the journey to the mountain began. As far as I could tell, none of the tribesmen said a single word as we traveled. They each seemed to have their place in the caravan and just walked in silence. Jacob and Levi and two others were in front of the first sled. Each set of reindeer had several men and boys walking alongside them. The guards walked closely behind our group.

Twice during the morning, we stopped long enough to sit for a few minutes on the soft tundra and drink some fresh water from the bags. When we started moving again after the first rest stop, I noticed Levi dropped back in the caravan until he was even with the back of the first sled where Danny was sitting and Mom was walking. They were too far ahead for me to tell if he said anything, but I watched as he motioned for Mom to sit on the back of the sled next to Danny. She seemed surprised by the invitation and hesitated before climbing on. She then looked at Levi with a look that clearly asked, "Is this what you had in mind?" Levi responded by gently touching his hands together and bowing slightly. She returned a soft smile in his direction.

Levi then dropped back to where the rest of us were walking and gestured for Shauna, Jo, and Nancy to each take a place on the back of the other two sleds. Shauna and Nancy sat by Chelsea and Jo climbed on next to Meg. They all seemed tired and grateful for the ride. Once he had each of the women on one of the sleds, Levi returned to the front of the caravan where he stayed the rest of the morning.

A couple of times earlier in the day, two or three different people from our group briefly said something to someone else. Each of these attempts at conversation was immediately stopped by a grunt from one of our guards. The glare that followed made it clear that silence was to be the order of the trip. I couldn't tell if it was because we were trying to pass through this landscape as unnoticed as possible or if these guys just didn't believe in mixing pleasure with travel. All that could be done was to watch the changing scenery as we neared the base of the mountain. I noticed that the tribesmen seemed to be spending quite a bit of time scanning the rolling hills around us and the trail ahead as they walked. Maybe there was some kind of danger lurking that we weren't aware of. But whether it was danger or just custom, the result was the same either way: a long, boring, somewhat-tense walk.

For a while I was looking around, but the scenery all seemed the same to me; there was nothing but rolling hills covered with tundra. The mountains were getting closer, and at one point I looked backwards to see that the ocean was no longer in view, but other than this, nothing looked any different.

I was tired and starving by the time we stopped for lunch. We could tell that this stop was going to be longer than the first two because the animal skins were removed from the sleds and spread out on the ground. We quickly recognized the one that was intended for us because we had spent most of the previous two days sitting on it. It was a welcome sight at this point. Most groups spread out their animal skin some distance from the sleds and broke out the leftover cakes from breakfast. We were given a large stack for our group. I think they tasted better this time than ever before. Of course, our family had a blessing on the food first, but then I ate quickly and drank quite a bit of water. Within a moment or two, I felt myself getting sleepy, so I laid back and closed my eyes.

I couldn't have been asleep for more than a few minutes before I was jolted awake again. Dad was shaking me, and I saw that everyone was packing up in silence. Within minutes the caravan was moving once more. Jo tried to get Brandon and me to take her place on the sled, but this idea was quickly squelched by the guards. Apparently, small children always rode, women usually rode, and men and non-small boys walked—no exceptions. Everyone who had been riding on the sleds during the morning eventually took their same positions as before, but there were some looks of regret from our airplane friends thrown in our direction. I tried not to think about it. Instead I just tried to think about something else— anything else. But what was there to think about? Home and friends seemed so far from reality that I couldn't keep my mind there. It kept wandering back to this nightmare. I was starting to wonder if it would ever end.

We stopped two more times during the afternoon for short water breaks but immediately moved on again, just as we had in the morning. By the end of the first day, the landscape finally began changing a little. There were small bushes here and there, and the reindeer seemed to be intent in trying to get at them. They were obviously as tired and hungry as I was. The tribesmen had to work harder and harder to keep the heads of the reindeer up and the sleds moving forward. After struggling for a few minutes, it appeared they were ready to give in and stop for the night. I was more than ready to fall asleep right where I stood, but it was not to be. There was work to be done before anyone could sleep.

After the reindeer were released from their leather harnesses, the tent bundles were unloaded and set up. Again Neil just watched as the Executive Tent was assembled for him and again, after watching a single demonstration of this process, we were expected to set up ours on our own. It took Dad, Tom, and John all together to set up our other two tents. Brandon and I basically just stared blankly in their general direction as they did all the work.

Once the tents were up, we were herded one more time to our pew to watch the ritual. The smell of the fire and the burning bird awakened my stomach, and the rest of me quickly followed. I could hardly wait for our family's blessing on the food to be completed before diving into the meal.

"Coming ye with me," Aaron said to Brandon and me just as I was feeling content. Sleep had started to overtake me again, but I managed to struggle to my feet. Aaron had several empty water pouches on long, leather straps slung over his head and shoulders, making a huge "X" across his chest.

"Collecting we water for journey," Aaron explained as we followed him away from camp. We walked in silence for a couple of minutes around the side of one of the hills. As soon as we were out of sight of the camp, Aaron immediately peppered us with questions.

"Coming ye from United States America?" he asked first. We nodded.

"Allowing rulers of United States America all people freedom to choose religion?" Aaron asked next. We nodded again. Aaron began walking faster and faster and speaking with more animation.

"Speaking Christian to my father many times of this," Aaron continued with excitement. "Saying many people worshipping God of Israel, also worshipping many people Jesus Christ, also worshipping many people other gods or no gods." As he said this, I was reminded of the Book of Mormon prophecies about America being a promised land and that the people living there would be protected as long as they were righteous and worshipped the only true God.

Aaron suddenly started removing the water bags from his shoulders, handing two each to Brandon and me. Then he stooped down and began filling one of the bags from a small spring that was gurgling between his feet. I hadn't even noticed it as we approached. He obviously knew this place well because he went straight to it in the dim light. We each filled our bags by sinking the opening into the freezing water, then tied the tops closed with a short leather strap. I began to shiver as soon as my hands became wet.

"Believing the family my father in Jesus Christ," Aaron continued, still with excitement. "Worshipping we Jesus Christ."

Then his face clouded slightly as he said, "Worshipping we Jesus Christ . . . in secret."

"Because of Jacob?" I asked.

"Angered is Jacob because of Christian," continued Aaron with obvious sadness. Our bags were full now and so Aaron led us slowly back toward camp. We followed, but it was hard to walk with the water bags sloshing against my hips.

"So the Christian taught your people of Jesus Christ and now you believe and worship him?" I asked, rubbing my hands together to try to warm them up.

"Yes. Believing many people of my village in Messiah Jesus Christ," Aaron explained. "Believing father of Jacob not in Messiah. Believing father of Jacob in Law of Moses. Forcing father of Jacob all people my village no more worshipping of Messiah.

Returning my people to old ways. Returning my people to Law of Moses."

"Why does Jacob's father force everyone to follow the Law of Moses," Brandon asked, "and not worship Christ anymore?"

"Dying is father of Jacob—or Jacob's father—many years ago," Aaron said. "Following Jacob in ways of his father."

"Oh," I said, "so now that Jacob's father is dead, Jacob is the one that forces everybody to live the Law of Moses and not believe in Jesus Christ?"

"Believing people of my village in coming of Messiah," Aaron said. "Saying Christian to my people: Messiah coming long ago. Saying Christian to my people: Jesus Christ being name of Messiah." With that, he didn't say another word. His expression changed, and I noticed the camp was in view once again. I wanted to get more information, but Aaron just stared at the ground as he walked. Once the water bags were stored on the sled, Aaron gestured for us to return to our family, and he left to take care of other chores. Quietly, we told everyone what had happened.

"I'd sure like to know how this Christian got here," said Neil, uninterested in the religious discussion.

"And I'd like to get another look at those dog tags," agreed John.

Without warning, Levi's voice spoke from behind Neil and John. Because they were standing, none of us had noticed him approaching. "Flying Christian to here with airplane," Levi said. John and Neil turned quickly to face Levi after he spoke.

"An airplane?" Neil asked in shock, as if he couldn't believe this man would know the word. "Christian flew here in an airplane?"

"Flying Christian to here in much small airplane. Ye flying to here in much large airplane," Levi said, gesturing to Neil. The shock remained on Neil's face. His mouth opened as if he would speak, but no sound came out for at least a couple of seconds.

Finally, he could contain himself no longer, and every question in his head seemed to gush out at once.

"What kind of plane was it?" Neil asked. "One-seater, two-seater? How many props did it have? Was it a military plane? I mean . . . since he was obviously in the military, right? Did he come alone? Did he crash?"

"Seeing ye airplane of Christian near to village my people," Levi said.

Now Neil's lower jaw dropped like a rock. "You still have the plane after fifty-three years?"

Levi just nodded. I wondered if nodding meant "yes" or something else. Maybe he had learned it from Christian. "Sleeping ye now in preparation of morrow," he said and left.

I could *not* believe the change that occurred in Neil's attitude after that little tidbit of information. He was the one who had had absolutely no interest in leaving the shore as long as he thought there was any hope of a rescue plane showing up. But now we couldn't slow him down! I think he was the first one up each of the next two mornings. I think he was even taking down and bundling his own tent, but I'm not completely sure because it was done and on the sled before any of the rest of us ever stumbled out of ours. He didn't walk in the back with the rest of us anymore, either. He was up in front of the first reindeer sled. At first Jacob didn't seem too happy about it, but as always seemed to be the case, Levi talked calmly with him until he agreed.

Other than Neil walking up front, the next two days were pretty much like the first one. No talking, two rest stops each morning and afternoon, the girls get to ride and boys get to walk. We kept walking southward and gradually upward. There began to be more and more bushes, and on the third day there were even trees. We helped Aaron fill water bags again the second evening, but this time a small stream was only a short distance from where we were camped, and we were in full view of the others. I figured that was why Aaron didn't hit us this time with the same type of questions as the night before.

On the evening of the third day, we came up over the top of a steep rise to a scene that looked like it came from an old movie. There was a large meadow at the base of a steep, rocky mountain. At the edge of the meadow, next to more trees than I had seen in days, were dozens of tents just like the ones we had been sleeping in. Thin lines of smoke rose slowly into the air and became lost up the side of the mountain. Several groups of reindeer were roaming through the trees and chomping at small bushes in the meadow.

I heard Dad say under his breath in almost complete astonishment, "There must be a hundred huts here!"

"It's like a lost tribe of Israel," Tom said in amazement as he surveyed the huts.

As we neared the tents, children of various ages came running to meet us. First they approached with smiles and then stopped short, hesitation showing on their faces. Some turned and ran immediately back toward various huts. Some cautiously approached some of the men and boys walking next to the reindeer and began mumbling with curious questions and looking at each of us foreigners in turn. Soon adults gathered to meet us at a place that looked pretty much to be the center of the long string of huts along the base of the mountain. All communication was hushed. Some people immediately went about the work of unloading and distributing the meat and other supplies from the sleds, while avoiding our things. But most of the people were gathered around the tribesmen who had brought us here, obviously wanting more information before they did anything else.

Within a few minutes, many of the questions had apparently been answered, and people began taking the supplies to their various huts. We were shown where to set up our tents. Levi gave Tom and Jo each their own tents now and gave our family an extra one so we could spread out a little. All the other tent bundles remained on the sled. I was surprised that though the new people stared and watched us as they worked, they all stayed well away from us and looked away if they ever got close.

Soon Levi and Aaron approached. I could tell from their faces that something was wrong.

"Are we going to the river tomorrow?" John asked, not waiting for them to speak.

"I want to see that old *plane* first!" Neil said.

Levi looked stern and hesitated for several moments before speaking. "Going ye not for many days," Levi said finally. "Remaining ye yet for many days."

CHAPTER 10

The Feast of Weeks

"What?" Neil asked, suddenly no longer interested in the plane.

"Why?" John added. "You said we would go to the river tomorrow. You said the next day after the village. This is the village, right?"

Levi looked sad. He said slowly, "Remaining yet much snow in mountain. Going ye not for many days."

"How many is 'many'?" Dad asked, immediately going after the detail we all wanted.

Levi thought for a moment before stating, "Going ye not for five or six or seven days."

"A week," John said, interpreting for us. "You're saying we're stuck here for as much as a week." John bounced his head up and down and chomped his gum three or four times while we all took in the information. "I . . . I can . . . I can do a week," John said finally. "I'm okay with a week."

"Yes," Neil said. "A week sounds entirely acceptable given our circumstances." I looked at him in surprise because he had suddenly found his formal voice again. I'd almost forgotten about it. "But not eight days?" Neil asked for reassurance. "Just five or six or seven?"

"Going ye not in eight days," Levi affirmed. "Traveling no one on Sabbath."

"Oh-h-h," Neil answered. "Of course. Of course, we will not travel on the Sabbath."

"So," John asked, "if the Sabbath is in eight days, then it must also be in one day. So tomorrow is the Sabbath?"

"Honoring we the Sabbath on the morrow on evening," Levi explained.

"At sundown?" Nancy asked.

"The sun doesn't go down, remember?" John said.

"Oh, oops!" Nancy grimaced. "Right. 'On the morrow on evening.' Of course."

Levi looked at each of us, apparently to be sure there were no more questions. Then he said, "Preparing we now for sacrifice."

By that I thought he meant that we should all get ready to watch the ceremony at the altar that I had noticed not far from where we had unloaded the sleds. This altar was similar to the one Jacob had been using. But it turned out that "preparing" meant getting cleaned up from our journey. Aaron approached with a woman whom he introduced as his mother and the "wife of his father, Levi." Everyone immediately came to greet her. She was carrying a container of warm water and a number of small cloths, which Aaron said we were to use to wash with. Tom, Dad, and John quickly set up one of the huts and then, one by one, we each took a turn inside, washing as quickly as possible. Even with the warm water, it was way too cold to stay undressed for long. And, of course, we had no change of clothes, so the dirty ones went right back on.

About the time everyone had finished washing and the last of our huts had been set up, I noticed that people from the village were beginning to gather. Animal skins were laid out on the ground, and the villagers sat on them, facing an altar similar to the one we had carried back from the shore with us. It was uncovered, and a fire was started.

"So is tomorrow Sunday?" I asked Dad as Tom and John spread out our animal skin on the ground. "Or is it the next day?"

Dad looked at his watch because it shows what day of the week it is. "Hmm," he said. "Tomorrow's Friday, which means they honor the Sabbath from Friday evening to Saturday evening." Dad smiled. "I guess you could expect that from people following the Old Testament."

"But we crossed the international dateline," Tom reminded us.

"Oh, yeah," Dad smiled. "Good point."

"We were going west," Tom said slowly as he worked out the details in his head, "so it's actually a day later. It's like we lost a day. That means tomorrow is Saturday."

"Wait, what?" Shauna scowled. We all waited. "But . . . didn't the Israelites celebrate the Sabbath from sundown Friday to sundown Saturday? So shouldn't these people be starting the Sabbath now."

"Maybe when Christian taught them about Christ, they changed their Sabbath to Sunday," Dad suggested.

"Sh-h-h," Neil said. "It's starting."

We immediately quieted down and turned our attention to Jacob and the altar. The burnt offering proceeded as always, and when it was done, the tribesmen went back to their huts and fires and began eating their own meals.

As we walked back to our hut, Dad asked Shauna, "Do you know why we hold the Sabbath on Sunday instead of Saturday?"

"Because Christ was resurrected on Sunday," she answered. "And so the Apostles started meeting on Sunday and taking the sacrament then."

"Right," Dad smiled.

As we approached our huts, Aaron informed us that it was time to eat. It turned out that their family hut was the closest one to ours. I was sure Levi had arranged this on purpose, and I was glad for it. We all gathered around their family's fire. We had the same unleavened cakes, but for the first time since getting off of the plane, we had hot meat as well. I don't know what it was, but it was delicious. I heard Dad and Tom and a couple of others trying to figure it out from Levi's explanation, but I don't think they ever did.

The rest of the evening was spent around the fire talking about various things. This was the first relaxed time I think any of us had had since getting (I mean *jumping*) off the plane. It was great. Chelsea, Danny, and Meg began playing and running around our huts. This was the first time in days that they had been able to do anything fun.

Of course, Neil asked about the old plane that Christian had flown to the village, and we were promised that since we were not climbing the mountain the next day, we would be taken to see it sometime after breakfast. Aaron let us each have a closer look at the dog tags. It turned out that "C A MORTENSEN" had been in the U.S. Air Force. We started asking for more information about Christian. Aaron went to his family's hut and returned with Christian's Bible, which he handed to Dad. It was old and well-worn. The margins were full of notes, and passages were underlined all through it.

"I'm sorry we never got the chance to meet Christian," Dad said to Levi.

"How long ago did he die?" Jo asked.

"Dying Christian this season in camp of summer," Levi explained.

There was stunned silence at this answer.

"This season?" Jo asked.

"Where is your summer camp?" Mom asked.

Levi seemed a little unsure of how to answer the question. "Living we this place in camp of summer," he explained with his arms gesturing all around us.

"This is merely your summer camp?" Tom asked. "This is not where you live all the time?"

"Coming we this place when snow flows as river of water," Levi explained.

"So you're saying that this summer when you came here is when Christian died?" Tom asked.

"Yes," stated Levi. "Burying we Christian at place of airplane."

"So we will be able to see where he is buried when we see the plane?" Neil asked.

"Yes," repeated Levi, which was followed by silence.

"We barely missed him," Jo said quietly, gently shaking her head back and forth.

"Writing Christian words in Bible before dying," Levi explained, reaching over to the book in Dad's hands and turning it open to the back page. There was a handwritten message in dark-brown, watery ink covering two pages inside the back cover.

"This is dated just five weeks ago," Dad said, looking up at all of us.

"May we read it aloud?" Mom asked. Levi nodded his approval, so Dad read it for us.

> To whom it may concern:
>
> If the above date is reasonably accurate, and I believe it is, I have lived among this village of people for some fifty-three years. I am writing this now because I believe my death is near. I have not been well for some months now. But no matter, I have been well enough during most of my life here, and I have seen far less inhumanity among these people in fifty years than I saw in WWII in just five. Which is why I came here.
>
> When the war ended, I never returned home. I had no family but for a brother who was killed in the Pacific. I spent over a year in a hospital in Switzerland, after which I wandered through Europe for some months. Eventually, I discovered an old airplane hidden in the woods in southern Germany. It was damaged but repairable, and somewhere I got the idea to use it to leave the world and its problems behind. Being an Air Force mechanic, I was able to make necessary repairs, and after a few weeks, I was able to secure several cans of gasoline. It was summer, and so I determined just to fly as far as the gasoline would take me, landing where I could for short rests along the way. I have been with this people ever since.

I have learned their language, though I don't know its name. We were able to learn from each other fairly quickly because they have writings that match parts of the Old Testament. If you are reading this, be warned that most of these people do not want the rest of the world to know they are here, which was alright by me. I felt the same way. The men in one family have learned some English also. They read and understand well enough, but usually mix up their sentences ridiculously when they speak (as you may have found). To protect them from those here who did not believe, we would always use English when speaking of Jesus Christ.

They are good people. I love them. But whether you desire to live among them or to return to where you came from, be careful whom you trust. Their names may be a guide, if you know the Bible. God be with you.

Christian A. Mortensen

"Wow," said Jo. "I wish I had met that man."

"Speaking we 'ridiculously' as Christian has written?" Aaron asked. It made me smile.

"You speak very well," Dad said. "No worries." After a pause, he added, "And we trust you to help us get back to where we come from."

"Going ye back to United States America," Levi nodded. "Going ye back."

The rest of us sat in silence as Dad closed the Bible and said, "Thank you for sharing that with us." He stood and handed the book to Levi.

"Tomorrow we will see this man's plane and his grave," Neil said soberly.

"Yes," Levi agreed. That was all Neil wanted to hear. He promptly informed us that the meal was delicious but that he was going to bed. John left to check on Nancy, who had been too tired to eat, and also went to bed right after the evening sacrifice.

As John said "Good night," I saw a young villager approaching, who looked like he was a couple of years older than Aaron. Aaron stood and introduced him to us as "Moses." I had seen him often during the past few days, usually working closely with Aaron and Levi.

"*Moses?*" Jo asked, almost laughing. "Do you all have Bible names?" She smiled and shook her head slightly as she spoke. "Did Christian give you these names, or did he just tell you how to say them in English?"

"Speaking Christian how to say names in English," Levi said.

"So his name is really Moses?" Jo asked.

"Moses is prophet of Israel," Aaron explained. I noticed that he was beginning to speak a little more normally.

"I know," Jo responded, "but why do you call him that?" Then turning to Moses, she asked, "Why do they call you Moses? Do you speak English?"

From his reaction, it was obvious that he had no idea how to respond.

"Learning Moses—" Aaron began, but then corrected himself. "Moses learning English. Moses speaking English not well."

Aaron then explained to us that Moses' name at birth was something else that none of us could pronounce. Apparently Moses' parents died not long after he was born, and so he had been raised by Jacob for most of his life until two years earlier, when he had left Jacob's family and begun living with Levi's family. It sounded like he had basically been kicked out by Jacob, but I wasn't sure. Anyway, Levi named him "Moses" at that time, because he had joined a family of power that was not his own and then returned to a family that did not have power.

"Giving we names for important . . . happenings in life," Levi explained.

"Oh, I get it," Shauna said. "Moses . . . you know . . . from the Bible . . . was born Hebrew, but was raised by Pharaoh's daughter, but gave it all up to live as a Hebrew again."

I laughed, "I guess I'm not the only one who thinks Jacob acts like a Pharaoh. Maybe *that* should be Jacob's name."

I was looking for someone to laugh, but no one did.

"So when did you get your name?" Tom asked Levi.

"Giving Christian to me name of Levi at twelve years of age," Levi said.

"Did something important happen at that time?" Jo asked.

Levi glanced up and around at other huts before answering, "Age of helping father with ordinance of Messiah."

"What?" Tom asked. "You said that you believe Jesus is the Messiah. So you perform ordinances of Jesus Christ?"

"Giving we bread and wine to believers," said Levi.

"The sacrament!" I breathed.

"The sacrament of the Lord's supper," Tom agreed with his head bobbing slightly.

"So when did you get your name?" Jo asked Aaron.

"Also at age of helping father with ordinance of Messiah," Aaron said.

"Of course," Dad said. "Aaron was a Levite. So he had authority to do ordinances."

"Having we authority not," Levi said. "Believing we in Jesus Christ. Waiting we for authority of Jesus Christ. Preparing we for Jesus Christ. Having we authority not."

"Are you saying Jacob is the only one with authority?" Jo asked.

"Having no man authority," Levi answered. "Until return of Messiah. Following my people wickedness for many generations. Laying hands on no man. Having no man authority."

"So you're saying the authority was lost because your people stopped passing it on by the laying on of hands?" Tom asked.

"Yes," Levi answered.

"Does Jacob know that you are doing these ordinances?" Jo asked.

"Knowing Jacob nothing of this," Levi said soberly. "Being this bad." He shook his head back and forth several times while he apparently contemplated the idea. "Much bad," he said.

I looked at Moses and wondered what he was thinking.

"Speaking of Jacob," Tom said, "where did he get his name?"

"Giving father of Jacob this name," Levi explained. "Near death of father."

"So when Jacob's father was going to die, he gave him that name?" Tom asked. "Why?"

Levi gestured with one hand toward all the other huts in the village and said, "Being father of all tribes."

"Oh, you mean he's the ruler of your village now," Tom said. "So he's like Jacob in the Bible, or Israel, after his name was changed."

"Jacob and Israel are the same guy?" Jo asked.

"Yes," Tom replied.

"So this custom of changing names originated in the Bible?" Jo asked.

"Yes," Tom nodded. "So since they have biblical writings, according to Christian's note, it makes sense that they would still be following the practice."

"Calling we Jacob this name for other purpose," Levi said. We all listened as Levi explained to us that Levi's father had been the leader of the village until Jacob's father sort of took over. Jacob's father didn't want anyone to worship the Messiah anymore and made everyone go back to the Law of Moses. Since Levi's father believed that all authority from God had been lost anyway, he felt it was better to keep peace among the village than to fight to keep his place as ruler.

"So that's why you don't mind calling him Jacob," Tom said with a smile.

"I don't get it," I admitted.

"Try looking up 'Jacob' in the Bible Dictionary," Dad suggested. I knew from experience that's all he would say about it, so I headed for my book bag. "Later," Dad said. "You should stay and talk with us for a while still." I sat down again without a word but managed to smile. I figured I could wait.

"So what were you called before your name was changed to Aaron?" Jo asked.

"Being named Joseph at time of birth," Aaron said.

"Joseph?" Mom said. "Why Joseph?"

Levi thought for a few moments before answering. Then slowly he said, "Going Joseph away from family to bring salvation."

My eyes about popped out of my head. I couldn't believe what he had said.

"You're referring to the Joseph who was sold into Egypt by his brothers," Tom said.

"Yes," Levi nodded.

"Remind me," Jo said.

"Joseph was able to save his family from the famine because while he was in Egypt he was put in charge of the grain storage," Tom explained.

"Oh, I think I remember this," said Jo.

"Joseph interpreted Pharaoh's dream about seven years of plenty followed by seven years of famine," Tom continued. "And so Pharaoh put him in charge of storing the grain in preparation for the famine. When Joseph's brothers came to Egypt to buy grain, he was able to save his entire family."

I was just waiting for someone to ask what seemed to me to be the obvious question: Did Levi expect Aaron to go to another country in order to save his family? And was it to be saved physically? Or spiritually? And even more important, were *we* going to have anything to do with this? Maybe that was why Levi was committed to getting us to the river. Was he planning to send Aaron with us? I wanted to know. I wanted to ask because it looked like no one else was going to. Hadn't anyone else heard what I had heard?

The talking continued a while longer, but soon everyone agreed to go to bed. When we gathered for family prayer, I asked Dad every one of my questions.

"I don't know," was all he said.

"Why didn't you ask?" I questioned.

"It didn't seem appropriate," Dad answered. "And I don't think it's appropriate to talk about it either. Whatever happens, happens."

I didn't want to leave it there, but I obviously had no choice. We had two huts now, so after our family prayer, Chelsea and Danny stayed with Mom and Dad, while the rest of us headed for the new hut. Dad reminded me to look up "Jacob" in the Bible Dictionary, so I kept the flap open for light and sat by the opening for a few minutes thinking about everything that had gone on. After thinking about the "Joseph" thing for a few minutes, I decided to check out Dad's suggestion and found the word "Jacob."

"Supplanter!" I said out loud. "What does 'supplanter' mean?"

"What?" Shauna asked, apparently pretty groggy.

"Dad told me to look up 'Jacob' in the Bible Dictionary and it says that 'Jacob' means 'supplanter.' That doesn't help me," I admitted.

Shauna kept her eyes closed and said, "You still have *my* dictionary, don't you?"

"Oh, yeah," I said and pulled it from my bag. "Listen to this," I said after a moment. Shauna just grunted. "Brandon," I said, "listen to this." He didn't even move. "Are you guys asleep already?" I asked. "Meg?" She didn't move, either. "Whatever," I mumbled.

I now knew what Levi meant when he said that they called him Jacob for a different reason. I pulled out my own Bible Dictionary and added a new entry:

Supplanter—To take the place of; to remove or uproot in order to replace with something else.

"If you guys were awake," I said as loud as I dared, "I'd tell you that they call him 'Jacob' because he took the place of Levi's father as the leader." All was quiet. "But now you'll just have to figure it out for yourselves."

As long as I was there, I started thinking about everyone else's name. I read some interesting stuff. But the most interesting thing I read in the Bible Dictionary was actually under the title "Names of persons":

The numerous passages of holy scripture in which reasons are given for bestowing a particular name on any person show that the Hebrews attached great importance to the meanings *of their names.*

"No kidding," I said out loud. "Anybody doubt that these people are Hebrew?" I asked. Shauna, Brandon, and Meg all lay in silence. "Speak up if you disagree," I said.

The next morning after the burnt offering and breakfast, we went with Levi and Aaron to see the plane. Neil about went crazy. It turned out to be a U.S. Air Force plane with two seats. It was rusted and falling apart, but Neil didn't care. He thought it was the coolest thing he'd ever seen.

"So do you think you can use it?" Brandon asked Neil.

"Use it for what?" Neil asked with a perplexed look.

"To *fly*," Brandon replied. "I thought you wanted to use it to fly out of here and find someone to rescue us. I thought that's why you were so excited."

"Oh," Neil said. It was obvious that this was something he had never considered. "No," he said finally, shaking his head from side to side. "There's no way that engine would start up again after fifty years of just sitting here. And if there's any fuel left, it's certainly contaminated. I knew the plane wouldn't be useable."

Brandon's face showed complete disgust. "Then what were you so excited about?" he asked.

"Well," Neil stammered a little, "just the idea of seeing something that is so much a part of the world's history. You know. Don't you think it's fascinating?"

Brandon tried to answer but just couldn't seem to come up with anything to say other than, "I guess so."

Not far from the plane was Christian's grave. The mound was still mostly bare with just a few small tufts of grass growing here and there. Once Neil quit talking about the plane, nobody else said much. On the way back to the village, Levi informed us that the following day, the Sabbath, was to be a day of feast and that all the men over the age of twelve would be going to a sacred place. Apparently, he hadn't mentioned it before because we were supposed to have gone to the "river of travelers" that day. He said it had been fifty days since the last feast. We would leave after lunch in order to be at the sacred place before the Sabbath officially began that evening. Levi said that we were welcome to join them but not obligated.

"That's the Feast of Pentecost," Tom said to Dad after Levi finished his explanation and Dad and Tom had agreed to go. "Pentecost is fifty days after Passover." Neil and John decided they would rather skip the feast and stay in the village with the women and children. *Wherever you think you fit in,* I thought.

Tom continued, "It seems like Passover and Pentecost are usually earlier in the year, but maybe with the different climate here, they don't have much choice."

"I don't know much about Pentecost," Dad admitted. "I guess that ought to be the subject of our family devotional today."

"Good idea," Tom said.

"You're welcome to join us," Dad said to Tom.

"Thank you," Tom smiled. "As always, thank you. I will. I'm grateful to be with you."

Well, our devotional turned out to be simply reading everything under the heading "Feasts" in the Bible Dictionary. It was pretty amazing. I ended up underlining several parts of it. There were lots of different feasts for various things. It turned out that the Feast of Pentecost was also called the Feast of Weeks or firstfruits. It was supposed to celebrate the harvest. The only scripture we actually read was Leviticus 23:18, where all the required animal sacrifices are listed.

"Do they have all those lambs and rams and stuff?" Shauna asked.

"I haven't seen anything like that," Dad said.

"It'll be interesting to see what they come up with, won't it?" said Tom.

"They are following other things in here, though," I said. "Like where it says that 'all the males of the covenant were to appear before the Lord.' Sorry, Shauna."

"It's okay," she smiled. "I'm seriously sort of tired of animals and dirty clothes and hiking all over the place."

Mom said, "Thank you for joining with us, Thomas. You're always welcome."

She still insisted on calling him "Thomas."

"My pleasure, Sarah," Tom said. "Thank you."

After lunch the reindeer sleds were again loaded up with the altar and other supplies. And out of nowhere, there suddenly came some boys with a group of what Tom called mountain goats. They were mostly white and had really long fur. At first I thought it might be where that dreadlock animal skin had come from, but that one was dark brown, not white. Most of the goats were quite small, but there were also several large ones. In addition there were several bird cages. Obviously, the morning and evening burnt offerings would continue even though the feast would also include lots of other sacrifices as well.

Once everything was collected, we gathered for a prayer to begin our journey. Aaron told us that we were all expected to fast from food and water until the feast the next day. After the prayer, we hiked practically straight up the mountain for about three hours with no break for water or anything else. I was glad the air was cool, but I still had a terrible time trying to catch my breath. Finally, we arrived at a large, flat meadow. Huts were set up around the edges of the area. We had learned by now to look at the other huts and be sure that we set ours up with the opening facing the same direction: east. The altar was put in a central place on top of stones that had obviously been arranged for that purpose some time long before.

After the evening ritual, the animals to be sacrificed were distributed to various men to be brought to the feast the next day. Levi was given one of the large goats, which he tied to a scruffy little tree near his hut. We did not eat as part of the ritual because we were fasting. I noticed that Jacob and his helpers had plenty to eat, though. I asked Aaron about it and learned that the two oldest helpers were actually Jacob's sons. Brandon and I watched them for a while and noticed that they always seemed to have the same expressions: one always seemed to look like he was just happy to be there, and the other always left his mouth half open. I'm not sure which one of us thought of it, but we started calling them "Tweedle Dee" and "Tweedle Dum."

The long afternoon hike left us all too tired for anything other than immediate sleep. I woke up in the morning to the sound of a native yelling at the top of his lungs just outside our hut. Even in the darkness of the tent, I could tell that Dad and Brandon were also awake, but we all just listened to the constant yelling for several moments before Dad finally got brave enough to go outside. Brandon and I quickly followed. Our fire from the night before had gone out, and the air was freezing.

We soon discovered what this man was yelling about: Levi's goat lay dead in a pool of blood, still tied to the tree. Levi and Aaron were inspecting the animal as if trying to decide what had happened. I noticed Moses stumble out of Levi's tent as if he had just been awakened by all the noise, like we had. Other men were now arriving, including Jacob. Jacob and Levi had an exchange like I hadn't seen since the first couple of days: Jacob was yelling, and Levi was responding with a quiet voice. But he didn't look very calm. I could tell that he was upset. Soon Jacob stormed back to his own hut, and the other men quietly returned to theirs.

"What happened?" Dad asked Levi when we were alone.

"Requiring feast each animal from village," Levi said.

"So because this one was killed, the feast will not be correct?" asked Tom.

"Yes," Levi nodded.

"Can we find another animal in the mountains?" Tom asked.

"Hunting no animal on Sabbath," Levi said, "but . . ." Levi acted like he didn't know how to explain what he wanted to say— or like he was afraid to say it.

"But what?" asked Dad.

Aaron answered the question, "Jacob saying our family not worthy to sacrifice. Jacob saying God sending sign our family performing ordinances without authority."

My throat caught as I heard his words. Levi and Aaron stared at each other. They had so few expressions, I couldn't tell if they were afraid or not—but it kind of looked like it.

"Do you think," Dad asked, "he has learned of your bread and wine ordinance for the Messiah?" Levi stared at Dad but didn't answer.

"How did he find out?" Tom asked. "How could he know?"

Levi said nothing for several moments, but eventually he summed it up perfectly. "Much bad," he said quietly. "Much bad."

CHAPTER 11

No More Strangers

"How was it killed?" Tom asked. "Was there a wild animal?"

Levi answered the question by rolling the animal on its side, revealing a small knife. The length of the handle had been tightly wrapped with a thin vine. It was well worn.

"Someone here killed it," Dad said. "Someone who wanted us to know they did."

Moses said something to Levi and Aaron that we did not understand. Both looked at him as if they didn't like what he had said.

"What is it?" Dad asked.

"Moses knowing this knife from family of Jacob," Aaron explained.

"Oh, that's right," Dad said. "You told us that he lived with Jacob for many years."

"Yes," said Aaron, looking at Moses. Moses said nothing else but went back inside the tent.

"So do you think Jacob saw you performing the Messiah sacrament ordinance?" Tom asked.

"No," answered Levi. "Performing always within home."

"Is anyone else ever there with you?" Dad asked. Quietly, he added, "Like Moses?"

"Moses waiting outside of home," Aaron said. "Father and I and family within home."

"What about other families?" Tom asked. "You said that there were other families who believed in the Messiah. Do they perform the Messiah sacrament?"

"Father and I going into homes of believers on Sabbath day," explained Aaron, "for praying and giving sacrament."

"That sounds like home teaching," Brandon said wryly.

Aaron said, "Yes. Home teaching."

I managed not to laugh, but I had a pretty big smile, and so did Brandon.

"So you go from home to home of the believers on the Sabbath and perform the sacrament?" Dad asked. "And Moses always goes with you?"

"Moses coming with us not always," said Aaron. "Moses coming not into home."

"What about Jacob?" Dad asked. "Doesn't Jacob see you do this?"

"Jacob going also to many homes on Sabbath day," Aaron explained. "Two other men going also to many homes on Sabbath day."

"Oh, so there are four men who visit the homes of all the village on the Sabbath?" Tom asked.

"Hey, Dad," Brandon said. "Did you notice how there were four men who walked at the front of the sleds when we came to the village? Jacob and Levi and two other guys?"

"These must be leaders of various groups in the village," Tom said.

"Yes," said Aaron, "nevertheless, Jacob is leader of all leaders."

"So what happens now?" Tom asked. "You're supposed to have certain animals for this feast, but you're not allowed to hunt on the Sabbath, right?"

"Praying we," Levi said. "Praying we for offering for feast."

With that, he turned and went inside his hut. Moses came out again and built the morning fire while Aaron took the dead goat and buried it not far from the huts. Then Aaron said, "We praying now for offering for feast. We needing animal for offering before evening. Ye helping us pray also." Then he and Moses joined Levi inside their hut. We could hear Levi's soft, rhythmic chanting as he prayed.

"I guess we had better pray, too," Dad said.

"Yes," Tom agreed and climbed into our hut with us.

"So we're supposed to pray for an animal to be delivered to us or what?" Brandon asked.

"I think that's the idea," Dad said.

"What if nothing shows up?" I asked.

"I don't know," Dad admitted.

"Hopefully we won't have to fast too much longer," Tom said. "Are you two all right?"

"I'm fine," I said. Brandon agreed.

"Our church teaches us to fast regularly," Dad said. "Usually twenty-four hours, once a month, so we're used to it."

"Wow," responded Tom. "Your church may never cease to amaze me."

Dad offered to say a prayer aloud for all of us and then suggested that we each take a turn. Brandon and I didn't pray for too long, but Dad and Tom must have gone on for ten or fifteen minutes each. My back was starting to hurt. After that Tom suggested that we each spend time praying silently. When we weren't praying out loud, I could hear Levi from inside his hut. This went on all morning. Every hour or so, Dad let us get out of the tent and stretch our legs a little, before returning to our assigned task.

One time when we came out, Moses was stoking the fire, and Aaron was scanning the mountainside. Other than the reindeer we saw the first day, I had yet to see any large animals just come waltzing up to anybody. I was trying to have faith, but the whole thing was beginning to seem hopeless.

"What if we don't get an animal?" I asked Aaron. "What about the feast?"

"Feast beginning at midday," Aaron said. "Needing offering before supper."

"Oh, great," I mumbled to Brandon as we climbed back inside our hut. "So everybody else is out feasting while we sit in here fasting and praying—and all because Jacob got our goat."

"And who knows what Jacob will do if we don't come up with one," Brandon agreed, "and end up ruining his feast?"

"C'mon, guys," Dad encouraged us. "I have faith that the Lord will protect us."

"Sorry, Dad," we said. Then I added, "By protecting us, you mean he'll keep us safe, right? But that doesn't necessarily mean we'll get to eat anytime soon, does it?"

Dad didn't answer for a moment, but I heard him sigh in the near darkness. "We'll be all right. I feel peace." No one responded. "How do you feel?" he asked.

"I don't know," I admitted.

"Me either," Brandon said. "But I don't feel afraid."

"Good," Dad said. "You two are welcome to rest or sleep if you want to."

"Thanks," we said in unison.

I laid down but tried to keep a prayer in my mind as I lay there. I think I did for a while, but some time later, I was awakened by the smell of cooking meat. It was wonderful. My stomach growled as I continued to lay with my eyes closed. My throat hurt as I tried to swallow. I heard Dad's voice outside, so I climbed out to see what was going on.

Apparently, the feast had been going on for quite a while, but we were not invited until we had an animal to sacrifice. Moses, Aaron, and Levi were still in their hut praying. I had slept most of the afternoon. Things were not looking good. The four of us had been sitting in silence around the fire for a few minutes when Tom quietly said, "Nobody move."

I looked at him and saw that he was staring into the trees.

"We may be in luck," Tom said. "Or, more accurately, our prayers may have been answered." I looked where he was looking and saw the weirdest animal I had ever seen. It was the dreadlock animal, the kind whose skin we first saw covering the altar at the shore. It was about the same size as the large goat that had been killed, but it was much smaller than the animal that the hide over the altar had come from. It looked sort of like a buffalo, but its fur was long and knotted.

Very slowly and almost without a sound, Brandon asked, "What . . . is . . . that?"

"It's a musk ox," Tom softly answered. "Just like the hide they use to cover the altar with. But that is definitely a young one."

"Young?" I asked.

"Oh, yeah," Tom said. "They get as big as cows. It must have wandered away from its mother."

"Or was prayed away from its mother," Dad said.

Tom nodded. As we whispered, the animal slowly moved closer and closer to where we sat. Its dreadlocks swayed gently back and forth as it moved unsteadily through the trees. I wanted to tell Levi to come out and catch this thing, but I wasn't sure how to do it without scaring it away. Just as I was about to stand up and go over to their hut, the flap opened and the three of them came out. The opening was exactly on the opposite side from where the musk ox was standing, only a few feet from their hut.

Making as little movement as possible, I pointed at the animal. Aaron and Moses turned to see it, almost as if they were expecting to see what they did and would have been more surprised to see no animal at all. Quickly and quietly, Moses moved in front of the musk ox, holding his hands out to the sides. At the same time, Aaron picked up the rope that had been tied around the goat's neck and circled around behind. He placed the loop of the rope on the ground just a couple of feet behind the musk ox and then backed away, still holding the other end of the rope.

Then Moses waved his hands around in circles and started moving forward. The musk ox immediately began snorting, shifting its weight from side to side and backing away from him. Keeping his eye on the loop on the ground, Moses continued to move slowly forward, and the animal continued backward. As soon as it stepped inside the loop, Aaron pulled the rope in a swift motion that caught the leg and threw the animal to the ground. Before it could even begin to try to get up again, Aaron was sitting on it. It snorted and kicked, but Aaron sat on it as calmly as if he had just claimed the pumpkin he planned to carve for Halloween.

Levi brought another rope, which Moses tied around the ox's neck. With that done, Aaron stood and let the animal return to its feet.

"Going now we to feast," Levi announced, and he led the way to the altar. Moses followed with the rope tied around the musk ox's neck while Aaron held tight to the rope that was still tied to its hind leg.

"I think we're in business," Tom said, and we fell in line behind Aaron.

"Good," I whispered, "because I'm starving."

"Me, too," Brandon agreed.

When we approached the altar where all the men and boys had joined together to feast, everyone became quiet. Jacob looked mad. He just stood and stared as Moses, Aaron, and Levi presented him with the animal. Levi spoke to Jacob in a hushed voice and waited for him to respond.

Jacob didn't seem to like what Levi had said. After a moment, Jacob mumbled something and gestured in our direction. This was the first time I'd seen Levi respond strongly back at Jacob. He spoke in a loud voice and gestured several times back and forth between us and the animal and everyone else who was eating. This was also the first time I had seen Jacob not have a comeback.

Instead, Levi called several young men over to help him, and he began preparing the musk ox to be cooked for the feast. No one said anything as they went about their work. After a few minutes, Levi said something to Aaron, who told us to go with him back to the huts.

"What happened?" I asked Aaron when I figured we were out of Jacob's hearing range.

"My father saying to Jacob, God providing animal for feast," said Aaron, still walking. "Sign from God that family of Levi being right with God."

"I got the feeling Jacob didn't like *that*," Brandon said.

"Yes," Aaron agreed. Then he added, "Jacob saying also no strangers eating in feast."

I gulped as I thought about what this probably meant. I was used to fasting for twenty-four hours but not while making a three-hour, straight-uphill hike. My mouth was dry, and my throat still hurt. "So how much longer do we have to keep fasting?" I asked. "Until we're back at the village?"

"My father saying word of Jacob not Law of Moses," Aaron replied. "Strangers also making Sabbath holy under Law of Moses."

"So does that mean we get to eat?" Brandon asked what we all wanted to know.

"Eating ye with family of Levi after cooking of animal."

"So we have to wait until the ox is cooked?" Tom asked.

"Yes," Aaron answered.

"Why does everyone else still get to eat?" Brandon asked, perturbed at the obvious injustice.

"Jacob being leader," Aaron said flatly. None of us had a response for that. Dad and Tom just slowly nodded their heads up and down. Once we all seemed to understand, Aaron and Moses went inside their hut while Tom, Dad, Brandon, and I sat around the fire. Dad added a couple of broken branches to the blaze.

"So he didn't want us to eat in the feast just because we're strangers?" I asked. "Then why did he let us hike up here in the first place! What a wannabe-Pharaoh-power-hungry . . . !"

"Jeff," Dad said quickly, stopping me before I had a chance to think up anything else to add to my description. "Remember, to these people 'stranger' doesn't just mean somebody they don't know."

"It doesn't?" I asked. "Then what does it mean?"

"Did you bring your scriptures?" he asked. "I did ask you to, didn't I?"

"I've got them," I answered.

Dad said, "Why don't you see what it says in the—"

I interrupted by saying, "Bible Dictionary, right?"

Dad just smiled. I climbed into our tent, grabbed my scriptures, and returned to the fire. I sat in a different place, though, because the smoke had been getting in my eyes. I found the reference for "Stranger" and read it aloud.

Stranger. The word is frequently used to denote a man of non-Israelite birth, resident in the promised land with the permission of the Israelite authorities.

"So just because we're not Israelites, he didn't want us to eat?" I asked.

"Do you know what it means to this people to be Israelite?" Tom asked. He answered his own question. "It means they are the covenant people. They know God, and God knows them."

"He knows we have scriptures about Christ," Dad explained, "which means our beliefs are different from what they believe."

"But Aaron said that that's not the Law of Moses," Brandon complained.

"Well, he's right," Dad said. "Does the Bible Dictionary list any scripture references about strangers?" he asked me.

"Yeah, a bunch," I said.

"Anything in Exodus, chapter 20?" Dad asked.

"Yeah," I answered, after scanning down through the entry. "Verse 10."

"Why don't you read it?" Dad suggested.

I found the scripture and read it out loud:

But the seventh day is the Sabbath of the Lord thy God: in it thou shalt not do any work, thou, nor thy son, nor thy daughter, thy man-servant, nor thy maidservant, nor thy cattle, nor thy stranger that is within thy gates.

"That's the scripture that Aaron was talking about!" Brandon said. "Even strangers are supposed to keep the Sabbath day holy, huh?"

"When they're within the home of the covenant people," Dad said. "That's right."

"How did you know it was in Exodus 20?" I asked, moving to avoid the smoke again.

"Those are the Ten Commandments," Tom answered.

"Do they have these scriptures?" Brandon asked. "They've got to."

"Well," said Tom, "I think that's what we decided after reading about burnt offerings. Everything they are doing is very accurate."

"When Aaron comes out, I'm going to ask him," I said.

"I think you should," Dad agreed. We all quit talking for a minute.

"Man!" I said, standing one more time to get away from the smoke. "What's the deal with the smoke today?"

"What's the matter?" Dad asked. "Don't you want to be turned into jerky?"

Brandon smiled and said, "Nobody likes turkey jerky!" His smug look said he was pretty proud of himself.

"Funny," I said, moving back to where I started from. Talking about jerky made me hungry. My stomach growled, but if I thought I was starving then, I was about ready to die by the time we actually got to eat. It must have been another three hours before Levi came to get us. Most everyone else had pretty much left the gathering area and returned to their own fires and huts.

After praying over the food to end our fast, I found a water bag and nearly drained it. As with all the other meals, we ate with our fingers. But the meat was hot, and we didn't have any cakes to wrap it or hold it with like before. I burned both my fingers and my mouth, but I didn't care. I could hardly eat fast enough. After everyone had pretty much had their fill, I thought to ask Aaron about the scriptures.

"Do you have the writings of Moses?" I asked. "Like the Christian Bible?"

Aaron and Levi looked around a little before Aaron answered, "Yes."

"Is there just one copy for everyone?" Tom wondered.

"Jacob having very old writings of Prophets from his father," Aaron said. "My father having old writings of Prophets from his father. My father also having new writings of his own hand."

"Do you mean he copied the writings for himself?" Dad asked.

"Yes," Levi answered.

"How long did that take?" Dad asked.

"I begin writing from twelve years of age," Levi said. "I finish writing at eighteen years of age."

"Six *years*?" I gasped in amazement. "It took you six years?"

"I writing also," Aaron said.

"Really?" Tom asked. "You're writing your own copy?"

"Yes," said Aaron.

Moses didn't say anything, but I saw him slowly turn and look carefully at Aaron, as if he thought he had understood but wasn't quite sure. I couldn't tell if he was pleased about what he had heard or not.

"Did you start at age twelve, like your father?" Tom asked.

"Yes," Aaron said again.

"Do all the boys copy the writings from age twelve to eighteen?"

Dad asked. I think he was looking for an idea of how to keep Brandon and me out of trouble for a few years.

"Family of Levi," Levi said with pride.

"So it's a tradition in your family for the boys to make their own copy of the scriptures?" Tom asked Levi. "Did this start with your father?"

"Writing we many hundreds of years," Levi said.

"Is Moses doing it, too?" Dad asked.

"Knowing Moses nothing of this," Levi answered.

"Can we see what you've done so far?" I asked.

"Yes," Aaron answered. "Christian seeing also my writings."

"Are they the same as Christian's Bible?" Tom wondered.

"Many writings being same, many writings being different," Aaron explained.

"Helping Christian learn language my people," Levi said. "Helping we learn language of English."

"Like a Rosetta stone!" Tom breathed.

"What's that?" I asked.

"It's a large, flat rock that some archaeologists found that has the same text written in three different languages," Tom explained. "And before they found this, no one had been able to translate one of the languages. But once they found the Rosetta stone, they were able to translate everything else in that language. It's quite amazing. I think it's in a British museum now."

We talked about it for a few more minutes, until Jacob and his helpers showed up for the evening burnt offering. He acted like we weren't even there. We just quietly backed away and watched as the sacrifice took place. Everyone else had supper afterwards, but since we had just eaten, we didn't bother. Apparently, the ritual marked the end of the Sabbath day, since the sun still didn't go down at night. And because the Sabbath had ended, everything except for the huts and altar was loaded up onto the sleds in preparation to leave in the morning.

Just as we were heading for bed, Aaron said to Dad, "My father wanting give gift to you."

Levi was standing just behind Aaron with his head bowed. Dad turned from the opening of our tent and faced them.

"Thank you very much, Aaron and Levi," Dad said, nodding at each of them as he said their names. "You have already given us many things. And we are very grateful."

I looked at Levi, trying to get an idea of what he might be giving Dad, but his hands were open against his knees as he leaned forward. It didn't look like he was holding anything.

"My father wanting give gift of gratitude to you," Aaron explained. "My father giving to you a name."

"A name?" Dad said. "You mean the way he gave Moses his name when he joined your family, and the way he gave you a name when you started helping with ordinances?"

"Yes," said Aaron and turned to his father.

Levi stepped forward and slowly said, "Calling I you Abraham." But he pronounced "Abraham" funny, with each *a* sounding the same. Then he looked at Aaron as if to ask if he had pronounced the name correctly. Aaron nodded his approval.

"Calling I you Abraham," Levi said again, "because we being blessed of God with animal for sacrificing at time of need."

Dad looked completely overwhelmed by the whole thing. "Do you mean as Abraham was given a ram to sacrifice instead of his son, Isaac?" Dad asked. He started shaking his head back and forth as if to say that he didn't deserve it, but then he thought better of it. "I am honored," he said, slightly bowing his head.

"And," Levi continued, "because of offspring." With that comment, he gestured toward me and Brandon.

"Thank you," Dad said softly. "I will always cherish and honor this name."

Levi bowed and returned to his hut. Aaron and Moses followed.

"Wow," Tom breathed. "That's incredible!"

"I can hardly believe it," Dad said quietly. "What an immense honor."

"What did he mean about your offspring?" I asked.

"I'm not sure," Dad admitted. Before anyone had the chance to suggest it, I went straight for my scriptures and found "Abraham" in the Bible Dictionary.

"Ha!" I laughed when I read the meaning. "It says 'father of a multitude.'"

Tom smiled and raised his eyebrows at Dad.

Dad smiled also. "I guess six children does seem like a lot to these people," he said.

"I haven't seen any family with more than one or two," Tom agreed. "That would explain why the population is still so small after so many generations."

Dad just nodded.

"Congratulations," Tom smiled, "and may you prosper with this name."

"Are you suggesting that we have more children?" Dad asked wryly. "Or that we will continue to require food to be miraculously provided?"

Tom's smiled got wider. Then Dad thanked him, and we all went to bed. I couldn't sleep very well, though. Probably partly because I'd slept during the day. At first I lay in the dark, smiling about Dad being the "father of a multitude," but then I started thinking about everything that had happened that day. Something still seemed funny about what was going on. We had gotten out of the mess with the feast because Heavenly Father had provided another animal for us to sacrifice, but we still didn't know how Jacob found out about the sacrament that Levi and Aaron had apparently been doing with other Christian believers in the village. All I could think was that one of those other people must have given it away. I wanted to get out of here. Had it really only been a week since we had been home? It seemed like a lifetime.

165

Morning came early. The burnt offering was made, the huts were taken down and loaded onto the sleds, and we all returned to the village. Going downhill on a full stomach made it seem like it took only half the time it had going uphill while fasting. I was glad to be back. I didn't even get annoyed by Neil's "having himself a situation" about every little thing or by John's constant chewing. I don't think he even had any gum anymore—but his jaw kept the rhythm going just the same.

We returned to find that Mom and Shauna were learning to prepare and cook some plants and roots—and the appropriate song to sing while doing it. It was soft and peaceful but nothing like I'd ever heard before. Meg, Chelsea, and Danny had each found friends at neighboring huts. It was amazing how they were able to play together without having a single word in common. Levi was still predicting three or four more days until the snow had melted enough for the mountain pass to be open. Apparently, this was a time of gathering food and supplies to be taken back to their winter home, where they spent most of their time. And we were going to be helping.

After the evening ritual, Aaron invited Brandon and me to see his copy of the scriptures. Moses was there also. The paper Aaron was writing on looked brownish and was thicker than construction paper and about twice as big as regular notebook paper. The edges were rough and uneven. Aaron said his father helped him make the paper at their winter home and that he also did most of his writing there. The ink was dark brown, similar to the writing Christian had added to his Bible shortly before he died. There were many lines of small writing on both sides of each sheet. Comparing Aaron's stack to his father's, it looked like he was about halfway done. The stack was already a couple of inches thick when laid out flat, though he kept it tied in a tight roll. I couldn't imagine how much time he had spent on this so far.

Moses seemed as amazed and interested in it as we were, but he didn't say much. Soon after the writings were put away, Moses left.

"Where is he going?" I asked.

"Moses sleeping near trees," Aaron explained. "Moses enjoying outside."

"Me, too," John said. "Is it all right if I sleep outside also?"

"I asking father," Aaron said. He returned in a couple of minutes and told John that Levi said he could but suggested that he stay near our huts. John agreed.

After Aaron went inside his family's hut for the night, John said to us, "I'm thinking that the sun is getting pretty close to going under the horizon for a short time during the night now. I don't know much about the constellations, but I'm thinking that if I copy down some star patterns each night, then once we get back home someone might be able to figure out exactly where we've been."

"It's worth a try," Neil said.

"If we get out of here," Tom said, "I don't think these people would want us to know how to find them again."

"This is the discovery of a millennium!" John said. "We need to try."

"I agree with Tom," Dad said. "I think it would be better if you didn't do it."

"I am responsible for a company aircraft," Neil said in his formal voice. "I have a duty to aid, however possible, in the locating and recovery of that aircraft."

"We don't have to find the people to find the plane," Tom countered.

"I will review that with my superiors upon our return," Neil said. "For now, I am asking my copilot to move ahead with his plan."

Dad and Tom gave up. Dad said it was time for bed, so we all gathered for family prayer. Shauna asked that the mountain pass might be opened as soon as possible so that we could go home. I couldn't have agreed more. After we bedded down, I had trouble getting to sleep again. Something in the back of my mind kept me from relaxing, but eventually I managed.

Some time later, though, I awoke in complete panic. I couldn't move, and I couldn't breathe. Someone was sitting on top of me. My arms and legs were being held, and a dirty cloth was being forced deep into my mouth. I thought I was going to throw up. I heard quiet thrashing elsewhere in the tent and got the impression that similar things must have been happening to Shauna, Brandon, and Meg, but I couldn't be sure. A leather strap was forced into my mouth and tied around the back of my head, holding the rag in place. Another cloth was wrapped around my face. I was then rolled over, and my wrists and ankles were tied.

I tried to scream or yell, but I couldn't even cough. I thought I was going to suffocate. I started feeling light-headed, as if I would soon faint. I felt myself being lifted, carried a short distance, and then dropped. I grunted as I landed and kicked my legs a few times. Within a few seconds, something else was dropped on top of me, which grunted when it landed. Now I really couldn't move. I tried to wriggle out from under whoever it was, but I just didn't have the strength. Sweat burst out on my upper lip and around my eyes, and my own heartbeat began to pound in my ears. I felt as though I was going to faint, and then everything went black.

CHAPTER 12

Sold into Egypt

I don't know how long it was before I woke up, but it felt like it could have been several hours. I was lying on my side, and the cloth had been removed from around my face, but I was still gagged. I took several deep breaths through my nose just to make sure that I had plenty of air. The smell of damp animal fur made me almost choke. My head was pounding, and the shoulder and arm that were underneath me ached horribly. When I tried to move, I realized that I was wedged in place. I soon found that my hands and feet were still tied. All I could do was move my head around a little.

The grunting blob that had landed on top of me just before I fainted turned out to be Brandon. He was now lying next to me flat on his back. He was gagged also. I was able to lift my head just enough to see that Aaron was with us and apparently in the same condition that we were.

Suddenly, there was a large jolt that caused my head to bounce against something hard. My head was really sore on that side, as if I had been repeatedly hit there. This was the first that I noticed we were moving. I could hear the sounds of birds rustling around and reindeer hooves tromping not far away. We were on a reindeer sled.

Lifting my head again, I looked past Aaron's feet and saw the sun shining dimly through thick trees. The trees were moving farther away. I knew from the last few days that the sun only got that low in the north. That meant that we were now moving even farther away from the ocean shoreline where this whole thing had started. The thought scared me. I wondered, *Who else is with us? Is Dad here? Or Tom?* Lifting my head again, I tried to see if there was another sled or if I could figure anything else out. I never once wondered who was doing this to us. I knew it had to be Jacob. My only question was what he had in mind.

My arm was killing me, so I tried one more time to move. I looked behind and decided that I was wedged between Brandon and a tent bundle. There was one on the other side of Aaron also. The only way I was going to get any more room was if Brandon moved. And the only way Brandon would move was if he was awake. He was still flat on his back with his mouth forced wide open by the rag.

I tried to wake him by calling his name, but with the rag stuck in my mouth, I think it sounded more like "Ann-onn!" I said it again. "Ann-onn!" This time I used my knees to emphasize each syllable. He snorted. I thought it was a little sick, and I planned on saying so once he woke up.

I tried again. "Ann-onn!" I tried to say, "Move over," but it came out, "Ooo o-er!" This time I used my feet and knees alternately to get his attention. "Ann-onn, ooo o-er!" I said again with another kick. This time instead of snorting, he just threw his head to one side—*my* side. And he whacked me right in the nose. I immediately decided I much preferred his snort over his flailing head move.

"Oowww!" I yelled. That came out clear enough I'm sure. But he still showed too few signs of waking up as far as I was concerned. My eyes started to water, and I couldn't tell if my nose was bleeding or not. It felt like it, though. Now I'd had it. I didn't have enough room to wind up and kick hard, so I opted for rapid-fire instead. I kicked him in the ankle about twenty times in a row within about fifteen seconds before he finally began to stir.

"Oowww," Brandon moaned. He looked over at me and blinked several times.

"Yeah, oowww!" I agreed. "Ooo o-er!"

"Ut?" he asked.

"Ooooo o-er!" I said again.

He grunted and tried to pull his hands out from behind his back.

"I an't," he said.

"Uh-huh," I said and started kicking again.

"Oowww!" Brandon said.

"Yeah, ow!" I said again. "Ooo o-er!"

Brandon squinted at me with half a scowl, but he finally tried to move. I think he decided his hands needed a break, and so he pushed himself over on one side, facing Aaron.

"Ank oo!" I said as I wriggled around and finally got mostly onto my back. My shoulder still hurt, but this was a lot better. All the commotion apparently woke up Aaron, and he moved around, too, making a little more room for Brandon.

Once we settled in again, I watched both Brandon and Aaron alternately lift their heads and look around, trying to see what was going on. Nobody tried to talk. For the next couple of hours, we continued to be bounced around. Occasionally, we did some adjusting of our positions, but there was only so much that we could do. I watched as the sun gradually moved higher until it was just above the trees.

Eventually, the sled stopped. We waited and watched. Soon I heard footsteps, and Jacob and his two sons appeared at the foot of the sled. Jacob said something I didn't understand, but his sons immediately began untying the straps around our heads and removed the rags. Brandon and I were helped first. We each coughed and gagged as the rags were removed. When Aaron's rags were pulled from his mouth, he didn't make a sound. He just stared

171

at Jacob. I wondered how he could possibly keep from gagging or coughing.

Jacob's sons then helped each of us into a sitting position on the tent bundles. Water was brought to us, and since we each still had our hands and feet tied, they poured the water into our mouths. Well, mostly, anyway. Part of it went down the side of my neck and into my shirt. It actually felt pretty good.

Finally being able to look around, I saw that ours was the only sled. There were six reindeer pulling it. The altar was strapped to the front with what looked like food and water bags on either side. There were also bird cages with several birds in each. It looked like there was only a single tent strapped to each side of the sled. Jacob and his sons were apparently the only kidnappers.

"Ye being all right?" Aaron asked Brandon and me after the Tweedles moved away and found themselves a place to rest. They were drinking water and chomping on dried meat.

"Yes," I said. "I'm okay."

"Okay being fine?" Aaron asked.

"Okay is the same as fine," I replied.

"I'm fine, too," Brandon said. "But one of my ankles is pretty sore." He winced a little as he said it. I wondered if he was referring to the ankle that was on the side of my rapid-fire.

"Is there blood on my nose?" I asked, getting ready to show that he wasn't the only one who had been mysteriously injured.

"No," Brandon said. Then turning to Aaron, he asked, "Do you know why they're doing this?"

"No," said Aaron.

"Do you have any idea where they might be taking us?" I asked.

"South," Aaron said.

"Yes, I know we're going south," I said, "but do you know where?"

"The people of my village traveling this trail to winter home," Aaron said.

"Do you think we're going there?" Brandon asked.

"I knowing not," Aaron admitted.

"How far is it?" I asked.

"We traveling six days with all people of my village," Aaron said.

"He *better* not be taking us that far," Brandon moaned.

"Wherever we're going," I said, "they are planning on being gone for a while." Aaron and Brandon just looked at me. "Did you see how many birds they brought?" I asked. "At two burnt offerings a day, there are enough there for a *lot* of days."

They both looked at the cages. Brandon looked sick. Aaron clenched his jaw.

"Won't your father come looking for us?" I asked Aaron.

Aaron thought for a moment before saying, "Jacob sending my father to place of many waters in night. He catching birds for sacrificing. My father returning not for many days."

"So first he sends your father off on a wild goose—or bird—chase . . . and . . . and then he kidnaps us?" I said. "Who does he think he is?"

"Jacob being leader of my people," Aaron said, as if this should answer all my questions. "We talking later," Aaron said quietly. Jacob and his sons were approaching.

The reindeer were taken off of their harnesses and allowed to graze a little as Jacob and his sons took care of the morning ritual. We watched as they unloaded the altar and performed a burnt offering. It seemed a little hurried, but I guess they covered all the important parts. We were offered cakes to eat, but Aaron refused, so Brandon and I did the same. Jacob didn't seem to care. When the ritual was done, the ashes were immediately dumped out and the altar was loaded onto the sled once more.

At one point, Aaron said something to Jacob. Jacob looked over at us, so I know that he heard him, but he just walked away without saying anything.

"What did you say?" I asked.

"I wanting Jacob saying where we going," Aaron said.

"I guess he figures we'll find out soon enough," Brandon suggested.

As the reindeer were being hooked up again, one at a time we were untied and escorted into some nearby trees where we could take care of anything we needed to, after which we were taken to the front of the sled where we would be riding now that we were awake. It felt great to move my legs, but as soon as we were in position, the straps went around our wrists and ankles again. Since we had apparently been traveling most of the night, Jacob laid down to get some sleep where we had been, while his sons led the reindeer further south.

The three of us rode in the same place for the rest of the morning. Jacob and his sons took turns leading the reindeer or sleeping at the back of the sled. We were given water a couple more times but nothing to eat. I thought about trying to get to the food bags and find some of the meat that I had seen the Tweedles eating, but I didn't see how I could do it without getting caught.

About noon we stopped, and Jacob came back and said something to Aaron. Aaron gave just a short response, and Jacob walked away.

"What did he say?" Brandon asked.

"I making covenant with Jacob, we not escaping at time of midday meal," Aaron said.

"We're going to eat?" I asked. "You'll let us eat?"

"I eating nothing of burnt offering," said Aaron.

"But this won't be food from the burnt offering, so we can eat it, right?" I asked.

"Yes," said Aaron.

Our hands were untied, and we were given water and dried meat to eat. Aaron offered a prayer over the food before we ate it. I was absolutely starving, and so it tasted wonderful. When we were done, I asked Aaron if we were going to try to escape. He got a shocked look on his face.

"I believing in Jesus Christ," Aaron said emphatically. "I breaking not covenant."

I wasn't sure how to respond. "That is good," I said finally. "I wouldn't break a covenant, either."

"God helping his faithful people," Aaron said.

"You're right," Brandon agreed. "We need to stay faithful to what we believe."

After we each had a moment in the trees again, we were returned to our positions on the front of the sled. The afternoon went very much like the morning, except we talked on and off about what Jacob was up to. Aaron was convinced that it all was related to the fact that Jacob somehow knew about the ordinances they were performing.

"What about us?" Brandon asked. "We haven't had anything to do with that. So why did he kidnap us?"

"I knowing not," Aaron admitted.

"Aaron," I said after a few moments, "you never told us what Christian's trespass was that he had to pay for."

Aaron didn't respond.

"Did everyone think that Christian had trespassed?" I asked. "Or was it just Jacob's father?"

Aaron still didn't say anything.

"Is it something that Jacob might think about us also?" I wanted to know.

Aaron's expression changed a little, but he didn't speak.

"If it is," I said, "then I think you should tell us because Jacob might have the same thing in mind for us now."

"We deserve to know," Brandon agreed.

Aaron acted like he wasn't quite sure what that meant, but I think he got the general idea.

It was slow with lots of pauses, but eventually Aaron told us that Christian's trespass had been coming to this land that had been given to these people from God. He had no right being there. God wanted his people to stay unknown from the rest of the world. I felt myself getting scared.

"So how did he have to pay for trespassing?" Brandon asked.

"Christian making covenant never leaving my people until time of his death," Aaron said.

I felt my face getting hot even in the cool air. It was obvious that we were "guilty" of the exact same "trespass" that Christian had been. Aaron surely saw that, too, otherwise he wouldn't have tried to keep it from us.

"He promised never to leave?" I asked, my voice quivering a little. "How could he make such a promise when you couldn't even understand each other? Didn't you say that it took a long time before you could talk to each other?"

"Christian remaining bound for many days," Aaron said.

"So they kept him tied up the whole time you learned each other's languages?" Brandon asked in near disbelief. "So that might be what's happening to us now, then, isn't it?"

"No," Aaron said strongly. "Jacob wanting something else. Jacob binding not John, not Neil, not family of Jeff and of Brandon."

"Well, we hope not," I said. "We can't be sure."

Aaron didn't really respond to that. He did tell us that Levi was convinced that their time of being isolated from the world was nearly over. Each winter they saw more and more lights moving through the night skies. The people thought that they were all airplanes, but Brandon and I figured some of them were probably satellites as well. We tried to explain satellites to Aaron, but he just didn't get it. He said that they saw more and more travelers on the rivers in other places and that it was getting harder and harder to stay hidden.

Apparently, though, Jacob said the people were supposed to stay away from the rest of the world until either their salt supply ran out or until the Messiah came so they didn't need all the salt for sacrifices anymore. Brandon and I immediately looked at each other when we heard that, obviously both thinking the same thing.

"So that's why he was so mad about us destroying all your salt, huh?" Brandon asked.

Aaron thought for a moment.

"We having also much salt at winter home," Aaron said.

"Do you mean that you have it stored in bags or do you mean that you can get more from the earth there?" I asked.

"We gathering much salt at winter home," Aaron replied. "We storing in bags."

I said, "Oh," but nothing more. I was thinking that if they had another large supply of salt at their winter home, then maybe it wasn't such a big deal after all that we had ruined some of the salt up by the shore. I wanted to ask Aaron about it, but didn't quite know how to phrase it.

That evening after the ritual, Aaron again refused to eat anything. Later Jacob came and spoke with Aaron. At first they both seemed calm, but after a couple of minutes, Aaron obviously said something that made Jacob really mad. He began yelling and waving his arms much like he had done the first time we saw him. Aaron again responded calmly, but Jacob continued to be extremely angry. This continued for several moments until Jacob stomped away over to the sled.

"What happened?" I asked quietly, almost afraid to know the truth.

"Jacob saying again I performing ordinances without authority," Aaron whispered. "Jacob saying only family of Jacob having authority for ordinances of Law of Moses."

"The Law of Moses?" I asked. "You're not doing that, are you? Aren't you only performing the Messiah sacrament?"

"Yes," said Aaron.

"What did he say?" Brandon asked.

"Jacob angry. Jacob saying again I performing ordinances of Law of Moses. I saying I not performing ordinances of Law of Moses."

"So he thinks you're lying," Brandon said.

"Yes," Aaron nodded. "Jacob angry more."

Just then Jacob returned, yelling at Aaron as he approached. Aaron's face had a look of shock and fear. As Jacob came closer, I realized that he was holding Aaron's hand-copied scriptures. He carelessly unrolled them and held them open two inches from Aaron's face, making sure that Aaron knew exactly what he was holding. Aaron turned his face away and stared at the ground.

Jacob continued yelling as he rolled up the writings and threw them to the ground. At this point, Aaron's expression changed from fear to intense determination—almost hate. He looked narrowly at Jacob, and I saw his jaw clench. Aaron waited patiently for Jacob to finish his tirade, then he looked directly into Jacob's eyes and said something very quietly and slowly. Continuing to stare him down, Aaron waited for a response. Brandon and I waited, too.

For the first time in my life, I understood those silly cartoons that show someone's face go red from bottom to top and then show smoke exploding out of their ears. Other than the smoke, that's exactly what happened. First Jacob's neck turned red. Then his cheeks turned red. Next were his ears, followed by his forehead. I was just *waiting* for the smoke.

Jacob lunged toward Aaron as if he was going to hit him with both fists at once, but he stopped just short of Aaron's head and yelled something instead. Though his hands were tied behind his back and he was totally defenseless, Aaron never took his eyes from Jacob. I don't think he even blinked. He responded softly but with conviction. Jacob yelled something again, still as mad as ever. This time Aaron said nothing but continued to stare at Jacob. Jacob glared back for a few moments and then snatched up Aaron's scripture writings and stomped back to the sled. Aaron's face never relaxed as he continued to watch Jacob.

Neither Brandon nor I dared to say anything. We just waited until Aaron was ready to tell us what had happened. Eventually, Aaron looked at us and realized that we had no clue what was going on.

"Jacob saying my writings proving I performing ordinances of Law of Moses," Aaron said after his jaw finally relaxed a little. "I saying I believing in Messiah Jesus Christ. Law of Moses being signs for Jesus Christ. Law of Moses being dead."

"Is that when he got so mad—so angry?" I asked, thinking of the red face and smoke.

"Yes," Aaron nodded. "Jacob much angry I not believing in Law of Moses."

"So I guess he just figured out that you don't think his burnt offerings are worth anything," Brandon said.

"Law of Moses showing signs of Messiah Jesus," Aaron corrected him.

"We study the Old Testament for the same reason," I said.

"But how did he get your writings?" Brandon asked. "And how did he even know about them?"

Aaron's face tightened again. "I knowing not," he said.

"That explains why you're here," I said, "but what about us?"

"I knowing not," Aaron said again.

"Didn't he say anything about us?" Brandon asked.

Aaron paused for a moment before finally admitting, "Jacob saying strangers paying for sins."

"Sins?" Brandon asked. "What sins?"

"Jacob saying not," Aaron answered.

We quit talking about it at this point because Jacob's sons came close to where we were sitting and began setting up one of the tents. Aaron said something to them, causing them both to look over at him. The three of them exchanged a few words until Jacob returned a few moments later. Then the Tweedles apparently explained to their father what Aaron had said. Jacob thought for a moment, said something gruffly, and walked away. The Tweedles then came and untied us and sat down on the back of the sled staring at us. Brandon and I just looked at each other in amazement.

"We building huts," Aaron said to Brandon and me. He stood and set to work on the tent, so we went to help.

"Why did they untie us?" I asked, rubbing my wrists. "Do you think we could try to escape this time?"

"No," said Aaron as he worked. "I saying we building huts. I saying we wanting writings of Prophets. We searching writings of Prophets."

"You made a deal with them?" Brandon asked.

"Yes," said Aaron.

"And they trust us?" I asked.

"I making covenant running we away not," Aaron said. "I speaking for you also." He stopped what he was doing for a moment and looked straight at me. "You running away not." Aaron waited, making sure I understood what he expected.

"Okay," I said, "I won't run away." I glanced over at Brandon. "We won't run away. But I'm still surprised that he trusts us."

"I saying you bringing Bible of God like Christian," Aaron explained. "I saying you fearing God. You breaking covenant not. Like Christian."

"I'm glad Christian never broke his covenant then," I said. "But don't expect us to make the same one." Aaron just looked at me. I said, "I'm not staying here for the rest of my life. Don't make that covenant for me."

"Not for me, either," Brandon agreed.

Aaron nodded and returned to his work. When both tents were set up with their flaps open to the east, we sat down in front of ours. Tweedle Dee brought Aaron his writings and carelessly dropped them at his side. Aaron gently picked them up and began to unroll them. Brandon and I were watching Aaron, so neither of us noticed Tweedle Dum until he dropped our scripture cases between us. I was so shocked, I probably looked as dumb as he did. I'm sure my mouth was open for several moments as my eyes jumped back and forth between him and my scriptures. His mouth was half-open as always, but he just returned to the sled and plopped down.

Brandon and I each picked up our scripture cases and opened them probably as carefully as Aaron had unrolled his writings. I had never felt so much appreciation for them as I did right now. I couldn't imagine why these bozos had stolen our scriptures. All of a sudden, I felt more afraid now than ever before. We were caught up in some religious power struggle, and these guys obviously hated what we represented. It was scary.

Aaron began to turn sheets of paper and read silently from his writings. For ten or fifteen minutes, none of us spoke.

"Aaron," Brandon said finally. "Can I tell you a story that we have in our scriptures that you probably don't have in yours?"

"Yes," Aaron agreed. "You telling story." After speaking, he closed his eyes, bent his head downward, and waited. I glanced over and saw that Brandon had the Book of Mormon open to Jacob chapter 5. I turned there in my own scriptures, remembering that this was a prophecy by the prophet Zenos.

Brandon began telling the story of the olive tree in a vineyard. He said that the tree represented the house of Israel. Many of the branches were good and healthy and had good fruit. But after a while some of the branches began to die.

I was following along in my scriptures as Brandon spoke. Dad had spent two or three family devotionals with us a few months earlier talking about this prophecy, and so we both had tons of notes in the margins explaining what everything meant.

Brandon told Aaron that the master of the vineyard took away some of the good branches to other places and grafted wild branches into the original tree.

Aaron looked up and said, "My people being branch of Israel taken to other place."

"We thought so," I nodded. Brandon raised his eyebrows and glanced in my direction.

Brandon continued by telling how the master of the vineyard worked with all the branches wherever they were. He said that some of the original branches stayed good longer than others, but that all of the branches that had been moved to other places eventually only gave bad fruit and no good fruit. He said that the original tree eventually only gave bad fruit and no good fruit.

Then Brandon said all the trees would bring only bad fruit until the master of the vineyard visited again. He said the master of the vineyard would bring the natural branches back to the original tree and that good fruit would come again. And then would be the end of the world when all the fruit would be gathered in.

"My people returning to original olive tree someday," Aaron said. We smiled.

"This story not in Bible of Christian," Aaron said. "This story not in writings of Prophets. Who prophet telling this story?"

I said, "Well, the prophet Jacob from the Book of Mormon is telling the words of the prophet Zenos from old writings that he had."

"Book of Mor-mon?" Aaron asked.

"Yes," we said. Brandon added, "The Book of Mormon contains writings from prophets in America a long time before the United States."

"These people were another one of the branches taken from the original olive tree," I explained. Aaron nodded as though he understood. Brandon and I used the notes in our margins to point out the Nephite people who were the natural branch that was taken to a good spot of ground. We showed Aaron where it said that in this place, part of the tree brought forth good fruit, while part brought forth wild fruit. We told him that the Book of Mormon was a record of this branch.

Then Aaron asked, "How having ye this Book of Mormon?"

Brandon immediately turned to his index.

"The Prophet Joseph Smith," I said. "He was visited by the Messiah Jesus Christ and Heavenly Father and given authority and given the Book of Mormon."

"Prophet Joseph-Smith," Aaron repeated, running the first and last names together.

Looking up "Joseph" in the Index, Brandon had found 2 Nephi 3 where it states that Joseph of Egypt prophesied that a man named Joseph, whose father was also named Joseph, would be raised up in the last days. He read it to us. I looked at him in disbelief, wondering how he had found or even remembered this scripture.

"We talked about this just a couple weeks ago in deacons quorum," Brandon explained to me. "I thought of it because Brother Stemmons said that it was too bad that this prophecy wasn't part of the Old Testament."

Brandon began reading from 2 Nephi as he spoke. When he got to verse 12 where it states that the writings of Judah and the writings of Joseph "shall grow together," I held up my quad and wiggled it a little bit at Brandon. Brandon smiled.

"The Christian's Bible is the writings of Judah," I said. "Now we have both together."

When Brandon finished reading to us, Aaron said, "Book of Mormon telling of . . ."

"The Nephites," I said. "And they are descendants of Joseph."

"Nephites," Aaron repeated. "Nephites being piece of coat of colors of Joseph."

"That's right," Brandon nodded. I stared blankly back at both of them. "Jeff, remember the play I was in last year? It was the story of Joseph's coat of many colors. Joseph's brothers took a part of his coat and gave it to their father."

"So . . . ?" I said, still not understanding what he was saying.

"Well," Brandon continued, "we just read in verse 5 where

Joseph was promised that a righteous branch would come from his descendants."

"Oh, yeah," I said. "I remember."

Brandon turned to his index again and said, "Brother Stemmons had us look up 'remnant' in the Index and mark the prophecy. Here it is."

Brandon read Alma 46:23–24 out loud. In the middle of verse 24 are the words:

> . . . *the remnant of the coat of Joseph was preserved and had not decayed. And he said—Even as this remnant of garment of my son hath been preserved, so shall a remnant of the seed of my son be preserved by the hand of God. . . .*

When Brandon finished reading, I saw a look on Aaron's face that I had never seen before. He was staring at my scriptures. No one said anything for several moments.

"Prophet Joseph-Smith receiving authority of Messiah Jesus Christ," Aaron said.

"Yes," I replied.

"Prophet Joseph-Smith laying hands on heads of others to give authority?" Aaron asked.

"Yes," I answered.

"Prophet Joseph-Smith laying hands on head of Brandon and Jeff?" Aaron asked.

"No," I shook my head back and forth. "The Prophet Joseph Smith is dead. But he laid his hands on the heads of the Apostles and many others. They have laid their hands on the heads of many others. We got the priesthood authority from our father."

"Ye helping with sacrament of Jesus Christ?" Aaron asked.

"Yes," we answered, both nodding.

"Ye having authority of Messiah," Aaron said. It was a statement, not a question. Finally, he said, "My people remaining wild branch of olive tree."

I paused as I thought about what he was saying. "For now,"

I agreed, "but Zenos promised that all the natural branches would return to the tree someday."

"Someday," repeated Aaron.

"Maybe our dad can give you the authority," I said. "I don't know how that works, but we'll ask him."

Aaron nodded. We sat in silence for several minutes until it was broken by the Tweedles. They were still lounging on the sled, but they made it clear that we were done. They wanted Aaron's writings and our scriptures. Brandon and Aaron immediately stood and headed toward the sled. Before I moved, I sat and stared at my open scriptures for a moment. *Aaron and Levi should have these*, I thought. They had Christian's Bible, which told them about Jesus Christ— but the Book of Mormon would tell them even more about Jesus Christ.

The Tweedles grunted at me, and so I stood to return my scriptures to them. I had trouble closing my quad because it felt like a pencil had fallen into the back binding. As Brandon and Aaron stood and walked to the sled, I pushed my finger inside the binding. I twitched as something sharp stuck me. Luckily the Tweedles didn't notice—probably because Brandon and Aaron were walking between me and them. Reaching in slowly from the other side, I soon discovered a small knife that I had never seen before. It looked similar to other knives I'd seen being used by the tribesmen.

My mind raced as I thought about who might have put it there and why. I got excited as I realized that someone was probably trying to help us. *But who could it be?* I thought.

I quickly hid the knife inside my coat sleeve, hoping I might still be able to reach it after my hands were tied again. I was sure Jacob wouldn't let us stay untied during the night, and I was right. As soon as our scriptures had been handed over, we were escorted to our hut where our hands and feet were tied once more.

I could hardly contain my combination of both fear and excitement as I waited for the sounds of Jacob and his sons to die down.

I'm sure I waited at least another thirty minutes before daring to attempt removing the knife and cutting the straps on my wrists. Luckily they weren't as tight this time as they had been in the past. I didn't dare say anything to Brandon or Aaron yet. I waited until I was free and then gently woke them one at a time. I cut Aaron's straps, after which he took the knife and freed Brandon. As soon as we were all loose, we opened the flap and sneaked out of our tent to find the sun just dropping below the northwest horizon.

CHAPTER 13

Pillar of Salt

The first thing Aaron did after closing the flap behind us and making sure that neither Jacob nor his sons were anywhere in sight was to head for the reindeer sled. He went to the front of the sled where we had watched the Tweedles stash his writings and our scriptures. Almost instantly he found our scripture cases and handed Brandon's to him and mine to me. At first Aaron moved around the various bags carefully, but within a few seconds he began to act more and more frantic as it became obvious that his writings were not to be found.

"Maybe they took it into their tent with them," Brandon whispered.

Aaron looked quickly over at Brandon with an expression that said that the very thought hit him like a fist in the stomach. Then, almost as quickly, he turned his attention to Jacob's tent and his expression changed to determination and resolve. He still had the small knife in his hand after having cut Brandon free.

"*No!*" I said, probably too loud for the circumstances. But I had no intention of standing around watching while Aaron tried to sneak into a hut that held three guys that were not only bigger and stronger than each of us, but who had already kidnapped us and had who-knows-what-else still in their plans for us.

Aaron looked at me like he knew he should feel the same way I did, but he was still determined to go through with it. He wanted his writings and that was that. I'm sure I would have felt the same about something I had worked on for three years already and was only half-finished. They were irreplaceable, but then so were our *lives*—and I was more concerned about those for the moment.

As Aaron started for the hut, I said, "What are we supposed to do when you get caught?" I was specific about saying "when" and not "if." He stopped to think about this for a minute, but I continued before he answered me. "There is *no* way that we can find our way back to the summer camp by ourselves without them catching us, too. *Please,* just come with us," I pleaded. Aaron took a deep breath but still didn't respond. "They will be more interested in catching us than doing anything to harm your writings," I said.

I could tell from his expression that his determination was fading. He felt an obligation to help us that was stronger than his desire to save his work.

"Let's say a prayer," suggested Brandon, "and then see how we feel."

It sounded like such a great idea that I offered to say it. Aaron agreed, while struggling to pull his eyes from Jacob's tent. This was probably the most fervent prayer I'd offered since this trip began. I asked Heavenly Father to protect us from harm and make it possible for us each to return home safely. I asked Heavenly Father to soften Jacob's heart and make him realize that what he was doing was completely against the Law of Moses that he said he was following. Then, almost more important than anything else, I asked Him to protect Aaron's writings from all harm and to make it possible for us to get them back at a later time when we could get them safely. I ended in the name of Jesus Christ and then slowly lifted my head and opened my eyes.

Aaron's head remained bowed for several moments. I noticed that instead of folding his arms like Brandon and I had done, Aaron held tight fists out in front of his stomach. As he stood there with his head still bowed, I watched as his fists gradually began to relax until his arms fell limp at his sides.

"Fine," Aaron said. "Okay. I retrieving writings not. We going summer home."

I was absolutely relieved to hear him say it. I was now starting to get an idea of what Jacob was capable of, and I feared what he might do to Aaron if he caught him again. The problem was that Jacob thought he had the right to do anything he wanted. And the way Aaron kept saying "Jacob being leader" in response to all my questions, it was obvious that he and everyone else thought Jacob had that right, too.

If Aaron had been caught again, I wouldn't even have known what to do. I couldn't imagine how Brandon and I would have a chance of either freeing Aaron or getting back to the summer camp on our own. That thought reminded me that it was cold, and I tightened my coat around me. Though I was relieved that Aaron was not going after his writings, I soon remembered that we were still in big trouble. We had traveled all the previous day and much of the night before to get as far as we were. Now we would be returning on foot and with very little sleep.

Hopefully, some one had figured out what must have happened and would be on his way with Dad to rescue us. They would if they were able to guess which way we had gone—and if they hadn't been kidnapped, too. It was impossible to know how many people were really loyal to Jacob and how many would be willing to help him with this crazy plot he had going. Aaron seemed sure that Jacob and his sons were the only ones involved. I hoped he was right.

We grabbed two animal skin water bags and a single bag of dried meat and headed back north on foot. The sun had gone down in front of us, but Aaron said it wouldn't be down for long. Aaron led the way, walking briskly down the trail with one of the water bags. Brandon followed with the food bag. I came last, struggling to keep up and also keep my water bag from being so noisy as it sloshed against my hip. Aaron showed us how to keep our footsteps inside the tracks of one of the six sled runners. Each runner track was wider than our shoes, so it should have been easy—but as fast as we were trying to go, plus the awkward weight of the water bag, it was a lot harder than it looked.

"Jeff, can't you be quiet?" Brandon hissed over his shoulder at me.

"Sorry, *Master,*" I hissed back, "but I never finished my Ninja training!"

I don't think Brandon appreciated my comment, but Aaron had figured out what was going on and turned back to help me. He took the water bag and opened it, squeezing it from the bottom until all the air was gone and water spilled out of the top. Then he quickly tied it up again and slung it back over my head and one shoulder. He also took my scripture case so I only had to worry about the water bag.

"Thanks," I whispered. He nodded and immediately charged down the trail again.

The water bag was much quieter now that all the air was gone from inside. It was heavy, though, and I still had trouble keeping up. After a while, Brandon was good enough to offer to trade me, which I really appreciated. The food bag was considerably lighter and easier to manage than the water. I stayed in the rear, though.

We continued for most of the night, pausing every hour or so to grab a quick drink of water, but Aaron became impatient if we sat down or tried to rest. He wanted us to keep moving, feeling sure that our absence would be discovered and that Jacob would soon be on our trail. But after several hours, it became obvious that we simply could go no further.

At this point, Aaron carefully chose a place to leave the trail where there were several jagged rocks that led into some thick trees. Once inside the trees, we followed him for at least a couple of minutes as he hiked further from the trail. We didn't have a tent to keep us warm, but the air was still within the tree-filled area, and we huddled close together in a place where we were mostly surrounded by thick bushes.

I must have fallen asleep almost instantly and stayed that way for several hours. I awoke to find Aaron stooped over me, gently shaking my shoulder.

"I sleeping," Aaron whispered. "You watching."

It took me a second to remember where I was, but I soon figured out what he meant.

"Have you been watching all this time?" I asked softly, sitting up and stretching.

"Yes," he answered. "You following me." With that he disappeared around the bushes.

I stumbled quickly to my feet and followed him to some thick trees where the trail could barely be seen.

"You watching for Jacob," Aaron explained, and he immediately returned to the bushes where Brandon was still asleep.

I was groggy and stared blankly through the dim light in the general direction of the trail. The more I woke up, the more I found myself trying to figure out what Jacob was up to. I kept thinking about the salt deposit they apparently used there. I wondered if it was a big open meadow like the one we had ruined or what. After at least half an hour, I was so tired and bored that I began to worry about falling asleep. I was sure that Aaron wouldn't be too happy with me if that happened, though I was equally sure that Jacob & Sons would never find us even if they did catch up.

I was getting more curious about the salt, so I went back up to where Aaron and Brandon were sleeping and got my scriptures. Sitting behind the tree where Aaron had put me, I looked up *salt* in the Bible Dictionary. I expected to find some long explanation about how important salt was to the Israelites and how it was used in each of the sacrifices of the Law of Moses. The only headings were "Salt Sea" and "Salt, Valley of," so I turned to the Topical Guide instead.

I looked up every reference listed, starting with Levitcus 2:13, which ends with:

. . . with all thine offerings thou shalt offer salt.

I remembered reading that before, when we looked up all the different sacrifices and offerings. I read a few more scriptures about a "covenant of salt" and about priests using salt for burnt offerings. I thought the most interesting scriptures were a couple in the New Testament and also in the Doctrine and Covenants about Christ's disciples being the "salt of the earth," or the people who make an everlasting covenant being "the savor of men."

This reminded me of what Dad had said about salt representing God's power to preserve and save us. I wondered if this was supposed to mean that the covenant people had the power and authority to bring salvation to all the people of the earth—at least to those who wanted to hear it.

After I had looked up all the scriptures and thought about some of them for a while, I looked back at the beginning of the listing. Somehow I had missed the very first reference. Probably because the next one was written in bold, and I already had Leviticus on my mind. I never have figured out why the first one is not bold, when all the other references are, but it looked like it was that way in every single listing. Anyway, the first reference is:

Gen. 19:26 she became a pillar of s.

I knew this story. This was talking about Lot's wife. Lot had been warned by angels that the evil place where he lived was going to be destroyed, and so he needed to get his family out. I went backwards in the chapter a little until I found in the middle of verse 17 where it says, "Escape for thy life; look not behind thee." But Lot's wife didn't listen. Verse 26 says:

But his wife looked back from behind him, and she became a pillar of salt.

I suddenly had the thought that this applied to us when we had escaped from Jacob and his sons during the night. I was sure now that we had done the right thing in not going after Aaron's writings—that would have been "looking back," after Heavenly Father had provided a way for us to escape. I sat thinking about this for quite a long time. I think I was almost in a daydream when suddenly I realized that there was something moving along the trail in the same direction we had been going. It was mid-morning now, and the movement stood out easily in the sunlight, making me glad that I was still hidden within the thick trees.

Even so, my heart jumped into my throat, and I couldn't breathe. I soon made out the shapes of six reindeer pulling a sled. Jacob was walking along quickly next to the lead deer on the side closest to me. One of his sons was on the other side, close to the front end of the sled, and his other son was standing on the rear of the sled. I couldn't tell which one was which until I got a clear glimpse of the one at the back with his mouth hanging half open.

"Tweedle Dum," I whispered to myself.

I knew I was too far away for them to hear me, but hearing my own voice scared me a little anyway. Though they were moving quickly, Jacob seemed to be watching the ground in front of them while his sons scanned the sides of the trail. I tried to hold as still as possible. I remembered that both my coat and jeans were dark blue, but I instinctively looked down just the same. My shoes were mostly white, but with a bush in front of me, I knew they wouldn't be able to see them. I watched and waited until I couldn't see them anymore and then I sneaked as quickly and quietly as I could back up the hill.

"They just passed us," I whispered to Aaron after waking him. Brandon was awake, too, but seemed to be still trying to remember where he was and why. Aaron looked up at me but didn't say anything.

"They're still going up the trail," I said.

With that, Aaron stood and made his way through the trees. He seemed hesitant to get too close to the trail, but the sled was nowhere in sight. I told him how they were set up and which direction each of them was looking. Aaron told Brandon and me to go back to the bushes where we had slept and that he would return soon.

I wasn't sure what he meant by "soon," but I certainly wasn't expecting to wait for the fifteen or twenty minutes that it took him to get back. My mind raced wildly the longer he was gone, and I almost went crazy imagining what might have happened to him. Brandon and I both jumped when he reappeared around the bushes.

"We following," was all Aaron said as he picked up his water bag.

Brandon and I picked up our bags and scripture cases and tried to keep up with him. Aaron angled toward the trail until he was within about fifteen feet of it, and then he just moved parallel with it. I knew we were moving a lot faster than the reindeer sled, but it seemed like it took close to half an hour before Aaron stopped suddenly behind a tree and peered carefully around it. It took everything I had to keep from panting so loud that every wild animal within a mile could have heard it. Brandon looked as exhausted as I felt. I wondered why, though, because as far as I could tell, he had slept about twice as much as I had in the last twenty-four hours. I smirked at him between deep breaths, and he looked back with a puzzled expression—which I ignored, of course.

Aaron began moving again, and we continued following, only this time at a much more reasonable pace. Sometime later Aaron stopped and crouched down behind some bushes. Brandon and I immediately dropped to our hands and knees. After a minute or so, Aaron peeked around the side of the bush to check out what was happening. He returned to his crouched position and whispered, "They resting."

Good, I thought, *I'd like to do the same.*

I hung my head to relax, but my pleasure was short-lived when Aaron said, "I retrieving my writings."

The image of Lot's wife being turned into a pillar of salt flashed immediately into my mind. I wanted to grab him and yell, "*No!*" as quietly and intently as possible, but it was already too late. As soon as he had said it, he had left. Brandon and I looked at each other in total dismay and exasperation. We both knew that if Aaron got caught, we had no chance.

"What should we do?" Brandon mouthed.

I scrunched up my eyes, shook my head back and forth, and mouthed, "I don't know."

Either we silently agreed to stay put, or we were both too afraid to do anything. I'm really not sure which. But in any case, we just huddled right there behind the bush. Minutes seemed to pass like hours of suspense. I couldn't imagine how he could possibly get his writings without being caught. After what seemed like a really long time, I looked nervously at my watch, but it didn't do me any good since I didn't know what time he had left.

Suddenly, Brandon and I both jumped as the words, "Ye running!" pierced the air. It was Aaron. He yelled it again before either of us moved. "Ye running!" he called from some distance away.

We scrambled to our feet and turned to run in the opposite direction of Aaron and the sled. Before we had even stood completely straight up, we stopped short at the sight of Tweedle Dee and Tweedle Dum right in front of us. They grabbed us before we even had time to change directions. We were thrown face down on the ground and our hands were once more tied behind our backs. Brandon and I were facing each other as we lay on the ground with the Tweedles on our backs. His look showed exactly what I was feeling: a combination of disgust that we had allowed ourselves to be captured again, and fear about what they were going to do to us next.

"Ye running!" Aaron called again, but this time one of the Tweedles called something back. I'm sure he was informing Jacob of their success because we didn't hear anything else from Aaron.

We were gruffly escorted down to the stopped sled and thrown on the back of it where Aaron already lay. He looked sad and apologetic. I figured he was sorry for getting caught but not sorry he had tried; we all knew that he would do it again if he got the chance. I tried to smile to give Aaron some reassurance that it was okay. I don't know if he understood or not. None of us spoke as our ankles were then tied. We were each searched, and Aaron's knife was confiscated.

Without a word from our captors, the sled began moving almost immediately, and as soon as a suitable place was found for turning around, we were again headed south. For the next three days, we were constantly under guard. We were not allowed to talk or study our scriptures or anything else. We were untied three times each day, one at a time, and allowed to eat some dried meat and drink some water, followed by a trip behind a nearby tree. They weren't going to take any chances this time.

In late afternoon of the third day, we arrived at the winter home. It was a huge cave. The altar was set up near the opening, and we were taken inside. A fire was built, which revealed a large chamber where we would be sleeping. We could also see the openings into several other passageways or rooms. We were still not allowed to speak, as the Tweedles continued to trade off on guard duty at all times.

After spending a night in the cave, Jacob finally revealed what he had in mind. Following the morning burnt offering, which we witnessed from the mouth of the cave, we were taken through several passageways until we came to a chamber that was the largest we had seen. I looked upward to see how high the ceiling was but could only find blackness. Torches were set up along the walls, and Jacob now spoke to us for the first time since we had been recaptured. Aaron just stared blankly at Jacob for about a minute as he spoke, gesturing back and forth between us. The Tweedles looked like they were definitely enjoying this. When Jacob quit speaking, Aaron turned slowly toward us.

"This is room of salt," Aaron said, looking past us.

We turned and looked at the wall of the cave behind us. Running diagonally, from the floor, clear up past where the light from the torches reached, was a huge vein of white salt. It had to be at least ten feet wide. Much of the lower portion had been dug away such that several people could easily fit into the opening. It didn't look like they had yet reached the back of the vein.

"Jacob saying ye repaying trespass," Aaron said slowly. "Repaying salt from place of many waters."

We just stared at him in shock.

"We're supposed to dig out as much salt as was ruined by the plane's fuel?" I asked with my lips barely moving. "He can't be serious!" I whispered, knowing full well that Jacob was serious about everything.

I heard Brandon gulp before he said, "It will take forever to dig out that much salt!"

"Six parts for five," Aaron said.

CHAPTER 14

Trespass Offering

We just stared at Aaron in disbelief. Jacob stood several feet away with a smug look, the Tweedles standing at his sides.

"Just me and Brandon?" I gasped. "We'll never be able to replace all that! Is he going after everybody else, too?"

"I knowing not. I working also," Aaron said. "I helping ye."

"You didn't ruin any salt," I said to Aaron. "You don't have to do it."

"Yes," Aaron corrected me. "Jacob saying I must work also."

"Why?" I asked. "Just because you've been our friend?"

"Jacob saying I performing Messiah sacrament no more," said Aaron. "Jacob saying I covenanting no more Messiah sacrament."

"So if you don't covenant not to do the sacrament, then you have to work, too?" I asked.

"Yes," Aaron answered.

"You shouldn't have to help us," I said, shaking my head from side to side. "What did you tell Jacob?"

"I covenanting with my father," said Aaron forcefully. "I covenanting with people of my village—*Christians* of my village. I helping Christians coming more close to Messiah with sacrament."

"But they will understand," I said. "We will understand."

"I believing in Jesus Christ. I Christian," Aaron said emphatically. "I breaking not covenant. Many people trusting me, bringing

198

them closer to God. I taking place of my father at the time of my father's death. I showing now—I proving—I living trustworthy."

I wasn't sure how to respond. He was right, of course. I had the same obligation. I had made promises when I was baptized and when I received the priesthood. I thought of the many people that I watched take the sacrament each week at church. They were there to receive forgiveness and come closer to Jesus Christ and Heavenly Father. I thought about how they would feel if they knew that I had helped to prepare or pass the sacrament and was unworthy to do it. I didn't think it was quite the same, but I knew what Aaron meant.

"That's good," I said finally. "I wouldn't break a covenant, either."

No one said anything for a moment. I looked over at Brandon. He apparently hadn't really been listening to our conversation. He was staring up at the huge vein of salt with a defiant look. I heard him taking several deep breaths, each becoming gradually louder than the last. Finally, he spun around with fire in his eyes, enhanced by the reflection of the many torches along the walls.

"It's not our fault," Brandon said sternly to Aaron, through clenched teeth. Then apparently realizing that it wasn't Aaron's fault either, he turned to Jacob and his sons and this time yelled, "It's not our fault!"

Jacob looked surprised. I got the impression he was thinking something like, "What are you yelling at us for? We can't understand you." I thought, *Well, hello-o-o! Welcome to our reality from the first time we saw you!* This guy was amazing.

"*We* didn't *do* it!" Brandon continued. "*You* saw who was wearing the uniform! *You* know who was in charge! *We* didn't fly the plane! *We* didn't dump the fuel!"

Jacob was starting to look annoyed. His sons continued to look disinterested and dumb, respectively—but still strong and threatening, I might add.

Brandon had obviously had enough of this whole situation, and it was starting to look like he wasn't going to back down until he had his say—at least not for as long as they were willing to just stand there and keep listening.

"Look at all this!" Brandon yelled, gesturing at the vein of salt. "You have plenty of salt. There was plenty still up by the ocean, too. Only *part* of it was ruined." He paused to pant and think up a closing statement to summarize his feelings about the whole thing. At first I was thinking it didn't matter much that they couldn't understand his words, they certainly couldn't doubt his meaning. But what he said next, I was glad that they couldn't understand.

"You're just a big, fat *baby!*" Brandon yelled. "You're *all* just a bunch of *babies!* Grow up! Babies! Babies! *Babies!*"

Brandon was jerking his head back and forth and almost spitting with each time he said the word *babies*. I couldn't decide whether to laugh or run for my life. We had been untied so that we could begin digging salt and filling the animal skin bags with it. The entire company of Jacob & Sons was still looking so stunned by Brandon's incoherent outburst that I seriously thought I might be able to get away. But for how long? I figured it wasn't worth trying yet. We'd have to come up with a plan later on.

Still looking slightly stunned, Jacob said something to Aaron. As usual, I couldn't understand what he said—except for the last word. Whatever Jacob said sounded like it ended with *babies*. Aaron didn't reply. Jacob spoke again. This time I was listening for it, and this time it was definite. Whatever Jacob said to Aaron had to do with the word *babies*.

Aaron's look showed that he was uncertain how to respond, but eventually he did. The expression on the Tweedles' faces didn't change, but Jacob hadn't liked what he heard. He did the red-line-going-up-the-face thing again. And this time he started to shake and tremble, to the point that I was sure the smoke from his ears was not far behind. He was as mad about being called a "baby" as he was that Aaron didn't believe they should be following the Law of Moses anymore.

Slowly, with fire in his eyes, Jacob began lifting one fist that got tighter and tighter as he raised it. Then he started moving straight toward Brandon with their eyes locked together. Brandon's determined, defiant stare wavered just a little now, and his eyes darted briefly toward Aaron and me before returning to meet Jacob head-on once more. Jacob continued to approach with his fist held high in the air.

Brandon didn't back down, though. He leaned back slightly, and his eyes definitely got much wider, but his feet never moved. Obviously, he had had all he was going to take from this guy. Just as I thought I would surely witness Brandon's instantaneous death from a single blow, we all heard something that made everyone stop. Someone had yelled a single syllable from the passage opening that led into this chamber.

We all turned to see who had spoken. There, standing in the dim light, we saw about ten men bunched together in the opening. The single syllable yell was repeated by a man that I recognized as being one of the other group leaders who had walked in front of the reindeer sleds when we were traveling from the ocean to the village's summer camp. Next to him stood the other group leader. Jacob slowly dropped his arm and turned to face them with a defiant look that clearly communicated, "I am in charge here, this is *my* domain. What right do you have to challenge *me?*"

As the men moved from the small opening into the chamber where we were, I saw Levi and several other men I recognized from the village. The last two to come in were Dad and Tom. I looked over at Brandon and noticed that his face showed exactly what I felt: extreme and complete relief! *That* was a close one!

Jacob maintained his arrogant glare as the men from his village came and stood facing him and his sons, standing only a few feet away. Dad and Tom, however, came immediately over to us and quietly asked if we were all right.

"We're fine," I whispered. Brandon winced as he rubbed his wrists.

Dad took a hold of Brandon's hands and asked, "Have you been tied up this whole time?"

"Pretty much," Brandon nodded.

Dad reached over and looked at my wrists. His face was sad when he whispered, "I'm *so* sorry it took us so long to get here."

"It's okay, Dad," I said.

"Aaron took good care of us," Brandon said. I think he was fighting back some tears. I know I was. "It would have been a lot scarier without him," I managed to say.

While we talked to Dad, Tom was being especially attentive to Aaron, since his father was in a face-off with Jacob at the moment. The debate began in low, controlled voices, but Jacob was soon using all the force he had to try to make his point. But Levi and the other two group leaders refused to back down. The other leaders proved that they had the ability to face Jacob just as Levi did. Jacob continued to yell and scream, but the other three always answered in much quieter, yet firm, voices. This went on for at least fifteen minutes. No one spoke other than the four leaders. The Tweedles just stood on either side of their father, looking like bodyguards who had spent every spare minute working out. But the men who had arrived with Dad and Levi were just as tough-looking and just as committed to what they were doing.

Finally, Jacob decided it was time to make his final point, since he wasn't getting the respect he thought he deserved. He yelled and screamed and threw wild gestures around with both arms. Then he emphasized his last word by stomping his foot on the floor of the cave, kicking dust in the direction of the other men, and storming toward the opening to the passageway. But these guys had no intention of letting him leave.

The other group leaders didn't move, but the men behind them immediately stepped out and blocked Jacob's path. He stopped so abruptly that Tweedle Dum ran right into the back of him. Jacob was lost between annoyance at his son and utter shock that anyone of his people would dare to stand in his way. He did a doubletake back and forth from his sons behind him to the men in front of him. But if Jacob was shocked then, he was completely bewildered by what happened next.

One of the leaders came right up to his face and chewed him up one side and down the other. I only *wish* I could have known exactly what he was saying. Jacob's mouth just dropped halfway to his chest, and his eyes stretched wide open while this guy pointed at Aaron and then at his father and then at Brandon and me and Dad. His mouth was moving ninety miles an hour the whole time. He gestured toward the Tweedles and back at us and then at everyone else as he continued. He must have yelled for five minutes straight.

Then I saw something I had never seen before. Jacob actually looked sorry! His head fell forward. His eyes now stared at the ground. His shoulders slumped. That seemed to be enough for the man doing the chewing, because he soon finished and backed off a step or two. Jacob hadn't had all that was coming to him, though. The other group leader had something to say, too. And he was no less forceful than the first. He ranted and raved for almost as long and gestured even more emphatically. When he finished, he also moved back a step and stood next to the first man. During all this, Jacob never raised his eyes from the floor. His sons just stared at his back and acted a little perturbed by the whole experience.

Now it was Levi's turn. He walked slowly up to Jacob and the Tweedles. He looked stern yet calm at the same time. He stood looking at Jacob for several moments with nothing but silence all around. Finally, he quietly said a short sentence and then paused. No one moved or spoke. Levi repeated the short phrase and waited again. Then slowly, Jacob lifted his eyes gradually until they met Levi's constant gaze.

The two stood a foot apart with eyes locked for a good thirty seconds until Levi finally spoke. Whatever he said was calm and brief. His eyes never moved or even blinked as he continued to stare at Jacob. After a few moments, Jacob let his eyes and his head drop once more. Levi had apparently said all that he needed to, and he walked over to Aaron. They hugged each other, saying nothing for several moments. Jacob continued to stare at the ground and soon his sons were doing the same, their shoulders slumped and their heads bowed. After a time, the three of them were quietly escorted back out the way we had all come in. I heard Aaron and Levi begin whispering to one another. Tom came and joined with us.

"Are Meg and Shauna okay?" Brandon asked.

"Yeah," I agreed, "and everyone else?"

"Everyone is fine," Dad reassured us. "Shauna and Meg were tied up half the night until we figured out something was going on."

"It took us a while to put all the pieces together," said Tom.

"We're so sorry that it took us so long to catch up with you," Dad said again. Tom nodded in agreement.

"It really is okay," I answered.

Brandon added, "But I'm sure glad you showed up when you did!"

"Yeah," said Tom. "It looked like Jacob was about ready to put you out of his misery."

"That's for sure," I laughed.

"What was going on?" Dad asked. "Did they hit any of you before this?"

"No," we said in unison. I said, "Jacob threatened a couple of times, but this would have been the first time he actually went through with it."

"So what was going on?" Dad asked again.

"Well . . . " Brandon said. He was looking a little embarrassed and even swayed from side to side just a bit. "I sort of lost my cool," he admitted. "I started yelling about how the jet fuel wasn't our fault and how they obviously still had plenty of salt." He gestured toward the vein again.

"So that's what all this is about?" Tom asked. "They were expecting you to make some sort of restitution for the salt?"

"Yeah," Brandon replied. "But at the end I got a little frustrated, and I called them a bunch of . . . babies . . . and I guess he didn't care for that too much."

"First you called him 'a big, fat baby' and then you called them all 'a bunch of babies,'" I corrected him.

Dad looked a little confused. "And they understood the word *baby?*" he asked.

"Well, no," Brandon said. "At least not until Aaron translated it for them."

"Why did he do that?" Tom asked. "If he had to translate something, why didn't he just leave that part out of it?"

"That's the only word he *did* translate," Brandon explained.

"What?" Dad asked. "*Why?*"

"Well, it would have helped," I laughed, "if Brandon hadn't jumped up and down and yelled 'babies, babies, babies' four times!"

Tom and Dad started to laugh. "I didn't jump up and down," Brandon whined. "And I only said it three times, I think." Now Dad and Tom really were laughing. "Well, maybe it was four," Brandon said. "But this whole thing made me *mad!*"

"Did it make you mad *two times?*" I asked.

Over the next few minutes, we told Tom and Dad everything that had happened, and Aaron was apparently doing the same for Levi. They were all amazed when they heard it. Dad and Tom were as perplexed as we were about the knife I found in my scripture case though.

"Who could have possibly put it in there?" Dad asked.

"It's as though," Tom said slowly, "someone who knew what was going to happen wanted to try to help you out."

"That's what we thought," I said. "But who? Do you know of anyone who knew about this ahead of time? I mean other than Jacob and the Tweedles?"

"The *who?*" Dad asked. Brandon and I both started to laugh. "Did you say 'the Tweedles'? What's that all about?"

"You know," Brandon smiled. "Tweedle Dee and Tweedle Dum! We just call them 'the Tweedles' for short! Jeff came up with it."

I tried to smirk at Brandon, but I was smiling too big.

"Tweedle Dum wouldn't be the one whose mouth is always half open, would it?" Tom asked. *Tom's quick,* I thought, but I just smiled and nodded.

Now that we had finally relaxed a little, Dad and Tom told us what they had been going through. Apparently, it wasn't until morning that anyone discovered that anything was wrong.

When Dad came to our hut to wake us up, he found the two of us missing and both Shauna and Meg tied and gagged just like we had been. He immediately went to Levi's hut, but his wife was the only one there.

"Neil was trying to convince me that Levi and Aaron must have done it, but I couldn't believe that," Dad said. "I kept saying, 'Moses, go get Moses' to Levi's wife, and finally she figured out what I meant. I was hoping she had heard us using the name 'Moses' enough that she would get it. *And* I was hoping that Moses knew more English than he had showed so far. Luckily, I was right."

"So did Moses know anything about it?" Brandon asked.

"No," Dad said, "but Levi's wife said that Jacob had come during the night and sent Levi and Aaron back north to collect more birds for burnt offerings. She thought Aaron had gone with him. So Moses agreed to take Tom and me to try to catch up with them. Levi had a reindeer sled, so he was going slower than we could on foot, but still, he had a several-hours head start on us, and it wasn't until late afternoon that we finally caught up with him. He was obviously really upset to learn that the three of you were missing."

"At that point," Tom continued, "Levi said that his reindeer were too tired to begin the return trip until the next morning, since they had already traveled most of the night and day. Instead, he felt it would be better to spend time praying for you. So that's what we did."

"That was the night we got away," I said, "when I found the knife."

Dad and Tom just nodded. "So we left early the next morning and managed to make it back late in the evening," Dad explained.

"So how did you figure out where to find us?" Brandon asked.

"Well, by the time we got back, Levi's wife had told the other tribe leaders that the two of you were missing," Tom said. "They learned that Jacob and his sons were gone, too."

"That would be the Tweedles," I said. Tom smiled.

"R-r-right," said Dad. "I guess they spent the day checking things out and discovered fresh sled tracks heading south, but not until late in the afternoon. So they decided to wait for us to get back, hoping it would be soon."

"Then we left first thing the next morning and got down here as soon as we could," Tom said. "We only stopped for a couple of hours each night."

"And I'm beginning to feel it," Dad admitted. "I'm beat."

Aaron and Levi had finished telling each other their versions of the last four days and stood quietly watching us.

"Are you okay?" Dad asked Aaron.

"Okay—fine, yes," said Aaron.

"Thank you for taking care of my sons," Dad said.

"I making mistake," Aaron admitted. "We getting catched again. I wanting my writings." Suddenly, as he said it, he remembered his writings and immediately started to head out of the cave.

Levi called him back reassuringly. Aaron's worried look turned quickly to relief.

"My father finding my writings," Aaron smiled as he returned to where we stood. "Everything being well."

That statement reminded me of the first time he had spoken English to us when he sneaked into our tent the first night and said, "Being everything well." I thought about how he was now switching things around and not saying the verb first nearly so often anymore.

We asked Levi and Aaron what had happened between all the men and Jacob—what the big argument was about. It turned out that Jacob was indeed planning to force us to perform a trespass offering, but only after we had made restitution for the ruined salt—plus 20 percent, of course. The other leaders told him that it would take months for us to gather that much salt, but apparently he didn't care. He said that was the law and that we would be able to go home the next summer after we'd paid for our trespass.

Levi had argued that a trespass was disrespect for things that we *knew* were sacred. And since we had not done anything on purpose, we could not be held accountable. So I guess Jacob said then that we would at least have to make a sin offering, because that was for sins committed accidentally. But then he still wanted us to at least gather enough salt to pay for all the food and water that we were using. Levi and the other leaders argued that we had done absolutely nothing wrong. That's when Jacob began to stomp out of the cave.

"So what changed him from being mean and mad to being quiet and sad?" I asked.

"Other leaders telling Jacob, he committing many sins," Aaron said. "Jacob hearing such words before never."

"I don't imagine he cared for that too much," Tom said.

Aaron said, "Leaders telling Jacob, he having . . ." Aaron paused as he tried to come up with the word. We all waited as he tried to explain what he meant, "Leaders judging Jacob."

"He's going to have a trial?" Tom asked. Neither Aaron nor Levi understood what he meant, so Tom asked, "Do you mean that his sins will be heard by other leaders, and he will be judged, and he might be punished?"

"Yes," said Aaron.

After speaking for a few more minutes, we went outside to see what was going on. I sort of expected to see Jacob and the Tweedles getting some of the same treatment that they had been inflicting on us ever since we got here. I figured they would essentially be arrested at this point, since they were going to have a trial. It would have been nice to see them tied up like Aaron and Brandon and I had been for the last four days or at least under guard like we all were when we first landed. But no. They were simply doing their own stuff around their tent while everyone else pretty much ignored them. I was amazed that after everything they had done, they were still trusted.

The first thing that Levi did was give Aaron's writings back to him. He was clearly ecstatic to have them safely in his possession once more, and he spent several minutes examining them very closely before putting them away. Brandon and I each got our scriptures back as well. We spent some time checking them out but not nearly so carefully as Aaron had. Of course I couldn't imagine having written out half of the Old Testament by hand and not being extremely protective of my work.

The other men who had come with Levi were busily taking care of the reindeer and the sled that they had brought with them. Apparently, even though it was still early morning, they had already been traveling for several hours. Once the tents were set up and the camp was settled, everyone climbed into their huts to get some rest.

I was tired, too, I guess, but much more than that, I was pretty anxious to get back to the summer camp. I guess I sort of wanted to see for myself that Mom and everyone else were okay. And I was anxious to head home. From what Levi had said a week earlier, the mountain pass should be open by now, and I figured that we were still three or four days away. I asked Aaron hopefully if we might be leaving in the afternoon, but he reminded me that the Sabbath was to begin at sundown. The next two days would be spent resting in preparation to leave first thing on the morning following the Sabbath. I was less than pleased with this news. I knew there was nothing I could do about it, though, so I tried to find something to occupy my mind.

Watching Aaron with his writings reminded me of my personal Bible dictionary, and I pulled the small notebook out of the back of my scripture case. I only had a few lines written in it. Remembering that *salt* was not listed in the Bible Dictionary, I reread a few *salt* scriptures from the Topical Guide and then added an entry to my own Bible dictionary:

Salt—the symbol of the covenant; possibly the most important possession of anyone following the Law of Moses.

Leviticus 2:13 With all thine offerings thou shalt offer salt.

Once I finished, I realized that I really was exhausted. I spent the rest of the day sleeping, entirely missing lunch. Brandon missed it, too. Dad woke us up for the evening burnt offering and supper. My stomach was churning and growling during the entire ritual.

To continue my amazement, Jacob was still the one who performed the sacrifice with his sons helping, along with a couple of other men. Everyone seemed to pretty much be acting as though nothing had happened. I was starting to worry that by the time we would get back, everyone would have forgotten about the whole thing, and Jacob would never end up having his trial. I asked Aaron about it, but he assured me that it would happen. Jacob had apparently covenanted not to go anywhere until after the Sabbath, and so no one was worried. Except for me. I didn't trust him for a minute.

At midday on the Sabbath, Jacob performed a peace offering, signifying that he and his sons had renewed their covenants. He told everyone that he had been wrong in wanting a trespass offering or a sin offering from us and asked for us to forgive him. We did, of course, but I decided that forgiving him didn't necessarily mean trusting him. The way I figured it, he wasn't convinced he had done anything wrong—he was simply outnumbered and basically had no chance of getting what he wanted. I wondered if he was being a good boy now just because he had more people in the village who would stand up for him once we got back. I thought about asking Aaron about it or asking Dad, but I didn't want to get talked into trusting him, so I just kept my mouth shut. I would find out soon enough.

Watching Jacob made me think about authority again. I asked Dad about whether he could give the priesthood to Levi so that they could have authority.

"Not without permission from someone with keys," Dad said. "And there are lots of things that would have to happen before that. First he would have to be a member of the Church. But we can't baptize him without permission, either. And before he could be baptized, he would have to be taught the gospel and receive a testimony of its restoration. Also, he would need to be interviewed by Church leaders to determine worthiness and readiness." Dad paused, shaking his head. "It's just not possible."

I nodded my understanding. A few minutes later, I went and found Aaron and told him what Dad had said. He seemed a little disappointed, but like that's what he had expected.

Once evening came and Jacob declared the official end of the Sabbath, Tom turned into a chemist. Apparently during the afternoon of the previous day, he had spent some time hiking and stumbled onto what he called a "rubber tree plant."

"What's that?" I asked.

"It's where we get rubber from," Tom explained. "These plants are indigenous to south and central Asia, but I was surprised to find one this far north."

"We're not as far north as we used to be," Brandon reminded him.

"Good point," Tom smiled. "Anyway," he continued, "I collected some of the sap in this animal skin bag and was planning to do some experiments with it tonight."

"So now you're a chemist, too?" I asked. "Are you sure your friends don't call you 'professor'?"

Tom smiled but also looked a little embarrassed. "If I remember right," Tom said, "you can heat this stuff for a while until it starts to get thick and then when it cools it's pretty much like a thick glue or paste."

We all just stared at him, not having a clue what he was up to.

"I was hoping," Tom explained, "that we might be able to use it to repair the raft. Since Levi is planning on taking us to a river, I thought we might have a better chance of being found if we have some way to float down it."

"That would be great!" Dad agreed.

Tom spent the rest of the evening trying to heat up rubber by placing it in the fire on rocks that were bowl-shaped on top. He was still working at it when Brandon and I went to bed. I didn't fall asleep for a long time. I was excited about finally getting to go back to the village. But there were lots of other things on my mind as well. I kept thinking about the fact that we had still never figured out how Jacob knew about the sacrament that Levi and Aaron had been performing for the Christians in the village. And no one had a decent explanation for how that small knife ended up in my scripture case, either. There were just too many things that didn't feel right about all of this and because of it, I ended up not sleeping very well at all.

The next morning, Dad shook me several times before I finally started to wake up.

"Come on," I heard Dad say somewhere through the fog. "We

need to take the tent down as fast as possible. Levi and the others want to leave immediately." He sounded *way* tense.

"What's going on?" I yawned. "What happened?"

"Jacob is gone," Dad said. "He and his sons sneaked away sometime during the night."

CHAPTER 15

New Star in
the Heavens

I jumped up as fast as I could. I was still pretty groggy, but I was definitely feeling motivated to get back to the village. One of the other leaders handled the morning burnt offering since Jacob wasn't around. I sort of wondered why we bothered doing it at all, but I didn't ask.

For the next three days, we traveled long and hard, only stopping for a few hours each night. In the evening, we didn't do the burnt offerings until much later than usual, and in the morning it was a lot earlier. I figured it didn't matter too much, because in the Old Testament it says to do them at sunup and sundown, so it was actually closer to what was right.

Along the way, we talked to Aaron and Levi about Jacob. I was pleased to learn that at this point they were feeling pretty much the same way I was: Jacob couldn't be trusted. They wanted to get back to the summer camp as soon as possible to make sure that the rest of our family and the airline crew were all safe.

Even though everyone was in a hurry to get back before Jacob did, the trip was certainly a lot less stressful than the way down had been. It was great to be with Dad and Tom again. Tom, the professor, always had something interesting to talk about. It turned out that he had done pretty well with his experiment. He had several little chunks of dark brown rubber, and he said that he thought he could make it work for patching the raft. Tom was hopeful, anyway, and so was Dad. My hope was just that we would be sure one way or another before we ended up on a river. I was tired of surprises.

When we finally arrived back at the summer camp, it was great to see everyone again. Shauna and Meg seemed to have pretty much forgotten about being tied up for half a night. Danny and Chelsea had each made friends that they apparently spent most of each day playing with. Mom, Jo, and Nancy had learned to sing some interesting songs and to cook some even more interesting food. Personally, I preferred sticking with the jerky. Neil was still talking about all the things that "we have ourselves," and John's chin hadn't lost its rhythm—I had the feeling he hadn't even missed a beat. I wondered if he might enjoy chewing one of Tom's little dark-brown chunks of cooked tree sap.

Aaron was happy to see Moses again, and we all spent the evening having a great reunion around Levi's family fire. Levi wasn't there, though. Right after supper, he had told us that the mountain pass was open and that we should plan to leave the next day. Apparently, it would be about a three-hour hike to get through the pass but then it would take another several hours from there to actually get down to the huge, wide river where they said they had seen travelers on big boats. Levi said he wasn't sure how long it would take but that it should be no problem to get there by late afternoon.

"Traveling we slow with women and small children," Levi had said.

After telling us this, Levi had left for the rest of the evening. He and the other tribe leaders were having discussions about Jacob. No one in the village had seen Jacob or his sons since the night we had been kidnapped.

Tom had his own fire going closer to his tent. He was working with some of the sap from the rubber tree plant. John was with him most of the evening. I think he thought he was helping, but it looked to me like he was just watching and talking. And chomping, of course. I wondered how long he was going to keep chewing nothing but the *memory* of gum. Sometime late in the evening, Tom came over and said that he was done with the raft but that he wanted to wait several hours before testing his patch job with air pressure. Then Tom started asking Aaron some questions about the hike. By this time, several of our group had already wandered off to bed, including Mom, with Danny and Chelsea.

"Is there a river that goes through the mountain pass?" Tom asked Aaron.

"No river of water," Aaron answered. "Water flowing other side to large river of water."

"So there's a smaller river or stream that flows down to the big river?" John asked.

"Yes," replied Aaron.

"Your father said that it would take about three hours to get to the pass," Tom continued. "How long would it take to get from the pass to the small river?" he asked.

Aaron thought for a moment before answering. I had the feeling he had never actually made the trip and was guessing. "We traveling one hour," Aaron said finally.

"Are you sure it's not more than that?" Tom asked.

"No more," Aaron said, shaking his head from side to side like a good American kid.

"Are you sure?" Tom asked. "You say that we can all make it to this small river in less than four hours?"

"Yes," Aaron said, nodding. It was obvious that something was spinning in Tom's head.

"Can you get us there by yourself?" Tom asked. "Or will you need help from your father?"

"I traveling," Aaron said confidently. "Father traveling not necessary."

I smiled as I realized that he still emphasized the second syllable in "necessary" just as he had done the very first night.

"Will our raft fit on the small river?" Tom asked, pointing to where he had left the raft.

"Yes," Aaron said confidently.

"What are you thinking?" Dad asked Tom.

Tom looked around as if to make sure he could trust everyone around the fire. "I'm thinking we shouldn't wait until tomorrow morning to leave. I think we should leave in the middle of the night." Then turning to Aaron, he asked, "Can we travel safely at night?"

"Yes," said Aaron.

"Why don't you want to wait till morning?" John asked.

"Because no one seems to know where Jacob is," Tom explained. "And we all know that he doesn't want us to ever leave here."

No one else spoke.

"I just have this fear that Jacob still has friends in this village," Tom said. "I'm sure that Levi has told the other tribe leaders about our plans to leave tomorrow. We just don't know whom we can trust. We have no idea where Jacob is, but he had a head start from the winter cave. I think we have to assume that he's not far off and is still going to do whatever he can to keep us here."

It was great to hear someone thinking the same way I was.

"You're right," Neil agreed. "We do still have ourselves a situation with regard to that Jacob fellow."

"I think," Tom continued, "that instead of hiking down to the main river, maybe we can use this raft on the tributary and get there a whole lot quicker. If we leave just after midnight when the sun is down for a couple of hours, we might be able to get on the water before anyone here even realizes we're gone."

Then turning to Aaron again, Tom asked, "Do you think we can ride this raft safely all the way to the big river?"

"Yes," Aaron said. "Ye riding boat to big river of water."

"I like it," Neil said. "I think it's a good plan."

217

"I agree," said John.

"Let's do it," Dad said. "Aaron, will you take us when the sun is down?"

"Yes," he answered. "Everything being well."

"It's going to take a while to fill that raft with air," Neil said.

"I thought about that," Tom replied. "Once we're out of sight of the village, I think we should take turns blowing into it. I'm hoping we can have it mostly full by the time we reach the water."

Everyone agreed to the plan and then we all went straight to bed, since it would only be two or three hours before we would be leaving. It felt great to be with the whole family again as we knelt for family prayer in Mom and Dad's hut. I was excited as I lay in the dark, thinking that we would finally be starting for home the next day. I thought for a long time about Aaron and Levi and all that had happened over the past week and a half. It seemed like forever since we had been home. As I lay in the dark, I heard whispering outside my tent. I wasn't the least bit sleepy, so after quickly pulling my shoes and coat back on, I crept outside to see who it was. Levi was back. He and Aaron were talking softly with Dad and Tom.

"Will you be coming with us?" Dad asked Levi. Just then Brandon stumbled out of our tent and came over to see what was going on. I guess he hadn't been able to sleep, either.

"No," answered Levi.

"My father having important work in village on morrow," said Aaron.

"Oh," Dad nodded. "Are the leaders preparing to meet together again about Jacob?"

"No," Levi said. "Leaders talking finished."

"So have you decided what to do with him?" I asked. "I mean, will he be punished for what he did to us?"

Levi looked carefully around on all sides to be sure we were alone. Then he nodded at Aaron as if to say, "Go ahead."

"Yes," Aaron spoke quietly. "Jacob being punished. People of my village not knowing of punishment of Jacob until on morrow."

"We understand," Dad said. "You don't need to tell us. We're just happy for your sake that he will be punished."

"No," Aaron said. "My father saying me telling you of punishment of Jacob. Leaders saying Jacob having now another name."

"Another name?" asked Dad.

"Different name," Aaron corrected himself. "We saying 'Jacob' for him not again."

"So after tomorrow, you will all call him something else?" I asked. "What's the name?"

Aaron scrunched his face slightly as he tried to think of how to say the name in English. "Jacob in writings of Prophets having older brother," Aaron said finally. "I remembering not name of brother used by Christian."

"You're talking about Jacob in the Old Testament," Dad said. "Do you mean Esau?"

"Yes!" said Aaron. "E-sau. Jacob having now name of E-sau."

"Why?" I asked. "What does that name mean to your people?"

"Esau was the older brother," Tom explained, "which means he had the birthright."

"What's that?" Brandon asked.

"Having the birthright meant that he would inherit his father's lands," Tom said, "and that he had the authority to preside."

"Oh," Brandon and I said in unison. I was stunned when Tom said that "he had the authority to preside." What kind of punishment was that? For Aaron's and Levi's sake, I was scared for what this would probably mean to them. If Jacob—or Esau now—was given authority to preside, would they have to give up their worship of Jesus Christ?

"That's right," said Dad, "but Esau sold his birthright to his younger brother when Esau was desperate for food. He sold it for a 'mess of pottage.'"

"What's pottage?" Brandon asked.

"It's like thick soup," Dad said. "Esau sold his birthright for a bowl of soup."

I was confused. "I don't get what this means," I said.

"Esau being leader of village no more," Aaron said. "My father being leader of village."

"No way!" said Brandon. "That's great!"

"Cool!" I agreed.

"Shh-h-h," Dad reminded us. "Keep it down." I noticed that Dad and Tom both had questioning looks on their faces.

"How do you feel about being the new leader?" Dad asked Levi.

"Having I great duty," Levi said. "Having I great responsibility."

"It's true," nodded Tom. "But you *understand* the great responsibility, and you will seek to follow God's will."

"You will do well," said Dad.

Levi just nodded. At the time I didn't know if it was the dim light or just not getting enough sleep like the rest of us for the last week, but suddenly Levi looked much older to me. I didn't realize until later that he was probably just feeling the weight of his new responsibility.

No one spoke for a few seconds as we all watched Levi. I found myself wondering how all this would work. Was Levi to be the leader for life now? How was Jacob—or Esau—going to take his sudden loss of power? I wondered if the village would now immediately begin worshipping Jesus Christ and stop performing the rituals and offerings.

"Saying ye nothing of E-sau," Levi reminded us.

"We understand," Tom said.

Levi nodded and then suggested that we all get some sleep before leaving. After returning to bed, I started thinking about all that had happened, reviewing each day in my mind and thinking about all the trouble that Jacob had caused us. If he had had his way, Brandon, Aaron, and I would still be slaving away, digging up enough salt for every ritual he would witness for the rest of his life. I thought it sure was a good thing that Moses knew enough English to be able to translate between Dad and Aaron's mother. Otherwise, we might still be down there in that cave. If we hadn't been found before the rest of the village returned for the winter, every one of us would have been stuck here for a year.

I smiled as I thought about the fact that Moses wouldn't know about Jacob's punishment until tomorrow with the rest of the village. I was sure that he'd be happy about the news. It was then that I realized that I had never even told Moses "thank you." We were planning to leave in a couple of hours, and I would never see him again and never get a chance to thank him. I knew that Moses slept by the trees, but I wasn't sure exactly where. I had seen the general direction that he had gone that first night that John said he wanted to sleep outside, too. That was the night we were kidnapped. I knew that finding Moses would be a long shot, but I had an uncontrollable urge to at least try. Quietly, I pulled my shoes and coat on one more time and slowly opened the tent flap. The sun was down just below the horizon. That meant that we would be leaving soon, so if I was going to do it, I'd better go fast.

"What are you up to?" came John's voice out of the darkness when I was just a few feet from our tent. I jumped like our cat does with the first fireworks on the Fourth of July.

"Whoa!" I gasped softly. I breathed deeply in and out several times before saying, "You scared me to death, John!"

"Sorry," he apologized. "I just wondered what you were up to. We'll be leaving soon, so if you go running off somewhere, I thought it might be a good idea for someone to know where you are."

"Of course, yeah," I agreed. "I just had no idea anyone would be awake. What are you doing out here?"

"Remember my star charts?" John asked with a little bit of excitement in his voice.

"Oh, yeah," I said. I felt a little annoyed as I remembered that John and Neil were planning to try to find their way back here using John's star drawings. "Are you still doing that?" I asked.

"Of course," John answered. "I just got started for tonight. I figure it'll be my last chance."

"We can hope so," I said. "But I'm glad you're awake. Can you tell me how to find where Moses sleeps? I want to go tell him thanks before I never get to see him again."

"Sure," said John. "Look up at the top of the mountain." I turned and looked. The ridge was clearly outlined because the sun had just gone down behind it. "Do you see how it's mostly smooth and even, but then there are three pretty sharp points together?"

"Yeah," I said.

"Well, if you head straight for the one on the right, you'll run almost smack into him," John said. "He may be actually a little farther to the left, but you should be able to find him okay."

"Thanks," I whispered and immediately took off toward the mountain.

There was about a half-moon, and it was bright, so I could see where I was going with no problem. It was only a few minutes before I was at the first trees. I walked up the slope a little way but couldn't see him. The trees were thick and things got dark really fast. I wondered if Moses was covered in a dark animal skin like our huts were, which would make him nearly impossible to find in the dark. Then I remembered John saying I might need to go to the left a little, so I turned and headed that way.

I stopped short when I heard someone hissing something in the dark. It sounded like it came from thirty or forty feet away. It was a villager saying something I didn't understand. But it didn't sound like Moses. I froze in my tracks, hoping that I was blocked from view by a couple of nearby trees that were between me and the sound. The two syllables came again, from a little closer. I still didn't move. A few seconds later I heard it again, even closer still. Because no one seemed to be answering this guy, I suddenly had the fear come over me that he had seen me and was talking to me. I didn't have any idea who it was, and I had absolutely no interest in meeting up with him.

Just as I was about to turn and run for all I was worth back to our huts, I heard something just a few feet in front of me on the other side of the trees that I had hoped were shielding me. It was Moses, sitting up. He grunted softly. The villager that I didn't know said the same two syllables again, and this time Moses responded in their language with a word that I had learned meant "hello" or "greetings."

I couldn't imagine what was going on. The two of them spoke for a minute, then Moses stood and went with the guy back in the direction he had come from. I didn't move for at least another three or four minutes. I decided to forget about saying anything to Moses and just ask Aaron to pass the message along for me. Once I was sure the two of them were gone, I sneaked carefully back the way I had come. I was trying to be quiet, but it didn't seem to be working very well. I was really nervous and could feel my knees beginning to shake a little, so as soon as I got out in the open enough that I thought I could make it without tripping over something, I set out on a dead run back to the huts. I was running so hard and fast that I think I scared John a little when I came charging in between the tents. It took a lot longer to get back than I expected. I guessed it must have been farther away than I had first thought.

"What's up? Are you all right?" John asked me.

"Yes," I gasped, between pants. "I'm fine. I just . . . didn't like being out there . . . in the dark . . . alone."

"Did you see Moses?" John asked.

"Yeah," I panted. "I saw him."

"Good," John said, but he sounded disinterested. I decided not to bother telling him what had happened. But I wanted to talk to

Aaron about it. I tiptoed carefully around the backside of Aaron's family's tent. I knew about where he slept.

"Aaron!" I hissed near the ground. Nothing happened. "Aaron!" I called again.

"I hearing you," came Aaron's voice as the bottom part of the animal skin was raised just a couple of inches.

"I need to ask you something," I whispered.

"Fine," said Aaron. "Okay."

I heard a short discussion between Aaron and Levi before Aaron came out. I'm sure Aaron's side of the conversation was the villagers' equivalent of, "Aw, Dad. It's Jeff's last night! Lemme go out for just a sec!" But whatever he said, it worked. And "just a sec" was all I needed. I told Aaron what had happened and then asked him what the word meant that the man had said when he was trying to find Moses.

"This being name," Aaron said.

"Oh!" I said. "Is that his name in your language?"

"No," said Aaron. "This being name of man from tribe of Judah in writings of Prophets."

"Really?" I asked. "Have you ever heard him called that before?"

"No," Aaron yawned. I thought, *How can you be yawning? Something weird is going on here!*

"Well, what does it mean?" I asked. "Do you know how to say it in English?"

"This man of tribe of Judah being good man," Aaron reassured me.

"How do you say it in English?" I asked again. "Do you know?"

"Christian saying name 'Kae-leb,'" Aaron said.

"Kaleb?" I repeated.

"Yes."

"Okay, thanks," I said. "You can go back to sleep now."

Without another word, Aaron nodded once and disappeared inside his family's tent. Once I found out that it was a name from the scriptures, I wanted to look it up and see what I could learn. I didn't remember the name from the Old Testament, so at first I was worried that maybe it was just in writings that Aaron had. But since Christian had an English pronunciation for it, I was hopeful I could find it.

I looked up at the moon and then down at my open hands to decide how well I might be able to read. It was worth a try. As quietly as possible, I sneaked back into our tent just long enough to find my quad and bring it back out. Now was when I was especially glad that we weren't still sharing a tent with Mom and Dad. They never would have let me take the time to check this out. They would have said something like, "Wait till tomorrow" or "Wait till we get home."

John was still working away on his star charts. "Are you going to join me?" he asked, looking back and forth between his paper and the night sky.

"Yeah," I said. "I just thought I'd study for a while."

"Fine with me," John said absently.

The first place I turned was to the Bible Dictionary. I was hoping there would be a definition of the name "Kaleb." There was nothing there. Next I turned to the Topical Guide, but again there was nothing. I let a little puff of air burst from my nose in frustration.

"What's going on?" asked John.

"I was hoping the name 'Kaleb' would be in the Bible," I said. "But I can't find anything."

John spelled the name out loud, wondering if that was the name I meant. "C-A-L-E-B?" he asked.

"No," I said, "K—"I paused a moment. "You're right!" I said. "It is spelled with a C, isn't it?"

"You never know how anybody's gonna spell any name these days," John said, still working. "Seems like the old way of spelling just isn't good enough for anybody giving a kid a name anymore."

I threw a puzzled glance in his direction. He sounded like somebody's grandpa. I thought it was a pretty weird thing to say for someone who didn't spend any time in a rocking chair.

I looked up *Caleb* with a C this time. I forgot that I was still in the Topical Guide and all it had was:

Caleb (see Dictionary: Caleb)

I sighed in frustration with myself and turned to the Bible Dictionary. At least I knew it was there, though, and I got more and more excited as I got close. The reference under "Caleb" filled about a third of a column. I read the whole thing through twice, trying to find any clues I could about what was meant when this guy called Moses by the name of "Caleb." I couldn't figure it out. There were about a dozen scripture references mixed in with the explanation of this man, Caleb. I read every single one of them—and a couple of them were pretty long. I still couldn't figure it out. John just kept working away at his star chart. Between his chart and his chewing, I was getting more and more annoyed each time I glanced over at him. I wanted to tell him to give it up. We should leave these people alone.

Looking back at the Bible Dictionary, I decided that whatever I was looking for had to be in there somewhere. I just needed to look harder. The first two references listed were both in chapter 13 of the book of Numbers, verses 6 and 30, so I decided to read everything in between as well. I was getting a little bored at first because I was just reading a big, long list of names of tribes and fathers and sons.

But when I got to verse 16, it hit me like a rock. One word seemed to jump off the page at me, even in the dim light. I read the verse three times before continuing. When I read verse 17, the exact same thing happened. The same word jumped out at me again. I now knew what it meant. I knew why that man had called him "Caleb."

I suddenly remembered the final warning from Christian's note in his Bible. I don't think I had thought about it since the first and only time I heard it. Hadn't it said, "Be careful whom you trust" or something like that? And it seemed like it had also said, "Use their names as a clue."

For several moments I felt everything spinning in my head. The puzzle was suddenly coming together. I felt my eyes dart about as I thought about all the things that had happened that I hadn't been able to explain. No one had. Now all of a sudden, they were starting to make sense—perfect sense. I shook my head slowly back and forth as I thought about what this all meant.

I needed to talk to Aaron or Dad—or both—as soon as possible. I didn't know if I dared get Aaron from his tent again or not. I had the feeling that we were going to be leaving really soon, but the thought of waiting even one more minute was scaring me to death. I just sat there, trying to decide what to do.

"Guess what," John said unexpectedly.

I looked over at him. He was staring at his paper with obvious satisfaction in his face. I could see it even in the dark.

"Something big just happened," I said.

"You're right," John replied. "Good guess." He stood and came over to sit next to me. "Look at this," he said, holding out the page of random dots for me to inspect. "See that one?" he asked, pointing to a large dot right at the edge of the paper. "That's a new star that I haven't seen before. It just appeared for the first time tonight above the western horizon." He beamed at me as he explained it. "That new star," John continued, "is going to lead us from the east to the west tonight—just like the wise men were led." He paused before smugly adding, "Because we were wise enough to make these maps. It's a good sign."

I just stared at his paper for a moment before finally saying, "It's a sign all right. It's definitely a sign."

CHAPTER 16

River of Water

"Are you two ready to go?" Tom asked from behind us. It made me jump because I was still lost in thought about what to do. I didn't know who was trustworthy anymore. Though the puzzle was coming together, one of my questions was still unanswered. I looked carefully back and forth at John and Tom. *I can trust Tom*, I thought. But I didn't know enough about John. I would have told Tom right then what I had discovered about Moses, but I didn't dare do it while John was around.

"Let's get moving," Tom said. "The sun will be up again soon, and we had better be out of here by then."

Tom sent me to wake up Aaron, while he went to wake up Mom and Dad. John went after the rest of the airline crew. I went around the back of Aaron's hut again, hoping to wake up Aaron and get him to come out before his parents woke up. I didn't know if I could trust Levi. I was pretty sure that it would be all right, but I just didn't want to take a chance. I think Aaron must have been as anxious about all this as I was because he answered after I had said his name only one time. He sounded wide awake and said he would be right out. I stood from my kneeling position and went around to the opening of the hut, but I stopped short at the sight of Moses standing right there.

I didn't know what to do. He just stared at me, and I stared right back at him. Neither of us said a word. It was only a second or two before Aaron came out, but it was pretty uncomfortable. Had he seen me running from the trees earlier? Did he suspect what I knew? Aaron immediately greeted Moses and then me. Moses then finally acknowledged me, too, and so I returned the greeting. I thought he was still looking at me pretty funny, though.

Dad came over to where we were standing. "Good morning," he whispered. Then glancing up over the mountain where the sun would be coming up in a little while he said, "Well, almost." To Aaron he asked, "Is Moses coming?"

"Yes," answered Aaron. "Moses traveling to river of water." Aaron reached over and gripped Moses' shoulder and gave him a look that said he was grateful for such a good friend. I thought *There's something you need to know about him!*

"Great," Dad whispered, nodding toward Moses. "We thank you for help."

Moses nodded. I still wondered how much he really understood. I had a feeling it was more than any of us thought. I wasn't sure how I felt about Moses coming along, especially if he was guiding the reindeer. Would he take us the right way? On the other hand, I thought it might be a good idea to keep an eye on him. And if he was out in front guiding the reindeer, that ought to be easy enough to do. I was still really nervous, though.

Levi came from his tent, and I found myself immediately wishing that he was coming to the river with us. Then the thought hit me that maybe the reason he was just sending Aaron was because he intended that Aaron would actually go with us. Did he see this as the opportunity for Aaron to go to another land in order to bring salvation to his people? That's what he said the name "Joseph" meant. I got excited as I thought about it. I looked at Levi again and wondered if maybe that was why he looked a little sad and tired. Maybe he didn't think he would see his son again for a long time—if ever. But what about Moses? Was he supposed to go, too?

"We had better get going," Dad said. Turning to Levi, he asked, "Are you sure we can't help you take down the huts?"

"No," Levi said. "Leaving ye at this time being best. Leaving ye with haste."

The plan was to use a four-reindeer sled up the mountain. The raft was unrolled and set up on the sled with all of our personal stuff in the middle. Tom's idea was that whoever was currently working on blowing up the raft could ride at the front of the sled. He thought that two people at a time could probably trade off. One would relax for a moment while the other blew several breaths of air into the raft and then they would switch. Meg, Chelsea, and Danny were asleep on the raft, wrapped up in blankets. They were also covered with a thick musk ox hide. Apparently, the hike would be steep enough that they would be the only ones allowed to ride on the sled, other than whoever was currently blowing up the raft.

I looked at my book bag and thought of my scriptures inside, remembering that I thought Aaron and his father should have a copy of the Book of Mormon. When it looked like no one was watching, I climbed onto the sled and quickly pulled my quad from inside my bag. I started rummaging through my scripture case for a moment just to give the impression that I was looking for something. I was glad I did, too, because otherwise I probably never would have thought to pull out my little purple notebook and stick it in my coat pocket. After determining that so far no one seemed to notice what I was up to, I slowly walked over to our tent and placed my quad just inside the opening, closing the flap again.

"I'm sorry you won't be coming with us," Dad said to Levi. "But I know that you have much work to do in the village. Thank you for all that you have done. Thank you for helping us to get back to the river."

"This bringing pleasure to me," nodded Levi.

"Our prayers are with you," said Mom. "I thank your good wife for all of her kindness and patience with me."

For the first time I noticed that Levi's wife was there also. Mom went to her and hugged her for a long time. "Thank you," she said. I wondered if the woman understood her. I thought I saw tears glistening in her eyes. Nancy and Jo also hugged her. Before they even let go, the sled was moving with Aaron walking at the front. I heard each of the men tell Levi and his wife "thank you" as they walked past.

I hung back so that I was the last one from our group to say something to Levi. Moses stood a few feet away, apparently waiting for me. I said "thank you" like everybody else and then, very quietly, I whispered to Levi, "I left a gift for you in the tent." He seemed to understand and with a small nod closed his eyes. It was strange, realizing that we would never see them again. I smiled and ran to catch up with everybody else. Moses looked at me narrowly as I ran past him. I think he was wondering what I had whispered to Levi. I just ignored him.

"Did your patch job work?" I heard John ask Tom as soon as we were out of earshot of Levi's hut.

"I really don't know," Tom admitted. "But it's definitely time to find out." Tom and Neil took the first turn at the front of the sled. After only about five minutes, they switched with John and Nancy.

"It seems to be okay so far," said Tom, "but we won't really know for sure until it's at least half full."

"We're a long way from that," Neil replied.

"Who would like to be next?" asked John a few minutes later. He was panting heavily.

"*I* want a turn," Mom whined. She said it like a little kid whose older siblings would never include her in their game.

"So let's go," Dad suggested, and he and Mom took the next few minutes.

"Whoa," Mom said, staggering a little when she climbed back off of the sled at the end of their turn. She acted like she was a little light-headed. "That's all you're getting out of me for a while," she said. Dad smiled.

Shauna and Jo were next, followed by Brandon and me. It turned out to be a lot harder than it looked. We were already breathing hard from the hike, so after only a couple of puffs into the raft, I already was feeling out of breath. We continued taking turns in pairs as we proceeded up the mountain. I was glad that Tom and John were apparently willing and able to do most of the work. Most of the rest of us pretty much quit helping very much at all after a while. As the raft continued to expand, it became obvious that it was bigger than the sled. It hung at least a foot or so over each side and several feet off of the back. We tried to keep it from dragging on the ground as much as possible until it got full enough to hold itself up.

Not long after we started up the mountain, the sun came up and shone on our backs. The warmth felt good. As we walked, I kept a close watch on Moses. He and Aaron just marched on in silence. Aaron stayed at the front, guiding one of the two lead reindeer. Moses was sort of walking next to one of the reindeer in back; it was starting to feel more like he was just staying close to *me*. If I moved more toward the back of the sled, Moses would drop back as well. As soon as I moved forward again, Moses would return to the side of the reindeer. He always seemed to be just close enough to me to be able to hear what I was saying. I didn't see how I was ever going to get a chance to tell Dad what I had figured out about Moses.

I wasn't having any luck getting with Aaron, either. One time I slowly moved around the opposite side of the sled from where Moses and Aaron were and then moved up next to the front reindeer. As soon as I was there, I saw that Moses had moved up so that he was right behind Aaron. Now I was absolutely sure about what I knew.

We finally stopped to let the reindeer rest after a couple of hours. Everyone turned to look back at the valley below us. It was beautiful. We couldn't see the village because it was too close to the base of the mountain, and the forest was too thick.

We all took the opportunity to drink from one of several water bags that we had with us. Levi wanted to make sure that we had plenty of food and water, not being certain how long we might have to wait before actually being rescued by one of these "boats of travelers." He had provided us with several bags of jerky along with the water. I had learned over the past couple of weeks that though they made their jerky from the meat of several different kinds of animals, because they used so much salt, it all tasted pretty much the same to me. We had most of the emergency meals still with us, too. Dad said he thought we probably had enough food and water to last three or four days if we had to.

"I hope we don't have to," I said, breathing hard again as we continued our climb up the mountain.

"So do I," he admitted. "But we'll just have to trust in the Lord." He paused before adding, "and these fine people."

Moses turned and glanced at us over his shoulder. I suddenly thought of the words "be careful who you trust" and it was as if I was hearing them in Christian's voice—even though I had never heard it before. A chill went up my spine. I knew I had to tell Dad soon. We were in trouble, and I could just feel it building. I felt a knot growing in the pit of my stomach.

"Are you all right?" Dad asked me a few minutes later. Moses looked back over his shoulder again. *He saw me in the trees*, I thought. *He knows that I know!*

"I'm okay," I said. "I'm just anxious to get home."

"I understand," Dad said. I thought, *No you don't! I only wish you did!*

A short time later we reached the mountain pass. There were still patches of snow here and there. We traveled through a narrow passage that wasn't much wider than the sled. The sides of the mountain were incredibly high and steep on either side. Not far above us, the entire rest of the mountain was covered in snow.

"I see now why this pass has so much snow," Tom said. "With these steep walls, I'm sure the snow ends up getting really deep in here."

The pass was narrow most of the way, but pretty much level, with only a slight upward slope. It took fifteen or twenty minutes to make it all the way through to the other side. Once we were through the pass, we stopped and rested the reindeer for a few minutes. The sun had lighted the trail quite well for the past couple of hours, but now that we were on the west side of the mountain, we were walking in its shadow and everything was pretty dark again. But there was enough light to see the huge river, far below us, off in the distance, running parallel to the mountain.

"Wow," said Tom. "That's got to be at least five miles away." Turning to Aaron, he asked, "Now which way do we go to get to the stream—the small river?"

"We traveling here," Aaron answered, gesturing south along the side of the mountain.

"And you think it will take about an hour from here?" Tom asked.

"Yes," said Aaron.

"So let me make sure I understand this right," John said. "We're going to hike along the side of the mountain here for about an hour. Then we're going to put this raft in the stream, and it will take us down to that big river out there, right?"

"Yes—right," said Aaron.

"How's the raft doing?" John asked Tom.

"I think it's going to work," Tom said. "It's more than half full and seems to be holding just fine." Tom went to the patched hole and put his cheek down next to it while pushing down on either side with both hands. He bounced on it with most of his weight two or three times. "It seems good," he said.

"I'm hungry," I announced, hoping to gain some support from anyone else that might be feeling the same way. The plan was to get to the stream and then eat while Tom and Dad and others made sure that everything looked safe enough, but I was hoping to convince enough people that we should eat now and not wait.

"Me, too," Brandon agreed, in response to my campaign for food.

"Can we eat now?" Meg asked, sitting up for the first time inside the raft. I didn't even know she was awake.

"No," said Moses sternly. I was shocked to hear him say something in English. This was the first time that I knew of since the day we first met. I think everyone else was just about as surprised as I was. "Eating ye not," Moses continued. "Traveling we to river of water."

"Yes," Aaron said. "We traveling first to river of water."

It was true that I was hungry, but more than that I wondered why Moses was so dead set on us getting to the river. What did he know that Aaron didn't know? Why didn't Aaron make the suggestion? I'm no detective, but it seemed to me that the only reason Moses would say such a thing was if he knew something that Aaron didn't know—and that fit perfectly with the name "Caleb." I tried to argue for a minute that it made no difference and it would only take a minute, but all the adults said I could wait.

"We'll be there in an hour," Mom said. "You can wait that long."

"I'd rather get there, get on the river, and just eat on the raft," said Jo.

"If that lunatic still intends trying to stop us," Neil said, "then I believe it is prudent to move forward as quickly as possible. If we dawdle long enough to let him catch up, then we'll definitely have ourselves a situation."

That was the first time I felt a violent reaction to hearing about something that we "have ourselves." Each time he had said it before, it had just been a gradually-growing annoyance, but this time I actually envisioned Neil in pain. I did my best to hide the smirk that was trying to expose itself across my face.

Before I could think of a response, Aaron had already started the reindeer moving forward again. Moses immediately followed. Something was going on, and I could just feel it getting closer and closer. I hung back a little as everyone else started moving. Moses glanced over his shoulder and immediately slowed down. I thought *How obvious can you get?*

The trail from the pass to the river was a much bigger pain than the first part of the hike had been. I think because there actually was no trail. Aaron was just trying to weave his way in and around the trees. Luckily, they weren't too thick here. I noticed that the raft seemed to be getting close to full. It was almost too much to hope that this would all soon be over. Within a few minutes, I could hear the sound of rushing water. It continued to grow louder and louder as we made our way along the side of the mountain. Then, suddenly, almost without warning, we came around a large rock, and we saw it. The sound of the water doubled almost immediately.

"This is the *small* river?" I asked. I said it loudly, but I don't think anyone heard me except for Brandon.

"This is the *safe* river?" Brandon asked.

I immediately saw what he meant. This looked like the type of thing that half of the guys at Scout camp would find and beg the Scoutmaster to take us on. To which the Scoutmaster would always reply, "Your parents would shoot me if they knew I took you guys on something like that!" And he would be right, of course. We were talking white-water rapids here.

Well, the others seemed to be pretty much as unsure about this as I was. Mom, Jo, and Nancy agreed to break out the food, while Aaron went with everyone else to check out the river. They said they would be back in just a few minutes. Moses, however, decided to stay with us. Surprise, surprise.

"Are we really going on that river?" Shauna asked, after they were gone.

"I don't know," Mom answered. "That's what they're trying to decide."

"I think it might be better to hike the rest of the way down," Nancy suggested.

"We may end up doing that yet," Jo replied.

That's what I would have voted for. I was typically *not* one of the Scouts who wanted to put my life at risk every time the rest of them found something they thought looked "fun." Brandon was, of course, but not me. I enjoyed my life and enjoyed the thought of keeping my body pretty much in the same condition it currently was, including having everything attached where it belonged!

Nobody really said anything else for the next few minutes—probably because we were all hungry and tired. Moses didn't eat anything. Instead, he started blowing into the raft. I figured he was just trying to act like he had a reason to stay behind, but I knew that he really just wanted to keep his eye on me. As I munched on the who-knows-what-kind-of jerky in my hand, I looked over at the raft and noticed the now beat-up box of emergency meals from the plane.

"Has anybody even tried those?" I asked.

"Tried what?" Mom asked.

"Those . . . boxes of food," I said. "Those meals."

"Uh-huh," Chelsea and Danny both giggled together. "We have," Chelsea added.

"What?" I said. "Are they good? Did you like them?"

They both laughed again. "Uh-huh," Danny smiled. "We like 'em, huh, Chelsea?"

"Yeah," she agreed, still giggling.

"Why are you laughing?" I asked. I looked over at Mom and noticed that she was smiling, too.

"Because they discovered something fun," Mom said. "You kids don't like to eat them, do you?"

"No!" Danny said, still giggling.

"But we know who *does!*" Chelsea offered.

"Who?" I asked.

"Can we show him, Mom?" Chelsea asked.

"Yeah," Danny agreed, jumping up and down at the thought. "Can we?"

"Sure," Mom said, chuckling just a little. "But only open one of them."

"We will," answered Chelsea, and the two of them jumped at the box and immediately grabbed one of the meals. Then Chelsea carefully opened it on just one side, and Danny watched her with sparkling eyes. Brandon and I watched in amazement as they carefully poured some water from one of the bags into the package and then used a twig to stir it around. They decided they needed just a little more water and then they each stirred it a few more times.

"Looks like you guys had fun while we were away," Brandon commented.

"Uh-huh," Danny said.

"Okay," said Chelsea, "I think it's ready now."

Then they started hunting for something. They walked slowly and carefully around several trees until Danny said finally, "Oh, there's one!" They both immediately fell to their knees. Using the stirring twig, they began making a small trail of the gooey stuff they had created from the emergency meal package. They kept the trail going until it was at least ten feet long, and they kept trading off, scooping more stuff out and alternately staring intently at the place where they had started.

"There's one!" Chelsea called. Danny jumped up from his work and looked over at the beginning of the trail. "There's another," Chelsea said after a moment. "Now there's three."

They both giggled and jumped up and down as they watched.

"What are you talking about?" I asked, moving closer to see what they were looking at.

"Lemmings!" they both chimed at once. "They love it."

Within a few minutes, the entire ten-foot trail was completely covered with the little mouse-like creatures. They loved it all right. They were climbing all over each other to get at it. Chelsea and Danny continued to just stare with delight.

"Do you have any more?" Brandon asked.

"Yeah," said Danny, "but it's not for them."

"Are you going to eat it?" Brandon asked, obviously nauseated by the very thought.

"Nope!" said Danny. "Watch!"

We watched as he ran over to the reindeer and, with his hand carefully placed under the bottom of the bag, held it up under the nose of one of them. I thought it would bite Danny's hand completely off. It grabbed the bag in its teeth and devoured the remaining goop. Danny jumped with simultaneous sheer terror and complete delight. He giggled almost uncontrollably, just like he had on the plane. He laughed so hard, he almost fell over. Everyone else started laughing, just watching him.

"They like it! Huh, Jeff?" Danny said, after regaining a little bit of his balance.

"They sure do," I agreed, shaking my head from side to side.

Chelsea and Danny of course begged to do it again, but Mom said we had to save the rest of the meals for our trip. If there were any left over, then of course they could have them. I noticed that she didn't bother to mention that there wouldn't be any lemmings or reindeer around by then.

Everyone else came back and announced that though the river looked really scary right where we were, that just a short distance further down, it looked a whole lot more calm. The plan was to hike down a half mile or so and take off from there.

"Traveling we now," Moses said.

What was going on with this guy? I decided it was time right then and there to tell everybody the truth about Moses, but I didn't get the chance. Instead, I spun around in horror when I heard a voice that was all too familiar. Just a few feet away and moving quickly toward us were Jacob and his sons.

Jacob immediately started yelling orders at Aaron and Moses that we obviously couldn't understand, while his sons, armed with those long spears, came running around the side of us. The next few minutes were a complete nightmare. Aaron was ordered to translate as Jacob told us that we would not be allowed to leave; we were returning to the village. I wondered if he knew that he was called Esau by his own people now—that he'd lost his authority in the village. Next he demanded that John hand over his star charts.

John's jaw dropped to his chest. Slowly he walked forward, pulling several sheets of paper from inside his coat. Jacob grabbed them and immediately ripped them to shreds.

"How did he even know about them?" John asked incredulously, returning to the group.

"Because *Moses* is a *spy!*" I yelled. "They call him 'Caleb'!"

"What?" Dad asked.

"He's a spy!" I yelled. "He came to live with Levi's family, but he's really just spying for them!" I thrust my finger at Jacob as I said it.

"What are you talking about?" asked Mom.

"Last night," I said, "I went out where he sleeps to tell him good-bye and thanks, and I saw someone else come get him, and they called him Caleb!"

"Caleb?" Dad asked.

"Yes!" I said knowingly. "Caleb is the name of a spy in the Bible who was sent to bring back a report about people in another land!" Moses' face had completely fallen by this time. I knew I was right. "That's how they knew about John's charts. That's how they knew about Aaron's writings. That's how they knew about the ordinances." I turned and looked at Moses, who stood staring at his feet.

"And that's how come they're here now," I said finally. "No one knew that we were leaving early except for Levi's family. You didn't see them talking to anyone last night, did you?" By now everyone was staring at Moses, the spy. "But Moses did," I said, "or should we just call you *Caleb?*"

No one said anything for several moments. Aaron, by far, looked the most flabbergasted by the news. Jacob and the Tweedles looked the most smug. Without a word, Jacob reached behind his back and pulled a knife out from the leather strap that went around his waist. He walked confidently over to Moses and gave it to him. Jacob also gave Moses a confident squeeze on the shoulder, throwing a smug look of defiance in my direction. Moses took the knife and backed up to stand in between the Tweedles. His head continued to hang. Now Aaron's face was the one that fell.

Shauna's soft voice finally broke the silence. "Moses," she said earnestly. She sounded like she was about to cry. "*Why?*"

Slowly Moses raised his head. He looked into her face for several moments before speaking. He looked at no one else. "Jacob being leader," Moses said finally.

"Not anymore," I said anxiously.

Moses looked confused.

"Jeff," Dad said. "We're not supposed to talk about it."

"Da-a-ad," I complained. "Are you *serious?*" Then turning back to Moses, I said firmly, "He's not your leader anymore. Just ask Aaron."

I couldn't tell if the confused look on Moses' face was because he wasn't sure he had understood me, or if he wasn't sure what it all meant. He stole a glance at Aaron who responded with a short quick nod. Moses immediately looked away again with a furrowed brow as if he were trying to comprehend the whole thing. Then, almost instantaneously, his entire countenance changed, and he held the knife up like he was ready to strike. That's when Jacob started ranting and raving like I'd never seen before. Aaron translated for us in between each phrase.

Jacob yelled that there would be no more talk of the United States. We would no longer wear the clothing of the United States. We would no longer eat the food of the United States. As that was said, he took the box of emergency meals and smashed it against a tree. He violently stomped on the remains of the meals several times, breaking everything open and smashing it all. It was a display that convinced us all that he was serious.

Aaron was told to turn the sled around and lead it back to the village. He obeyed slowly. I could no longer tell what Moses was thinking. He now seemed to be content at openly belonging to Jacob's team. Boldly, he went to the sled and pulled off one of the water bags and took a big drink as we all walked past. Jacob and the Tweedles were bringing up the rear. I glanced back and saw that Moses continued to drink as they passed him also. I couldn't believe this guy. He was a spy and a traitor. He had said that he did it all just because Jacob was the leader, but now that he knew differently, he was following Jacob just the same. I glanced back one more time just to sneer at him, but I was surprised by what I saw. He was stooped over the mess that Jacob had made and was scooping the remains of the emergency meals into the mostly empty water bag. He worked furiously to close it and stand up again before Jacob noticed. Then he hurriedly came forward and put the bag back with the other bags.

I watched with interest as Moses then moved quickly to the front of the sled and started to help steer the reindeer. He seemed to be forcing them in a little different direction than Aaron had intended. Aaron raised his eyes to him with a questioning look. I watched as Moses whispered frantically at Aaron, his eyes darting repeatedly toward Jacob. Aaron's face almost immediately turned to surprise. I looked back at Jacob to find that he was completely oblivious to everything Moses was doing. I turned back in time to see Moses whisper several more things, at which Aaron began glancing around at the trees and the river and the location of Jacob and his sons. He looked intense and excited.

As the sled continued to turn, I noticed Aaron was taking it in a little different direction now than before. Moses came back to where I was walking.

"Moses friend," he said sternly. "Moses friend always." I wasn't sure what to think. I didn't see how I could believe it. I just stared at him as the sled continued to move. Then Moses said something that caught me completely off guard. "Moses hiding knife in Bible of Jeff," he said.

"What?" I gasped. Without another word, he held out the knife that Jacob had just given to him. The handle was toward me and blade toward him. He wanted me to take it!

"Cutting you this," Moses said, running his hand across the straps that held the sled to the reindeer. We were heading uphill. I knew that if the reindeer were cut free, then the sled would immediately slide backward.

"Now?" I asked.

He shook his head from side to side. "Yelling Moses 'Jeff,'" he said quietly.

"So when you yell 'Jeff,' then you want me to cut the straps?" I asked.

"Yes," he said. I couldn't believe what was happening. Next he grabbed the water bag that he had stuffed full of the remains of the meals. He began kneading it between his hands, mixing up the meals with the water. Then he returned to the front of the sled, at which point Aaron came back to where we were walking and started whispering, "Ye riding. All riding." He started pushing Shauna into the raft on the sled. "All riding now," he said, loud enough for everyone to hear.

I looked back and saw that Jacob had just figured out that

something was going on. He yelled something but didn't move any closer. Luckily, he and his sons were now about thirty feet behind us. Suddenly I felt the sled jerk to the side. "All riding now," Aaron yelled again and began pushing everyone toward the sled. I looked at the reindeer to see what had made them jerk. Moses had the water bag open now and was waving it under the noses of the lead reindeer, who were intent on getting to it. He started running back toward us, and the reindeer charged after him.

"Je-e-effff!" he yelled, running for his life. I was so shocked by everything going on that I almost forgot what I was supposed to do. I started cutting the straps as fast as I could, but there were five or six of them. Luckily, the knife was incredibly sharp, and I was able to sever them with a single stroke each. Before I even got to the first strap, Moses had already passed me, heading down the hill. The reindeer were right behind, fumbling over each other. The sled instantly turned completely sideways with a single jerk.

"Get in!" Dad yelled. "Everybody into the raft! Quick!"

I jumped onto the front of the sled and kept cutting as fast as I could. One more jerk of the sled spun us completely around because I still had one strap left. We were headed down the slope at a pretty good clip when I finally got a hold of the last strap and cut us loose from the reindeer.

"I hope everyone is in!" I yelled, "'cause were goin' home!"

As I jumped from the front of the sled into the raft, I looked back and saw that everyone was indeed inside. But the raft was now barely still on the sled, and every face I could see had a look of shock and terror.

"Hold on!" I heard several people yell at once.

I faced forward again in time to see a sight that I will never forget as long as I live. Moses turned the water bag inside out and completely slimed Jacob all up the front, knocking him to the ground in the process. Suddenly, the reindeer were fighting with each other to be the one to get the most of this rare treat as they licked and bit at Jacob's face and clothing. Not much of the slime actually got on the Tweedles, but they were caught in the crossfire of reindeer mouths and hooves as they ended up trapped on the ground next to their father.

I heard several gasps from behind me as the sled barely missed the hind end of one of the reindeer standing over Tweedle Dum. I think that was the only time I ever saw him with his mouth completely closed.

Within a few bouncy seconds, we found ourselves sliding over the riverbank and right into the rapids. Neil and John yelled at all the adults to grab onto a strap with at least one hand as we splashed into the freezing water. The reindeer sled fell out from under the raft and began tumbling down the river behind us. I felt my throat go almost completely closed as I realized that this was a worse idea than any Scout could have *ever* dreamed up.

Brandon, on the other hand, was yelling, "Woo-hoo! We get to r-r-ride the r-r-rapids!" Sometimes I can hardly believe we came from the same genetic pool.

Ten terrifying minutes later, the river calmed down dramatically, and the ride was relatively smooth the rest of the way. In less than an hour, our smaller river merged into a much-larger, north-flowing river, and our raft gently floated out toward the middle.

CHAPTER 17

The Order of Aaron

The next three days were a blur. According to the days on Dad's watch, that's how long we floated in the raft down the river that eventually dumped us back into the Arctic Ocean. Everything was a dull glow the entire time because it was cloudy, and moving north, the sun never went below the horizon again. Everyone was so tired that we all slept most of the time. The food that Levi had given us was mostly gone.

Whenever I was awake, I found myself thinking about Aaron. By the time the rapids had calmed down enough that I had the courage to look back, Aaron and Moses and the slime-fest were no longer in sight. I had never really said "good-bye." My stomach twisted as I realized that Aaron wasn't coming with us. If he was indeed supposed to be like Joseph and go to another land in order to bring salvation to his people, it wouldn't be this time—and it wouldn't be with us. I wondered if Aaron had been planning to come with us but sacrificed the chance so that we would be sure to get away from Jacob. We would never know.

I thought about Moses, too. *Had he intended to come also?* I wondered. I felt really bad for the way I had treated him that last day. I realized that the guy was simply caught between a crazy man and trying to do what was right. I wished that I had had a chance to say I was sorry. I never said much of anything to anyone the entire trip down the river.

We only made occasional, quick stops along the shore in places where it looked like there were large rocks or small hills that would give a little bit of privacy to anyone who might need it. For all but the first few miles of the journey, the shorelines looked much like the place we had originally landed: rolling hills of tundra, with no trees or bushes anywhere. It was cold, too, so most of us spent every moment possible wrapped up in blankets or underneath the musk ox hide. Tom said that the moisture in the air made it feel much colder than it normally would have.

Tom was the hero, of course. It seemed like each time I was awake for more than just a few minutes, I heard someone say that his patch job seemed to be holding and what a great job he had done. When he was awake to hear it, he would just smile slightly and nod a humble acknowledgment at whomever had said it.

We were rescued just as a storm was beginning to kick up. The ocean was a little rough, and it was just starting to splash a freezing, misty spray over us when we heard a foghorn and saw a light in the distance. A huge ship pulled alongside us within a few minutes, and several men dressed in dark-green, waterproof jumpsuits threw a rope ladder down over the side to us. One of the men climbed down the ladder to try to help keep control of our raft as it bobbed up and down, repeatedly bouncing against the side of the ship. The men spoke English but with thick accents.

We were all taken immediately into a warm room where we were given dry blankets. Apparently, we were on a Russian military ship and, yes, we were indeed in the Arctic Ocean. They assured us that the United States Coast Guard had been contacted and that we would be transferred to a Coast Guard ship in a few hours. They got the airplane and flight information from John and Neil and said that they had been searching for us for almost three weeks. We huddled together with blankets, each clutching our backpacks and sipping warm, salty soup from metal mugs. I was sad to learn that Neil, who was the last one up the ladder, slipped when he was near the top and accidentally dropped the musk ox hide into the ocean. They tried to fish it out, but it sank quickly in the rough water before they could get to it. It would have been cool to have as a reminder of this whole trip.

It felt strange to be on a Russian ship. Everyone seemed a little tense. I wondered if Brandon still thought it was as cool as he had expressed when we first looked down from the airplane windows at what we thought was probably northeastern Russia. I have yet to ask him about it, though.

The feeling changed completely, however, after we transferred onto the Coast Guard ship. There's no way to explain how good it felt to take a shower and put on clean, dry clothing. Obviously, except for the adults, everyone's new clothes were too big. Mine weren't too bad, but Danny and Chelsea looked pretty silly. The jumpsuits they gave us were white, so they looked like a couple of marshmallow people. Danny was now convinced he wanted to be a marshmallow man for Halloween.

The Coast Guard told us all about everything that had been done to try to find us. Neil's long-awaited rescue plane had been delayed while the U. S. government tried to get permission from the Russians to fly in their airspace. We figured that by the time the plane finally got there, we were already heading south in the caravan.

"If we'd only just stayed one more day!" Neil groaned. I rolled my eyes. Had he forgotten Jacob's threat again already? I'm sure everyone else was thinking the same thing I was, but nobody thought it was worth bringing up. All the adults just nodded with half smiles.

Within a few hours, we were dropped off in Anchorage, Alaska, since that's what our original destination had been. All or most of the adults had to spend some time talking to United States and airline officials, because they apparently wanted all the information they could get about where we had been for the last three weeks.

Danny was sure to tell everyone that looked official that they needed to make airplanes be able to float from now on. I was glad that John's star charts had been destroyed. He tried to remember enough from his drawings that would be helpful but couldn't seem to make anything useful. I was hopeful that now that Levi was in charge, the tribe would be able to decide for themselves when it would be best to come out of isolation.

We were given special treatment by the airline. They had our luggage ready and waiting for us, because luckily, our *luggage* was smart enough to get on a different plane in Salt Lake, even though we weren't nearly that smart. We all got to stay for a night on the twentieth floor in the Marriott Hotel in downtown Anchorage. Mom and Dad shared a room with Chelsea and Danny, Shauna and Meg got to share their own room, and Brandon and I had one all to ourselves. It was really nice. Brandon took about a half hour shower, and when he finally got tired of me pounding on the door, I took a shower that was at least that long.

The next morning we all got to get on the plane before anyone else. This plane was taking us to Portland where we would have to change planes for Salt Lake City. We said good-bye to Tom and everyone else, because none of them were going on the plane with us. This time when we took off, no one screamed, no one giggled, and I got the impression that no one really even noticed we were taking off. In Portland we again got to get on before anyone else and probably a full hour before it was even supposed to take off.

It was warm, so before I sat down, I was cramming my coat into the overhead bin. As I did, my hand pushed against the little notebook in my coat pocket, so I decided to pull it out. I started reading through some of the things that I had written during our trip. The first thing there was the word *manifest*. I thought about the scripture where Christ healed the man who had been blind his whole life. I remembered Dad's prayer three weeks earlier when he asked for God's power to be "made manifest."

"Dad," I said, turning in my seat and looking across the aisle at the row behind.

"Hi, Jeff," Dad said, coming back from wherever he was. He calls it *pondering*, but it looked a lot like daydreaming to me.

"Remember the scripture about Christ healing the blind man?" I asked.

"Sure," he answered.

"You said that our situation could be like the blind man's," I said, "but he was healed immediately."

"Uh-huh," Dad nodded.

"So why did we have to go through all this stuff for the last three weeks?" I asked. "Why weren't we just rescued immediately?"

"He was healed immediately," Dad said, "when it was the right time. Remember that he was a man who was blind from birth. He'd already had a lifetime of affliction."

"But why?" I asked.

"Think about the time he spent being blind," Dad said. "Do you think being blind for most of his life had any effect on him? Do you think he was better or worse off because of the experience? Or would he have just been the same either way?"

I thought about it for a minute before suggesting, "Maybe he felt gratitude for those who helped him." I paused before adding, "I'll bet he had a lot more compassion for others who were sick or had problems."

"Anything else?" Dad asked.

"I've heard that people who are blind develop their other senses better," I said.

"That's true," Dad said. "Which senses do you think get better?"

"Probably hearing," I said. "And maybe touch, because they have to feel everything."

"What about spirituality?" Dad asked.

I wasn't sure what he meant by that.

"Maybe," I said.

"Some people might become bitter in affliction," Dad said, "and miss out on blessings—miss out on the manifestation of the works of God." He paused before asking me, "Are you a different person because of the last three weeks? Do you think that you're better or worse off? Or are you just the same, only three weeks older?"

"Definitely better," I answered.

"How?" Dad asked.

"Mostly," I said, "I guess I look at the Aaronic Priesthood a lot differently now than I used to. For the first time in my life, I've seen someone who wants to help perform ordinances and deserves to but doesn't have the authority."

Dad just smiled. I turned around and started thinking about getting home and what I would tell all my friends about the trip. I thought about Aaron and Moses and Levi. I knew people would ask about their names, and the thought made me smile. I thought about the fact that they now had a copy of the Book of Mormon. That also made me smile.

"Brandon," I said, "can I borrow your scriptures for a minute? I want to look something up."

"I . . . I don't have them," he admitted.

"Where are they?" Dad asked. He was getting something out of the overhead bin. Otherwise, I don't think he would have heard what we were saying.

"Well . . ." Brandon hesitated. "I left them."

"Left them where?" Dad asked. "Did you forget them?"

"No," Brandon answered, looking up over his shoulder at Dad. He hesitated again before saying, "I gave them to Moses."

Dad looked surprised. "Really?" he asked. "Why?"

"Because I thought somebody there should have a copy of the Book of Mormon," Brandon answered, "and so I gave them to him."

Dad just stared at him for a moment. "Okay," he said. "Can they read . . . ? I guess they can read English. Okay."

"And," Brandon added, "I wanted to be part of the prophecy

251

that the fulness of the gospel would be brought to the remnant of the house of Israel by the Gentiles."

Dad smiled.

"So can I borrow your scriptures instead, Dad?" I asked.

"Sure," Dad replied, pulling them out for me. It wasn't until he handed them to me that he thought to ask, "Where are yours?"

"Umm," I said, trying to keep from smiling. "I left them in the tent."

"Accidentally?" Dad asked, but before I could answer he said, "Let me guess; you both gave your scriptures away. You did it on purpose, too, didn't you?"

"Yeah," I smiled. "When we left, I told Levi there was a gift for him in my tent."

"So you two planned this?" Mom asked. She had seen Dad hand me his scriptures and stood up next to him so she could hear what was going on.

"No," we said in unison. "I had no clue Brandon was going to give his scriptures away," I said.

"I didn't know Jeff was going to, either," Brandon laughed.

"Good job, guys," Dad said. "I never even thought about it."

"We did," Shauna said.

"What?" Dad replied with a questioning look. "Who thought about it?"

"All of us!" Meg giggled.

"I gave mine to Levi's wife," Mom said.

"And I gave her mine for Aaron and Levi to share," Shauna added. "But since Jeff gave his to Levi, I guess that means they can each have their own!"

"And we gave ours to our friends," Meg smiled.

"The kids you played with every day?" Dad asked. "All three of you gave them your scriptures?"

"Uh-huh," Chelsea and Danny nodded. Meg just giggled.

"That's amazing," Dad said, shaking his head like he was trying to take it all in. "It's great! I'm proud of you—each one of you." Then he looked at Mom and asked, "Were you all thinking about the same prophecy?"

"Not really," Mom said.

"We just thought it would be a good thing," Shauna agreed.

"I gave my Book of Mormon away because I wanted room for *rocks!*" Danny said emphatically. With that he ripped open his backpack and pulled out three or four jagged stones. "See!" he said, showing them off to everyone.

As the laughter died down, Dad said to Mom, "Well, I guess we're going to be buying everyone a new set of scriptures when we get back."

"Do you know where that prophecy is?" Mom asked. I didn't, of course.

Dad helped me find 1 Nephi 15:13 where Nephi talks about the fullness of the gospel of the Messiah coming to the remnant of his seed from the Gentiles. In verse 18, he says that he has "not spoken of our seed alone, but also of all the house of Israel" getting the gospel from the Gentiles. It was pretty cool to think that we might be part of the fulfillment of that prophecy.

Remembering what had started this whole thing, I turned to the Bible Dictionary in Dad's scriptures and started looking for names and finding out what they meant. I smiled bigger and bigger each time I found a name that I thought I ought to use for someone I knew. I decided to add the names to my personal Bible dictionary, because I was also adding a new meaning for each one. Here's what I found:

Abraham—father of a multitude: Dad (Name given to him by Levi.)

Ahaz—professor: Tom (Or is it Thomas?)

Anna—prophetess: this is definitely Jo (She's the one who gave us all the "in case of emergency" demonstration.)

Asher—happy: Nancy (I had given her this name from the very start!)

Phili—lover of horses: Danny (They were actually reindeer, but I think it's close enough.)

Sarah—Princess: Mom (Sarah was the wife of Abraham, plus I figured Dad would agree.)

Seir—Shaggy: Brandon (That kid is always in desperate need of a serious haircut.)

I smiled at myself as I thought of having multiple names for people, like Aaron's village did. "Dad," I said, turning again in my seat to look at him, "it's funny how those people started using more than one name for each other and changing their names, just because of one example from the scriptures."

Dad raised his eyebrows. "One example?" he asked.

"I mean Jacob, whose name was changed to Israel, is the only one who had that happen, right?" I asked.

"No-o-o," Dad said slowly. "Abraham's name was originally Abram."

"Really?" I said.

"And his wife's name was changed from Sarai to Sarah," Dad added.

"Oh," I said. "I didn't know that." I paused before saying, "But that's all in the Old Testament, right? So I guess that's why Aaron's people do it."

"Do you remember Paul in the New Testament?" Mom asked. "His name was originally Saul."

"It was?" I said. "Oh, yeah, I think we talked about that in Sunday School." I thought for a moment. "But there wasn't anybody in the Book of Mormon with more than one name was there?"

Dad replied, "The most important person in the Book of Mormon is called dozens of different names! Do you remember when we were reading the Book of Mormon in our family devotionals a couple of years ago, and we wrote down every name we found for Jesus Christ?"

"Oh, yeah!" I remembered. "We had that big, huge list on the door, huh?"

"It's still there," Mom reminded me. "I think it has over seventy different names for Christ."

"And it seems like at least thirty of them are in First Nephi," Dad recalled.

"No way!" was the most intelligent thing I could come up with to say. I turned back around, opened Dad's Book of Mormon, and started scanning through First Nephi and writing down the names I found. Shauna and Brandon wanted to help, so they both looked over my shoulders, and between the three of us we skimmed through all of First Nephi in about forty-five minutes. We were going so fast that we probably missed some, but here's what we found:

Lord, Lord God Almighty, Messiah, Lord our God, God, God of Israel, God of Abraham, God of Isaac, God of Jacob, Savior of the World, Redeemer, Lamb of God, Son of God, Son of the Most High God, Son of the Eternal Father, Son of the Everlasting God, Redeemer of the World, Lamb, Lord God, Shepherd, Father, Almighty God, God of our Fathers, God of Nature, Holy One of Israel, Lord their Redeemer, Lord of Hosts, Holy One, Savior, Mighty One of Jacob, and *Mighty One of Israel.*

We were all amazed at how many different names are used for Jesus Christ, each one describing something important about him. Dad pointed out that the names *Christ* and *Eternal God* are also used in the title page of the Book of Mormon.

As we made the list, other people were boarding the plane, and everyone seemed to be just waiting to take off. It was starting to remind me of the plane in Salt Lake City. I had been sitting quietly, thinking about the list we had just made, when a crackling voice came from the speaker above my head. It was the pilot. "Please excuse the delay," he said. "We are apparently experiencing just a minor difficulty. There appears to be a slight problem with the plane's navigation system."

Brandon and I immediately whipped our heads toward each other in order to determine whether we had each heard what we thought we had heard. Then we froze in complete horror. Within two halves of a split second, I knew exactly what to do.

"No-o-o-o!!" I yelled, releasing my safety belt and jumping out of my seat all in a single motion. Brandon obviously felt the same way that I did, because he was right behind me in spirit, in voice, and in all other ways.

"We're outta here!" I yelled. "Dad! Mom! Everybody! Let's mo-o-o-ove! Go! Go! Go! This is NOT a drill! This is real! Repeat: This is NOT a drill."

"What's going on?" Dad said, apparently *completely* oblivious to the pilot's announcement.

"School starts in less than eight weeks, and there's *no way* I'm going to miss it!" I yelled.

"Me, either!" yelled Brandon with conviction.

I grabbed my coat and backpack.

"Danny," I said in response to his shocked gaze up at me. "You don't want to take a chance on missing your entire kindergarten school year, do you? This plane has the same problem our last plane had."

I have never seen Danny move so fast—either before or since. Everyone on the plane just stared as our entire family ran, practically in military formation, off the plane. They had no idea what we were thinking, but there was no way I was even going to slow down long enough to tell them.

"It would take too long to explain!" I said to the many stares and glares thrown my direction as I led the charge down the aisle.

Somewhere behind me I heard Dad say, "Please excuse my sons! That's why I call them 'Boanerges'!"

I didn't have any idea what he was talking about, but I didn't stop running until I was all the way up the ramp and back inside the airport. Well inside, as a matter of fact. We all dropped our carry-on bags in a huge heap on the floor. A very young and silly airline employee walked over to where we all stood.

"Is there a problem?" she asked.

"Well," Dad began. I could tell right from the way he started that he was not going to be able to give the explanation the dramatic impact it deserved. So I decided to answer her myself.

"There is absolutely *no way*," I said, whipping my head back and forth with the last two words, "that I'm sitting on *any* airplane where the pilot—or anyone else, for that matter—speaks the two words *navigation* and *problem* in the same sentence ever again!"

She just stared at me for a moment before responding. Then, turning to Dad, she asked, "Would it be all right if I find another flight for your family?"

"Thank you," Dad replied. "We would certainly appreciate that."

She smiled and went back to the counter, rapidly punching keys at the computer. Within just a few minutes we were rescheduled on a different plane that was supposed to leave just an hour after the first one.

"Anybody want to bet that we're not in the air before that other plane?" I asked.

Some time later, we found ourselves on a different airplane, patiently waiting to determine what, if any, flying capability *this* plane might have. My attention was caught by a flight attendant who approached Dad with a stack of papers and brochures.

"On behalf of the airline, I would like to apologize," she said. "Are you the family that had a small problem with a previous flight on our airline? You get first priority for anything you need. Just let me know." She flashed a plastic smile that I figured must have been given to her by the airline as part of her uniform.

I was going to call into question her choice of the word *small*, but I never got the chance before she continued.

"I understand you've had quite a series of unfortunate problems with some of our flights," she said. "I've been authorized to offer you all a free vacation with our sister company, which includes a seven-day Alaskan Cruise! How does that sound?"

My mouth fell open, and for at least fifteen seconds, I was trying to think of a way to ask something like, "Are you *completely insane?*" without sounding rude. Mom and Dad seemed as stunned by the offer as I was.

"The only requirement is that it must be used before June 23ᵈ next year," she added.

"Thank you for the offer," Dad smiled. "That's very kind of you. We'll think about it."

She handed Dad the papers and went back to the front of the plane, shaking her head as if she had no clue how we could be so dumb as to not *jump* at the chance for a free cruise. I was about to go explain it to her when I heard her begin her preflight routine. I listened intently to every word, thinking about how close to reality this little routine really was. I sort of stared into space for a while after watching her hold the oxygen mask as it swung back and forth in front of her face. My eyelids became heavy, and I could feel myself drifting off to sleep.

"Dad," I heard Brandon say, somewhere off in the distance, "what did you say that you call me and Jeff?"

"Boanerges," he answered.

I vaguely remember hearing Brandon laughing a few seconds later. I managed to move my head enough to see him through a slit in one eye. He had Dad's Bible open to the Bible Dictionary and was shaking his head back and forth as he laughed. I closed my eyes and snuggled in again.

"Thanks, Dad," Brandon said after a moment, with laughter still in his voice. "I'll take that as a compliment!"

"You're welcome!" I heard Dad say. "I meant it that way."

"What does it say?" I asked without opening my eyes. I don't know if they were ignoring me or if my question just hadn't made it out of my mouth far enough for them to hear me. They just continued chuckling softly, so I figured I'd have to check it out for myself. Later. I was too tired. I started thinking about Aaron and how committed he was to being completely trustworthy because of his responsibilities. I imagined myself being just as serious each time I helped with Aaronic Priesthood ordinances. I would probably never again hear the word *Aaronic* without thinking of Aaron and the power he seemed to have. The last thing I remember as the airplane continued to climb into the night sky was Aaron's voice repeating over and over the words, "Many people trusting me, bringing them closer to God."

About the Author

Carl Blaine Andersen holds a bachelor of science degree and a master's degree in mechanical engineering from Brigham Young University and is a software engineer at Novell. A former member of the Mormon Youth Symphony, Carl enjoys music and teaches cello. He has served in The Church of Jesus Christ of Latter-day Saints in various stake and ward callings and as a full-time missionary in the Switzerland Zurich Mission. Brother Andersen is married to Shari Lynn Tillery Andersen. They are the parents of six children and reside in Orem, Utah. *The Book of Mormon Sleuth 2: The Lost Tribe* is his second novel.